Snowed In at the Cat Café

About the Author

Rachel Rowlands lives in Manchester, England, with her husband and two cats. She grew up devouring any book she could get her hands on, and after earning her degree in English and Creative Writing, she built a career as a freelance editor while working on her own stories in her spare time. When she's not writing or editing, she enjoys playing video games and crying over romance Kdramas.

You can find her on Instagram @racheljrowlands and at racheljrowlands.com.

RACHEL ROWLANDS

Snowed In at the Cat Café

HODDER &
STOUGHTON

First published in Great Britain in 2024 by Hodder & Stoughton Limited
An Hachette UK company

The authorised representative in the EEA is Hachette Ireland, 8 Castlecourt
Centre, Dublin 15, D15 XTP3, Ireland (email: info@hbgi.ie)

4

A CIP catalogue record for this title is available from the British Library

Paperback ISBN 978 1 399 73795 1
ebook ISBN 978 1 399 73796 8

Typeset in Plantin light by Manipal Technologies Limited

Printed and bound in Great Britain by Clays Ltd, Elcograf S.p.A.

Hodder & Stoughton policy is to use papers that are natural, renewable
and recyclable products and made from wood grown in sustainable forests.
The logging and manufacturing processes are expected to conform to the
environmental regulations of the country of origin.

Hodder & Stoughton Limited
Carmelite House
50 Victoria Embankment
London EC4Y 0DZ

www.hodder.co.uk

In memory of Lily, a sweet and special cat

Catpurrcino Cat Café Rules

1. If a seat is occupied by a cat, do not move the cat.
2. Please do not pick up the cats, pull them away from equipment, or corner them. But feel free to make a fuss of them and pet them gently.
3. Sanitise your hands before and after touching the cats.
4. Photos welcome – but no flash!
5. No feeding. Cover your food with the covers provided to prevent grabbing paws.
6. Don't carry your hot drinks around. We will bring them to your table.
7. Walk, don't run! We don't want any trampled tails or paws!
8. Only children over the age of eleven are permitted. Supervise children closely, and don't let them play on or climb the cats' equipment.
9. No smoking, vaping, or laser pens.
10. No disturbing a napping cat. (We all like our sleep.)
11. You may fall in love with a cat.
12. Falling in love with a human is optional.

Chapter 1

Jared was so distracted by what he was seeing, he nearly crashed the car into the bollards as he pulled into the car park around the side of the café. He squeezed into a space, the radio blaring out a roar of music. He blinked, and told himself he simply hadn't had enough coffee this morning. Either that, or the grief was making him see things that weren't there.

Killing the car's engine and pushing a button on the side of his phone, he checked the time, feeling the wave of sadness he always felt when he saw his phone background. A whiskered tortoiseshell face stared back at him from the screen – Poppy, rolling in a patch of sunshine spilling in through the windows of his flat. Her loving feline eyes were enough to make his stomach clench, but he hadn't been able to bring himself to change the background.

Swallowing and shoving the phone in his pocket, he clicked the radio off and clambered out of the warmth of the car, into the cold air, making his way back round to the front of the café.

Jared stopped, his breath catching. He *hadn't* been seeing things at all.

Catpurrcino, the sign above the café proclaimed. The cartoonish logo to the side of the sign showed a wide-eyed cat poking its head from a cup of coffee. Its paws were pressed to its rosy cheeks in delight. The building was all red-brown brickwork, like much of Oakside, and gleaming Christmas fairy lights had been strung up on the trees outside, sparkling and winking. A beige-and-white awning drooped down over the windows, but there was no outdoor seating set out. It was far too cold to sit outside this close to Christmas, even with a hot drink and a million layers bundled on. A chalkboard sign, the top shaped like cat ears, proclaimed the cost of entry.

This *had* to be a joke. He should turn around and head straight back to his car, overdraft and unpaid bills be damned. The Christmas decorations were making his stomach hurt. He'd hoped she'd at least make it to Christmas before . . . But she hadn't.

Jared was about to spin on his heels when the café door jangled open, and a woman wearing an apron – decorated with chubby cats, because of course it was – stepped outside. Underneath the apron, she wore a long-sleeved turtleneck jumper and black trousers. Her curly auburn hair was piled high in a messy bun, held in place by a clip shaped like white-and-pink cat's paws.

'Jared Beck?' said the woman, beaming at him, her entire face lighting up and crinkling her cheeks and the corners of her eyes. She shivered in the cold, rubbing her hands together to keep the chill of winter at bay. 'I thought it must be you – I was sitting in the window.'

She pointed to the wide windows, where some customers were sitting hunched over hot chocolates laden with sprinkles and frothy coffees. Behind them was a complicated cat tower, rising in sections, so high it nearly reached the ceiling. A black cat was snoozing on top.

'I'm Sylvie Lindsay,' the woman continued. 'It's so nice to meet you in person. Have you been here before? It's quite relaxing inside – I'm sure we can find somewhere to sit and chat where we won't be disturbed.' She was talking fast, hardly pausing for breath, and he could barely process the words.

'Uh, hi. My brother . . .' Jared spluttered.

'Oh, Shane!' She grinned. 'His wife Danni comes in here all the time for our book club. I've only met him once or twice though – always busy, isn't he? He said you'd be perfect for the job. Why don't you come in? We'll catch our deaths out here. I can introduce you to Emmie, my niece – she's new here, living in the flat above the shop—'

Jared let her chatter on about her niece, talking fast, but he was barely listening. What was his brother thinking? He knew what had happened to Poppy, only weeks ago, and how hard the last few months dealing with his cat's decline had been. And his brother had sent him here?

'Actually . . .' he said slowly. 'My brother didn't even mention that this was a cat café.'

That finally made Sylvie slow down and take a breath. Her nose was turning red in the cold, as if she should be heading up Santa's sleigh rather than a café. She folded her arms, stuffing her fingers beneath her armpits to keep them warm. 'He didn't?'

'Nope.'

'Is that a problem?' she asked. 'I understand it's not for everyone . . . But our other driver left quite suddenly for personal reasons, and we're in a pinch, it being the holiday season and all . . .'

His teeth were grinding together so hard they'd be dust if he carried on. The unpaid overdraft, the bills, the financial mess he'd got himself into . . . The last thing he wanted was to end up evicted from his home, and the scraps of freelance work that his graphic design career had been reduced to weren't cutting it anymore. He hadn't even been able to land any other interviews recently – even the Christmas temp jobs had been snapped up. And he'd bought all his Christmas presents for his mum and brother, and extended family, on his credit card.

His eyes drifted to the café window. A cat had hopped up on one of the unoccupied armchairs and was perched on the back, watching the wind wave the bare branches of a tree around like a splayed hand. The cat looked so similar to Poppy, with its splotchy black and ginger face. The cat even had the same marking over her nose – a tiny ginger splodge – except she was a calico with an under-layer of white, rather than a tortoiseshell. His stomach performed a strange leap.

His mother – ever the mystic – would say it was a sign. He wasn't sure if he believed in them. The only sign that would be hanging over him soon would be an eviction notice and DEBT in big red letters, if he didn't sort himself out.

'Jared?' Sylvie prompted.

'Sorry,' he replied. He shuffled his feet to prompt some warmth. This was just delivery driving and the pay was enough to supplement his freelance income if he got the job; if he was clever here, maybe he didn't *have* to set foot inside at all?

The cat in the window fixed its pair of beautiful green eyes on him. The pull he felt in his chest was unmistakable; it was the same tug he got when he spotted a cat in the street and couldn't resist pausing to give it a rub behind the ears.

'Ah – that's Lilian. Rather beautiful, isn't she?' said Sylvie, glancing over to the window at the cat.

'She is,' he replied, and his heart twisted. It might not be so bad, so long as he could keep his distance. 'I'm actually . . . ah . . . allergic to cats,' he said.

'You're allergic . . . and your brother didn't tell you this was a cat café?' Sylvie said hesitantly.

'He always forgets,' said Jared.

When had he turned into such a liar? Immediately, he felt guilty, a prickling sensation starting in his scalp. Once, when he was still a chef, a customer had left a fancy watch on the table and he'd found it later that night when they were closing up. They'd waited to see if the guy came back, but he never did, and his boss said he could keep it, since the man was so complimentary about Jared's food anyway. Jared had felt so guilty about it that in the end, he'd given it to a charity shop.

It wasn't like he was lying about anything major today, though. Not like Megan . . .

There was no going back now, not if he wanted a job.

'We didn't have pets growing up, so it slips his mind. It's not severe enough that I wouldn't be able to handle deliveries,' he added quickly. His palms were warm now. 'I just can't come inside and be around the animals.'

'How awful – being allergic to cats! I can't think of anything worse, but I suppose you don't miss out, if you don't know what you're missing!' Sylvie said brightly, giving him a radiant smile. 'Why don't you come round the back?' She gestured back the way he'd come, round the side of the café. 'The cats don't come into the staffroom at all. We can chat in there.'

'Sure,' said Jared. He *knew* it was stupid; the words had just slipped out to make this situation more bearable.

They headed across the car park and to the area that was reserved for deliveries only, thick white lines painted on the concrete. He waited until Sylvie opened the back doors and waved him inside.

'This way,' she said, tugging off her apron.

He followed Sylvie out of the cold, through a narrow corridor and into a cheerful staffroom painted white and cream, where a break table was set up, surrounded by plastic chairs. Orchestral Christmas tunes were playing dimly somewhere in the distance. A bright blue fridge in the corner was decorated with an abundance of paw-shaped magnets, Christmas greetings cards, and sticky notes with scribbled reminders written on them.

Framed pictures of what Jared presumed were the café's cats were hanging on the walls: furry faces with long whiskers and wide eyes.

'Cup of tea?' Sylvie asked, motioning to a small kitchenette in the corner. 'Or maybe hot chocolate?'

'Tea's fine, with a sugar – thanks,' he agreed, and shuffled inside.

When she'd finished making the tea, Sylvie set about quizzing him – it was more of a casual chat than a formal job interview, asking about his driver's licence and explaining the job, which would involve delivering some of the café's most popular food to locals and businesses.

'People in Oakside and the surrounding areas love our cat-shaped biscuits, doughnuts, pastries . . .' Sylvie informed him. 'We make a lot of profit outside of the café itself, doing delivery orders. We have a very talented baker, Clem, working in the back. It's thanks to her that our deliveries really took off in the first place.' She gestured to a brown paper bag on the countertop behind her, stamped with the café's logo.

Jared raised his eyebrows. 'I'm surprised you get enough customers to stay open. Especially in the winter.'

'Oh, we do. Like Ambleside, we have a lot of amenities in Oakside, and this building is near enough to some of the most popular hotels, B&Bs and hostels, *and* a cracking Christmas tree farm that gets lots of custom this time of year. We do some activities too – quiet art nights, a book club. And . . .' She grinned, showing teeth. 'We have a wicked online presence. Tens of thousands of followers, actually. So, people visit us year-round, from all over.'

'That's impressive,' he said. He knew how much work that could be from trying to grow his presence online as a designer. 'Seems like an odd place to decide to open a cat café – in the Lake District – though. Rather than a city. If you don't mind me saying.'

'Ah, you would think so, but it worked out,' said Sylvie, leaning back in her seat with a nod. 'We don't just sell coffee and cake. We want to help people: ease their loneliness, relieve stress, give them a calming sanctuary, like we do for the animals who live here. The world is a hard, stressful place – and we aim to be a comfort. If you can get on board with that mission, you'll fit right in here.'

An unexpected emotion rose in Jared's chest that he couldn't quite untangle – a fullness of sorts. He cleared his throat, trying not to show it. 'Of course. I . . . ah, may have allergies, but I agree everyone needs something like that. Some relief from the frantic pace of things.'

'Exactly!'

Despite his misgivings about coming here at first, he couldn't help but appreciate what Sylvie was trying to do. They talked for another ten minutes or so, draining their cups of tea, Jared detailing his work background. Sylvie told him about their cat caretakers, Sophie and Miles. She also had cat care training, but since she was so busy running the place, they took care of things like enrichment activities for the cats, observing their behaviour to make sure they were happy and healthy, nutritional needs, and grooming and hygiene.

When she'd filled him in on all of that, Sylvie leaned back and said, 'You have the hospitality experience, certainly. What made you switch over to graphic design?'

'I always wanted to do something more creative. I fell into kitchen work after high school and did graphics on the side. It's nice to get out of the house sometimes though,' he said hurriedly, 'so I'm looking for something to do alongside freelancing.' This wasn't exactly a lie – the emptiness of the house had become unbearable on top of everything else. It almost took him back to . . . *No. Don't think about that.*

'I can understand that. If you're happy to take the job, we can sort the paperwork out now. We'll likely only need you about three days a week or so, on our busiest days. And we have a van for you to use on the job – there'll be no need to use your own car. Does that suit you? There might be more hours later, if you want them.'

Jared hadn't expected it to be so easy, after failing to get any other interviews. He thought longingly of another non-existent job that might crop up magically . . . but now really wasn't the time to be that picky.

'If you need to take some time to think about it—' Sylvie began.

'No, I don't. That works for me,' he said. 'Thanks, Sylvie.'

'Excellent! In that case, welcome aboard. It's such a shame you can't meet my niece, Emmie, but she's working the counter. I'm sure you'll bump into her soon enough, though.'

I don't need to bump into any women, either, Jared thought, as they got started on the paperwork. He wasn't in any kind of position for that – and besides, he knew where that sort of thing would lead.

Megan had taught him that.

★

'I can't believe you, Shane,' Jared said down the phone, but the words were half-hearted and punctuated with a sigh. Underneath his loss, which seemed to blanket everything lately, he recognised that his brother had given him a lifeline he desperately needed, and that meant a lot to him. Regardless, he almost felt guilty that he hadn't stormed out on Sylvie, as if he'd insulted Poppy's memory by accepting the job at Catpurrcino.

'Ah, did it go well, then?' said Shane, and Jared could hear the grin in his brother's tone.

'It went well, yes. You saved my arse.' He hesitated and added lightly, 'Arsehole.'

'Ah, is that a note of affection I detect? I'm a loving arsehole, if anything. If I'd told you the truth, you wouldn't have gone.'

'True.'

Jared had already driven away from the café, and had instead pulled in at a lay-by partway between Oakside and

Ambleside. The muted green countryside sprawled either side of him, the road framed by a stone wall that stretched on for miles into the hills. A thin layer of mist hung over distant clusters of trees and one of the sparkling lakes, and sheep dotted the landscape like flecks of snow. The sky was a wintry stretch of white and grey, thick with the promise of snowfall.

'I take it you took the job?' said Shane.

'I did take it,' Jared said. 'Look, thanks. I appreciate you looking out for me. It might not have been my first choice, but I needed it.'

'No prob. I don't want you to be stuck in a mess, not at this time of year.' His brother hesitated, and Jared could almost hear the unspoken line about how much money he'd spent on the vet bills. 'I just wanted to help you sort it out.'

'I know. Thanks, little bro.'

'Aside from the money, this could be good for you. Since what happened with Megan, you barely leave your flat. You need to get out there again. It's been six months! Sylvie has a niece—'

Jared snorted at hearing about the niece again. 'I'm delivery driving, Shane, I won't have time to stand around and flirt. Besides, Sylvie thinks I'm allergic to cats.'

There was a pause on the other end of the line, filled only with the *baa*-ing of sheep outside Jared's car and the whooshing of another vehicle driving through the towering green hills.

Then Shane laughed – the sound threaded with utter disbelief. 'She *what?*'

'Sylvie thinks I'm allergic to cats.'

'Okay . . . and why exactly does she think that?'

'I . . .' Jared hesitated, his ears burning in the aftermath of the lie, which seemed silly now. 'Well, I just panicked when I got there and told a fib, alright? You never told me it was a *cat* café and I just reacted.'

'You reacted? Are you kidding me? I don't think you can even walk down the street without stopping when you see a cat. A cat café should be your idea of heaven.'

'Maybe not right now,' Jared said slowly.

There was a long stretch of silence on the other end of the call. 'Don't you think you're being a bit . . .' Shane seemed to be struggling for words. Jared could sense what was coming like impending rain; he *knew* his brother was going to say something he didn't like. 'Well, overdramatic?'

'What?'

'I just mean—' Shane cut himself off, made a sound that was equal parts frustrated and thoughtful. 'I mean, you might be overreacting. You're acting like you've lost a *family member*. I know Poppy helped you through some rough times, but she was a cat, and you need to try to have some perspective if you—'

Jared's insides were burning like volcanic ash. He could barely hear the rest of his brother's sentence over the harsh pounding in his chest and the buzzing in his ears. 'Are you being serious?'

'I just meant—'

'No, wait, Shane. You're saying that I shouldn't be grieving because she wasn't a person? It's been *two weeks*. And it's nearly Christmas.' Jared tried to keep his voice level even though he felt like his bones were rattling. Why didn't he understand what a blow this was?

'Look, I know it's upsetting, but it's not the same as losing, say, a parent, is it? You have to put it behind you.'

Jared was clenching his phone so hard he was at risk of shattering the screen. 'Put it behind me, after two weeks? She was part of my family. I don't care that she wasn't a person. She meant a lot to me, and she declined and . . . I know you've never been an animal person, so you'll never understand that sometimes, they mean *just* as much to us as people do. But you could at least show a bit of tact here.'

Shane was silent. Jared didn't break the silence, either, allowing the words to sink in.

'Look, I'm sorry,' his brother said eventually. 'I may not understand, but I know she meant a lot to you. I was only trying to help.'

'I know,' Jared said. 'But this isn't me having a skewed perspective at all. I've learned the difference by now.'

Shane gave a thick sigh. 'I'm just trying to look out for you.'

'I get that. But you have to trust me when I say this is just life happening. I'm dealing with it. And you know I'd tell you if I felt like I couldn't cope.'

Another beat of silence. It was like they were dancing around the unspoken, ghostly words hovering between them.

'Good,' said Shane, sounding relieved.

'Listen, I'll talk to you later, yeah?' said Jared. 'I've got paperwork to send to Sylvie.'

'Okay. See ya.'

He swiped at the screen to end the call.

His brother cared, but he didn't get it. To *any* cat lover, they were family. He'd got Poppy as a tiny kitten, as soon as he moved out of home, into his very first flat, and she'd never left his side since – that is, right up until a few weeks ago. She'd been with him through all the big milestones. Through his depression, and the rise and fall of his mental health, and starting to work from home. Through a *pandemic* that saw everyone locked indoors. She was there on his bed every night, there every morning purring; she seemed to know when he felt bad, or was unwell, or when he needed her. She was his little partner in crime. She made the bad times easier to cope with.

Jared had begged his parents for a cat as a child. One of his best friends had one and he'd grown up enamoured with her: a gorgeous fluffy Maine Coon. His parents – well, his *dad*, actually, ever a grouchy old miser – refused to let him have a pet. *When you're older you can do what you like,* his dad would say. When his dad moved out when they were in high school, Jared decided not to keep pestering his mum, who now had to look after two boys on her own and was usually pennypinching to keep them fed and clothed. He'd decided to wait until he was older to get a pet. And he had.

Poppy's furry face looked back at him from the phone screen, and the gaping hole inside him grew wider, if that were even possible.

His phone screen flashed. A text message from his mum.

> *Mum:* Hope you're doing okay, love. Let me know if you need anything? Found some old photos of Poppy in a drawer if you want them xx

She'd attached a photo of the pictures she'd found. They were of Poppy as a kitten, when he'd first got her

– in his very first flat. She was playing with the shoe-laces on his trainers in one picture, and sitting inside his slipper in another. It had been a small flat, with ugly brown carpet that was stained and probably decades old, and cracked countertops in the kitchen. Little Poppy had brightened the place up like nothing else could. She'd made it feel like home. And his mum had visited all the time, bringing little toy mice and treats for her.

The back of his throat itched, his eyes burning, the sense of loss opening up inside him. His brother may not understand, but she did.

> *Jared:* Thanks, Mum, I'll grab them when I see you xxxxx

He shoved the phone in the glove compartment and tried to stow his thoughts in there along with it.

As he weaved around the twisting roads, through the hills back to Ambleside, he flicked on the radio to distract himself from his thoughts and memories, and a news bulletin echoed through the car.

Now for your ten-day trend weather update . . .

Jared struggled to focus as he drove through the hills, until a segment of the update caught his attention.

The slightly longer-term outlook is lively. A zone of stronger conditions known as a jet streak with an arched position will create an area of low pressure with some quite vicious features as it moves across the country. This will bring extremely strong winds, particularly across the north. With another area of low pressure expected to develop, and cold air sinking in, this is something we'll need to keep a close eye on. Initially, we have a warning in place for strong winds across northern parts of the country. Keep an eye on the forecast for more updates over the coming week.

'Great,' Jared mumbled. Bad weather was just what he needed the moment he'd landed a driving job.

Chapter 2

Emmie shook a dusting of chocolate over a cat-shaped stencil, adding a cute design to the latte. This was her favourite part of the job – making the drinks quirky and interesting, fitting them to the vibe and mood of the café. She mopped up some of the frothy mess she'd made while making the drink and stepped back to assess her work. A chocolatey cat waved back at her from the top of the milk froth, paw suspended in mid-air. Perfect. She smiled and took the latte and a pot of tea over to the customers, who were sitting by the wide front window. There was no giant Christmas tree to speak of here at the café – since the cats could easily climb it – but the walls had been stamped with peel-off festive snowflake stickers, and the regular cat beds swapped out for beds shaped like Christmas trees. Red and yellow lights had been installed across the ceiling, where the cats couldn't reach them.

The young woman on the receiving end of the latte beamed up at Emmie and cried, 'Thanks! It's *sooo* cute!'

'Emmie, the next one's an Earl Grey,' Faye, the part-timer, called from her position behind the till.

'Okay, I'm on it,' Emmie said, wandering back across to the drinks station behind the counter, dodging cat toys shaped like candy canes and snowmen. Her phone buzzed in her back pocket, like a persistent insect. She knew exactly who that would be. Dustin, her brother, calling for the hundredth time, no doubt.

She yanked the phone out and swiped to cancel the call. He hadn't stopped calling her – or Aunt Sylvie, for that matter – since she'd come here, even though she'd told him not to.

Working here at the café was calming. She didn't need her brother ruining that sense of peace.

Outside, the wind was roaring, a gathering of fat, black clouds spreading over the sky. In the gloom, the café was cosy and quiet: cat towers were interspersed with wooden tables and colourful, squashy chairs – some of the towers reached the ceiling, and there were shelves all around the highest parts of the walls and lower down. Baron, long-haired and a mix of brown and orange fur, sat on a top shelf, looking down on everything like a prince, his ears twitching back and forth. A TV built into one of the walls displayed silent videos for the cats, alternating between bright robins hopping from tree to tree, and heavy snow-fall. The cats were dotted everywhere: Thomas perched on a bookshelf, Jess snoozing in an egg-shaped chair meant for customers, Binx and Kitty weaving between table legs.

Emmie had found the rhythm of her new job fairly quickly, grateful for the retail jobs she'd worked at university – and after graduating. She knew how to work a till and a coffee machine, and memorising the cat café's various rules had been simple. Emmie also needed to be ready to enforce those rules, like some sort of cat police-woman. The thought made her smile. That could be a good illustration, or a concept for a picture book. She should jot it down later.

She set about making the Earl Grey that Faye had requested, trying to ignore thoughts about her art degree. It would do her no good to dwell on things – she had to keep moving forward.

With the tea made, she took it to the customer who had been waiting at a table – a woman with a teen girl in tow.

The rest of the morning passed swiftly, a blur of drinks and cat-shaped stencils.

'Nice job this morning, Em,' Faye said, placing a hand on her shoulder. Faye's dark eyes glittered and she gave a contented sigh. 'You have no idea how nice it is to have someone here who knows what they're doing – I mean, aside from Clem, obviously.' Faye smiled fondly. Clem was their baker, and she made the *best* cat-themed treats and desserts Emmie had ever seen – and tasted. She worked in the back, in the kitchen. 'Caroline only lasted a week. She was frightened of the cats,' Faye continued. 'I have no idea why she started working here.'

Emmie smiled. 'Aunt Sylvie told me.'

It was part of why Emmie had volunteered to move here and help. Aunt Sylvie needed someone capable to work here as a barista full-time when Caroline left – and Emmie was desperate to get away from Dustin's chaos. It was a win-win. Well, if you didn't count Dustin constantly phoning and texting them both, even as Emmie tried to cut him out of her – *their* – lives. It was only a matter of time before he showed up here. She wasn't looking forward to that.

'Hey, are you okay?' Faye asked her.

'Oh – yeah, I'm fine.' Realising that the bright expression had slipped from her face, Emmie gave Faye a reassuring smile again. 'Just tired. Long morning.'

'Why don't you take your lunch first? I have to post some photos on our socials anyway, and then I'll clock out.'

'Thanks, Faye.'

Faye nodded, waving Emmie off and fishing her phone from her back pocket. She was pretty, with sleek dark hair that fell to her shoulders in an angled cut, and big, dark eyes. Her family lived in Leeds, but she'd come here to study at the University of Cumbria and worked here on the side. Emmie was grateful she was here; they worked together well in tandem, like synchronised dancers. *And* they both loved video games and animation, so many a nerdy conversation had been had already, and they'd swapped favourites and recommendations.

'Oh, Emmie, before you go – have you seen Salem?' said Faye, as Emmie was turning to head towards the staffroom.

Emmie was still getting used to all the different cats that lived here – she went through their names every time she saw them – but Salem was their only black cat, with a tiny white diamond shape between his eyes. With a witchy name like that – she was pretty sure Sylvie had got it from *Sabrina the Teenage Witch* – and a sweet, affectionate temperament, Salem was hard to forget.

'I don't think so,' she replied.

'I haven't seen him since Jared came in with a delivery this morning,' said Faye, biting her lip. 'Has he ended up stuck somewhere again?'

Apparently, Salem had once managed to prise up a loose floorboard in the basement – a space for the cats to go and relax away from customers – and got stuck underneath it. The search to find him took all afternoon and it was Sophie, one of their cat caretakers, who finally found him.

Aunt Sylvie appeared from the back of the café, where she'd been holding a quick meeting in the kitchen with Clem. 'We'll find him, Faye, not to worry. He's always doing a disappearing act. He's like a little magician,' she said kindly, and checked her watch. 'You sign out, now, your shift's about over.'

'Emmie was about to go on lunch break—'

'That's okay. I'll take over the counter.'

'Okay. Will you text me if you find Salem?'

Sylvie and Emmie both nodded, and Faye said her goodbyes and headed to the staffroom to collect her things.

At least there was no way for Salem to get outside. Catpurrcino operated a strict triple-door policy. When you entered the café through the front door, you stepped into the tiny entrance space, two windows each side, one with a giant poster covering the rules. There was a boxed-off reception desk there, with a built-in window to chat to anyone who came in, and another door, leading directly into reception and the tacked-on gift shop to the side, where they sold little trinkets, cat toys, T-shirts and jumpers, bits of jewellery and mugs. Next, you passed through another door, where you were greeted by a latched gate. On the other side of that gate was the first café room – where drinks and food could be ordered – another room called the Cat Lounge, and the stairs to the second floor.

'I'll have a look round for Salem before I take my break,' Emmie told her aunt.

'Thanks, Em.' Sylvie smiled.

Her aunt's auburn hair was in a long braid today, hanging over her shoulder, exposing her ears, where she wore a pair of paw-shaped earrings. Emmie had been admiring

20

her ability to accessorise in coordination with the café since she got here. She really needed to step up her game herself – maybe buy a few things from the gift shop.

'If you can't find him, I'll take a look,' said her aunt.

Emmie nodded, but she was glad to be useful. It was the least she could do for Aunt Sylvie, who had given her a place to live in the flat above the café, and a job, when she'd needed to get away from Dustin.

She had to keep her brother where he belonged: in the past. If he did call back, she'd have to tell him that. Even if the thought did make her palms sweat. She didn't like treating anyone badly, least of all family, but she needed to put her foot down with him.

She scoured the main room, searching for Salem behind the furniture and making *chh, chh* noises when calling out his name didn't bring much success. She even checked the basement, which was for the cats only – there was an alcove in the floor, and some steps for the cats to retreat down there if they needed space to rest after all the interaction with visitors. Eric was there, a stripy tom-cat with a bobbed tail, curled on a cushion, and Duchess, their ragdoll, was grooming her fur nearby. No Salem.

When she returned unsuccessful, Jess – a large and often hungry black-and-white cat – came padding over to her from a cat flap built into the cupboard under the stairs. She smiled down at the cat, who gave a long mewl, her big green eyes wide and searching.

'Hi, Jess,' said Emmie, bending down to scratch her behind the ears.

Her search for Salem led her into the Cat Lounge, which was through another door close to the counter. It was cosier than the main room, with a grey-brick fireplace and wood burner, a large sofa, an armchair, and a wicker basket laden with woolly blankets. Logs were crackling inside the burner, bright and red. It was popular with customers in here, but those who had occupied it had left just after lunch, and now it was littered with empty coffee mugs and a plate holding the remnants of a chocolate cake. She was sure she'd heard a meow coming from this room, but now she wasn't sure if she'd been hearing things.

'Salem?' she called, making more *chh, chh* sounds. 'Are you in here?'

After a quick search for Salem, Emmie took some empty cups and mugs through to the kitchen and decided to search elsewhere. She could still hear faint meowing coming from somewhere. *What if he's outside?* The triple-door system was effective, but if he'd somehow got under the floorboards . . . it was worth checking.

Emmie headed out to the front of the café, circling the building to the wall around the side, where a huge colourful mural was painted. It had been done by children from one of the local hospitals – a display of tall, colourful poppies and sunflowers and roses, with stick-like cats wandering between the stems, tails raised. Salem was nowhere to be seen and she hadn't heard any more meowing. Thankfully, he didn't seem to be outside.

When she turned to head back inside, her heart caught in her chest – but it wasn't Salem. A bedraggled-looking black cat was standing across the street. The poor thing was terribly skinny, all bones, its coat dull rather than shiny, a few loose twigs caught in its fur. She knew it wasn't Salem because it had a white tuft below its chin, like an old man's beard, but it was matted and clumped. Was it a stray?

'Hey, you,' Emmie called softly, taking a tentative step forward. 'You okay over there?'

It looked to have been approaching her, but when she spoke, it halted, then turned and darted away into the trees at the side of the road, vanishing from view.

She'd never seen it around here before and the poor animal looked malnourished and mangy. Maybe she should contact the cat shelter, or at least suggest it to her aunt?

She headed back inside to continue her search for Salem, although she couldn't get her mind off the possible stray.

Where are you, Salem? Emmie banged her way through the triple-door system. She weaved her way to the customer toilets, which had been wallpapered with cute little smiling snowmen for the holidays. When she opened the door, a tiny black blob came shooting out, nearly tripping her up and making her shriek in surprise.

'Salem!' she cried, laughing at his antics. 'You silly thing!'

She followed him, smiling at herself for nearly ending up on her behind. Some customers were sitting near the counter, watching Kitty – their beautiful Bengal – leap up to the top of the cat tower. When Emmie had made a sufficient fuss of Salem, Sylvie approached her with a smile.

'I see you found him.'

'He was locked in the bathroom! He nearly broke my neck rushing out! He's lucky he's so cute.'

Sylvie burst out laughing. 'Sounds like him. I swear that's how I'm going to end my days now: death by cat.'

'How did no one notice him in there?'

'He probably darted in as they were leaving.'

'Have you seen that stray black cat outside?' Emmie asked her aunt, still crouching down and scratching Salem on the back of his neck.

'No?'

'It was over the road. Really skinny, and it looked scruffy. It didn't have a collar on, either.'

A fresh line of wrinkles appeared between Sylvie's brows. 'I'll have to check some of the local groups, see if someone's reported him missing.'

Emmie gave her more of a description of the cat, including the beard-like white fur.

'If he's not on any of the local groups, I can let the shelter know, so they can check for a microchip,' Sylvie said. 'We'll leave some food out for him in case he's hungry.'

'Good idea. I'll do it now.'

★

Emmie left the promised food out for the stray, but he didn't show his little face again. At the end of the day, when Sylvie flipped the café sign to closed, Emmie felt as though her mind had been put through a cat-shaped wringer. She'd spent most of the afternoon brushing up on the different cats that lived here – some of whom had different medical needs – and researching the cat shelter Sylvie often worked alongside to run special events and raise money. Sylvie got many of her cats from registered breeders; however, she'd also adopted cats from the shelter when the original owners had become unable to keep them because of declining health or other circumstances. She hoped that hadn't been what happened to the stray outside. Why would someone just leave a cat in the street like that, rather than taking them to a shelter?

'Why don't you come and sit in the Cat Lounge with me for five minutes, love?' said Aunt Sylvie, who had just finished cleaning up the drinks and till area, and was now tugging off her apron. The rest of the staff had already gone home.

Emmie was tidying up some of the cat toys, stuffing them into their dedicated baskets around the room. 'Oh, I was just going to head upstairs and do some sketching, maybe some digital stuff on my tablet—'

'You've just finished your shift! And weren't you up late doing your art last night?'

'Yep—'

'Emmie, you need to learn to take a break. Come on, sit with me for a bit. Your art isn't going anywhere. The fire's lit. I'll make you a hot chocolate – the minty one you like – and how about some food?' When Emmie hesitated, she added, 'You can't do good work on an empty stomach.'

'That sounds nice,' said Emmie, smiling back at her. 'Thanks.'

Sylvie vanished to make the drinks. As Emmie headed into the Cat Lounge, her phone vibrated against her back pocket again. She took a deep breath and checked the screen, where the word DUSTIN screamed at her in block letters. Her stomach turned over, churning with anxiety at the mere thought of talking to her brother, and her heart pounded at the base of her throat. Lilian appeared, weaving around Emmie's ankles, and Emmie bent down to stroke the calico, who pushed her cheek into her fingers.

She'd have to talk to him. She hadn't been firm enough when she left; she knew that. If she didn't answer him soon, he'd keep bugging her.

She straightened up and swiped to accept the call, pressing the phone to her ear, and she'd barely finished saying the word 'hello' when her brother cut across her.

'*Finally!* Why weren't you answering?' he demanded, the words slightly slurred. 'Have you fallen out with me?'

'What? Are you drunk?' She tried to think, but her brain seemed to have scrambled. It was always so hard to talk to him. So many things she wanted to say, yet the words wouldn't come, because she always anticipated how he'd twist them.

'No!'

'The slur says otherwise. Listen, we should talk when you're *not* drunk. You should sober up and we can talk when you have a clear head, okay?'

'You won't talk to me anyway! And you *left*—'

'I just needed some space, Dustin—'

'There was no need for you to go stay with Sylvie.'

'I had to,' she said. 'I really tried, Dustin, but I had to go.'

She'd moved all her things out of the flat when he spent another long afternoon drinking in the pub. That was *after* another bender a few evenings before – the one that had been the last straw for Emmie. He'd been failing to pay his half of the rent for months – instead gambling what money he had away. And then he'd done the one thing that had crossed the line. The thing that made her feel sick to even contemplate.

His punch to the wall between the kitchen and his bedroom had put a hole in it. She'd never seen him do anything like that, and it had frightened her. All she'd done was suggest, yet again, that he should get some help, go to the doctor, see a counsellor. That she cared about him and didn't want to see him like this, that it wasn't good for him. And that was how he'd reacted. And so, she hadn't wanted to be around him – not for Christmas, not like that.

She hadn't told him she was going until the last moment, the day she left. He was probably too wasted to remember half of that conversation as he stood swaying in front of Sylvie's fully packed car. But she was done trying to help him, trying to get him to help himself. He kept promising that he'd get help, and she'd held out hope that he *would*. That someday he'd become the brother she remembered. The brother who protected her and didn't hit things.

'You were drunk, so you weren't listening to me,' Emmie added. 'Dustin—'

'I said sorry for that, for being drunk!' His voice was rising, the slur becoming more pronounced. 'I don't even remember half of what I said or did! You always overreact like this—'

'I'm not overreacting—'

'I told you I'd get help when I'm good and ready and you're always pushing me!'

Empty words. She'd heard them before. And yet she struggled to put her foot down with him more firmly, to cut him off like her parents had. Because the good moments remained: the times they'd stayed up late, playing video games and eating pizza, when he'd tell her spooky stories he'd read on the Internet and they'd talk about whether ghosts were real, and how the universe worked and whether they were alone in it or not. When they'd drawn

27

silly pictures together, drawn faces on each other's chins, hung baubles on the Christmas tree as children. The time he'd confronted a group of girls who were picking on her in primary school, scolded them, and they'd never bothered her again. With her parents living in Spain, she was so reluctant to remove him from her life. He was her brother. He was family. Could she really cut him out like that? What she truly wanted was for him to get *better*.

'You hit the wall,' she said quietly. 'I suppose you don't remember that, either?'

He was silent for a while. Maybe she could get through to him?

'Dustin, please. I know you can do this – you don't have to live like this, and you can improve things for yourself if you try. You can't be happy with the way things are? We can work together, get you some help so you can recover, okay?'

'You don't care about me, do you?' he said, his volume ramping up even more. 'What about the rent here?' he went on. 'How am I supposed to pay it on my own? You wouldn't have left me like that if you cared!'

'Dustin, I do care,' she said, hurt at the accusation, a lump rising in her throat that she had to fight to swallow down.

Sylvie stepped into the Cat Lounge carrying two hot chocolates laden down with pink marshmallows and chocolate sprinkles, both in mugs shaped like black cats, with white faces painted on the sides. She dodged around Lilian and raised a questioning eyebrow. Emmie mouthed, *Dustin*. Her aunt frowned, setting the mugs on the table in front of the leather sofa and crouching to give Lilian some attention, scratching near her tail. The cat gave a happy mew.

'Dustin, are you listening?' said Emmie. He'd gone quiet. Not a good sign; he was probably stewing, mired in some dark thoughts. 'I do care about you, but neither of us could live that way anymore. And I can't help you if you don't want to help yourself.'

'No, you don't give a shit about me!' he roared suddenly, making her jump. 'You left me . . . just like . . . just like . . . you're just a stupid, selfish bitch who only cares about herself!'

Tears sprang to her eyes. Stupid and selfish, after all she'd done, tried to do, for him? *Bitch?* This was the drink talking but it didn't hurt any less. She was tired of it, tired of fighting for his happiness and wellbeing. She needed to think of her own now.

She tried hard to keep her voice even. 'Dustin. I don't want you to contact me again. I love you, but I think it's for the best for a while. I have to go now. I'm sorry. I can't watch you do this to yourself. You can't function, and you're going to either end up on the streets or hospitalised at this rate.'

The word 'sorry' had slipped out before she could stop it. She stabbed at the screen to end the call, partly annoyed with herself for caving and apologising.

She was bone-tired. Hurt. As she always did at the end of a conversation with her brother, she was left feeling a strange mix of emotions, and didn't know which one was most legitimate.

Aunt Sylvie was sitting on the sofa now, her hot chocolate in hand. She'd already demolished some of the marshmallows on top, a sinking, sticky residue remaining in the chocolate. She was scowling. Lilian had hopped up onto the arm of the sofa beside her and settled there, paws tucked underneath her.

'What happened?' her auntie asked.

Emmie took a seat beside her on the squashy leather. 'He was drunk – hurled insults around, as he tends to do.'

'I know it's hard for you, love, but you did the right thing.'

Emmie hoped so. She remembered the trips to the cinema, some of those with Sylvie *and* Dustin, the home-movie nights, the fish and chips at midnight and the scary video games and building forts out of pillows and blankets. She remembered the time *before* her brother drank too much, before the gambling. Did she disregard him because of his flaws? Then again, when his 'flaws' included getting drunk and being cruel, constantly asking for money, and the recent hint of violence – was that something she could really accept? No, she couldn't let it continue.

Sylvie drank some of her chocolate and wiped her mouth. 'I know he's your brother. But you have to do what's best for you.'

'I know,' Emmie repeated. 'You're right.' She snatched at her phone, took a deep breath, and blocked his number before he could flood her with text messages. He still had her email address but at least he couldn't phone her and throw insults around anymore. 'I need to move on. Focus on the future.'

'And on that note . . . How are you getting on here?'

Emmie kicked off her shoes; they dropped onto the rug below, making Lilian's ears bend back. She wiggled her socked toes in the fire's warmth. 'I like it here,' she said. 'I prefer working for you than a random stranger, and I love the cats. And it's so relaxed.'

'That's good to hear.' Sylvie hesitated, and Emmie could tell she was thinking of Dustin, even though she'd changed the subject.

Emmie gulped down some of her chocolate, which was sweet and sticky and tasted faintly of mint Aero – her favourite. 'Something on your mind?'

'Mmm.' Sylvie tilted her mug of hot chocolate in her hands.

'If you need to talk about Dustin, you can. I can tell you're still thinking about him.'

'Your mum had a hard enough time with him, and he still pesters them sometimes,' said Sylvie. 'Did you tell them what happened?'

Emmie shook her head. 'Just that we argued. They're lucky they live in a different country,' Emmie pointed out, thinking of her parents and their sunny English school in Spain. 'It's easier for them, I mean,' she added. 'They don't have to worry about him knocking on their door. And it's more expensive for him to call them to rant.'

Her parents had visited the UK for Christmas last year; this year, they were spending it with neighbours and friends in Spain. And Emmie was okay with that, now that she was here with Sylvie, and not at home with Dustin. It was shaping up to be a far better place to be.

'It doesn't matter if he comes knocking on our door,' Sylvie said, her voice steely and her pale skin aglow with firelight. 'If you decide you don't want him around, he won't be coming in to see you.' The determination in her voice was replaced by a cheeky lilt as she nudged Emmie's leg with her foot. 'We have a triple-door system and I can use it to keep him out if necessary.'

Emmie snorted. 'That's to keep the cats inside, not to keep people out.'

Sylvie shrugged, and Emmie laughed. Another cat shoved its way through the cat flap to join them – Thomas.

He was huge and ginger, and loved cuddling up whenever anyone sat on the sofa in here. He leaped up beside Emmie and she patted her knee.

'Okay, I really am done talking about him now,' said Emmie, as Thomas circled her lap. She set her hot chocolate on the side table. 'I've had enough negativity for one day. Got to keep moving forward.'

Sylvie smiled, the corners of her sparkly green eyes crinkling, her auburn hair aglow in the light of the fire. 'I wanted to ask you about something.'

'What is it?'

'There's a winter arts and crafts fair happening this weekend at the Crescent Wood Country House. It's just outside Oakside. I have a stall for the café – we sell cupcakes, doughnuts, you know, the baked goods Clem makes, to raise money for the shelter. I was going to go, but I wondered if you wanted to go in my place? I've asked Clem a few times in the past, but she's a bit shy – so I thought you might like to?'

'Me?' said Emmie, running her fingers over Thomas's soft fur and eliciting a rumble of loud purrs. She'd been looking forward to doing some of the café's wider events since she got here, but nothing had come up yet. She sat up straighter, beaming. 'Really?'

'Yep. I was thinking you could take some of your illustrations. You still have those pieces for *The Cat and the Cauldron*. You could frame them, sell them off on the stall?'

Emmie had worked hard to obtain her illustration degree six years ago, but since then, she'd had lots of internship rejections, and one failed contract. Still, she worked on her art like it was a second job, because she was sure that if she worked hard enough, she'd make it somehow, be able to do what she loved. She'd cracked six hundred followers on Instagram recently, and although she barely made back what she spent when she sold prints and stickers online, it gave her a buzz to see people receiving what she'd made.

After six years, she did occasionally feel that she was standing on the same stretch of road she'd always stood on, wondering if things would ever really take off in the way she wanted. Perhaps taking Sylvie up on her offer would be a good thing, give her something fresh and fun to do with her art.

'I'd love to,' said Emmie brightly.

Salem padded into the room and hopped up onto the arm of the sofa beside Emmie, his black tail swishing. She smiled at him and tickled his chin. 'Hello, trouble.' Turning back to Sylvie, she said, 'The pieces I have are a bit autumnal, but I'm sure I can work with that.'

'The picture book illustrations?'

The letter she'd received from the publishing house last year crashed back into her mind. The words were imprinted on her psyche: *We regret to inform you that we will be terminating the contract for your picture book* The Cat and the Cauldron . . . Dustin's frowning face followed, swimming into her memory, his mouth curled and his comments equally as biting. He'd got drunk one night, and said: *Well, didn't you only graduate with a two-one, not a first? They probably got someone better than you. You should have studied something more useful, Em. Art? Everyone wants something more useful these days.*

She'd been determined to prove him wrong.

'Yep,' said Emmie, shoving aside thoughts of her brother. *I can do this.* 'You're right, I might as well make use of them.'

'It's just a small, local event so it's a good starting point,' said Sylvie. 'You're a good artist, Emmie. They'll love them.'

'I hope so,' said Emmie. Aunt Sylvie was always so supportive of her – such a contrast to her brother. 'You better load me up with plenty of Clem's doughnuts!'

'Of course.' Sylvie winked at her. 'Plenty for selling and plenty for you to eat while you work! Just like your Uncle Bennie used to do – scoffing doughnuts at his desk.'

Emmie grinned. 'Can't argue with that. How about I make you a drink after this one?'

Sylvie clapped a hand to her forehead. 'Oh my God, I've just realised, when I heard you talking on the phone, I came straight in, and forgot I said I'd feed you. What kind of aunt am I?'

'The *best* kind, since you make drinks like this,' Emmie told her, waving at her drink. 'We can always eat in the flat? I can cook.'

She still felt awkward about calling it *her* flat, even though she was paying Sylvie some rent. There were two flats upstairs – Sylvie rented the other one out to tourists. There were separate doors and stairways leading to the flats, and a connecting door between those and the café itself, but Sylvie kept that locked so customers didn't accidentally find themselves heading upstairs, and so tenants didn't bother the animals.

'That sounds lovely – but you don't have to cook. We can always order pizza,' said Sylvie. 'I phoned the shelter earlier, by the way. About that cat outside. I couldn't find him on any of the local groups.'

'What did they say?'

'They'll see if anyone reported a cat with his description as being missing. Failing that, they'll collect him and scan for a microchip.' Sylvie shook her head. 'It's terrible, how many pets are abandoned this time of year . . . I hope he's only missing.'

Emmie looked down at Thomas and his faint ginger stripes, content in her lap, and at Salem, black as night and sitting on the arm of the sofa. 'I hope he has a home he can go back to as well.'

'Not to worry, though – the shelter will see he's looked after either way. They're a good bunch.' A mischievous grin crinkled the corners of Aunt Sylvie's green eyes. 'Have you met Jared yet, by the way?'

'No, Faye took all the takeout orders out back to him today.'

'He's not much older than you . . .' She trailed off, raising her eyebrows at Emmie. 'He looks a bit like that actor you like, actually. What was his name . . . ?'

Emmie snorted. 'Sylvie! I'm really not in the market for a boyfriend right now. And I'm sure he's probably seeing someone already.'

'Even so, this is a new adventure for you, Em – away from your brother. You should be having fun, going on some dates. You work too hard.'

Emmie shrugged. 'I have to work hard to get what I want.'

Even though she sometimes wondered *why* she worked so hard, what the endgame was for 'success', she also couldn't bring herself to stop. Was it a bad thing, to work hard at what you loved and to hope it would be recognised? If she quit, stopped working so hard, maybe she'd miss her chance. How could she slow down? If she took her foot off the brakes, she might miss her one big opportunity to be the successful artist she'd always wanted to be.

And besides, she couldn't stay in Sylvie's flat forever. This was a temporary situation; she didn't even know if she'd be working at the café in another six months. She hoped she'd have a proper art job by then, or a successful business of her own, even.

'Anyway, Jared's your employee – you can't talk about him like that!' she told Sylvie playfully.

'If you say so,' said Sylvie, laughing.

Salem weaved his way onto the back of the sofa behind Sylvie's head. Sylvie reached round to tickle his back, and he settled down contentedly, tail tucked around his side.

As she stared into the fire inside the wood burner, Emmie couldn't help but wonder which actor Sylvie had been referring to, and what Jared might look like. *Not that it matters*, she thought. If he was that much of a catch, surely there was a woman in his life already.

★

During Emmie's next shift, Faye offered to be on the tills while Emmie cleaned up after the cats and the customers, and took orders to tables. On her lunch break, Emmie curled in one of the armchairs in a corner by the window, sketchpad in her lap and the cloudy grey skies outside for company. Clem had brought her a doughnut – a new blueberry flavour she was testing out – which she'd already devoured and given her approval on. Over by the window, Binx was engaged in his favourite activity: watching the soft rain fall outside the window and trying to swat the drops as they hit the glass, his pupils wide. Sylvie had put snowman window stickers either side of the glass, and tiny stickers of snowflakes higher up. Sophie was organising some new dangly toys for the cats in a basket nearby.

Emmie's fingers were itchy to draw, to create, as they were whenever she had some downtime. She'd been so intent on quitting after the publisher cancelled her contract for the picture book, so sure that was it, the last time she'd put herself and her work out there. But even when she refused to hold a pencil, or to touch her iPad, the ideas swirled in her mind, a kaleidoscope of colours and shapes demanding her attention. And she realised that she couldn't let other people dictate what she did – she didn't want to give up, not on something she loved so much. And the cat café? It had her mind bursting with ideas for cute and colourful creations. It was a place that whispered to the imagination.

Kitty, their gorgeous Bengal, was snoozing on a chair nearby, a flood of light illuminating her orange-brown fur. She was twitching in her sleep, her tail flicking from side to side. Emmie smiled, settling in to draw her on her pad. She turned Kitty's tail into a magic wand, crackling with sparks, and gave her a wizard's hat. She'd sketched her in her trademark cute and cartoonish style, with massive glittering eyes.

When she settled back to admire her work, her smile faded. It looked just like something from *The Cat and the Cauldron*. If her contract hadn't been cancelled, she'd have an entire book like this. She could have walked into a bookshop and touched it, run her fingers over the spine, turned the pages, seen the glossy images on the cover.

One day, I will, she thought, picturing an imaginary panel of people seeing her newfound success and regretting their choice to cancel her book. *You'll see. I'll show you, and Dustin, that I can make it with my art.*

An idea sparked – she could do cute portraits of all the café's cats, minus the magical element. They would be different to what she did for the picture book – no Halloween themes or mini cat witches or ghosts – and she was sure Sylvie would like them, too. With that in mind, she was about to turn to a blank page when a faint dinging sound startled her so much she almost drew a line through her sketch.

'That's Jared with a delivery,' Faye called from behind the counter, where she was still making a latte, her long pink-and-white nails like claws as she clacked buttons on the machines. 'Could you grab it for me, Emmie? And tell him I have one coming up now, for him to take with him.'

'On it!' Emmie said.

Sylvie had nipped out for a quick break – and to leave some more food across the street for the apparent stray cat – so they were on their own for a short while. Emmie folded the pages of her sketchbook back; she'd continue this drawing when she got back. She clutched the pad to her chest as she hurried up the hallway, past the kitchen, staffroom and storeroom.

She shoved open the back door, and was met with a blast of wintry, cold air and blustering wind. She shuddered. Inside the café, it could get warm with all the coffee machines and tea brewing, so she was wearing a thin long-sleeved top, a Catpurrcino apron, and jeggings. Her hair whipped around her shoulders, and she shifted, struggling to acclimatise to the icy cold of the air after the heat of the café. Her drawing came loose from the sketchpad and breezed across the staff car park.

She cried out as it blustered free, hurrying after the scrap of paper. She didn't want to lose it.

A man had his back to her, on the way to a white van stamped with the café's logo. He turned, and she was so floored that she almost slipped on the ice-coated gravel. He saw the paper billowing in the air, and when it slapped against the windscreen of his van, he strode over and lifted it free, the edges fluttering around his fingers like a bird's wings.

He turned to look at her, with a lifted eyebrow, as she steadied herself.

The cold was stinging Emmie's cheeks, so why did she feel so unnaturally warm? Jared's golden-brown hair was fairly long, falling to the bottom of his ears, and he had a rough-looking beard and stubble. He wore a long, grey woollen coat, falling smoothly to his knees. How was it possible for someone to look both rugged and polished at the same time? It did something to her insides that she wasn't expecting, and she found herself catching her breath as threads coiled in her belly. He glanced up at her, his eyes brown and warm like hot chocolate, then studied the drawing.

Did she see a smile ghost across his mouth? Did he like her work? Her heart leaped, and she wasn't sure if it was the thought of someone assessing her work again, or how absolutely gorgeous he was.

When he looked up again, she was certain she'd imagined it, because now she couldn't decipher his expression. He looked almost . . . sad? Why was that?

Jared crossed the car park, holding the paper out towards her. He was dressed mostly in black beneath his coat, and had a grey, stripy scarf tucked into his jacket. *Greyscale perfection*, she found herself thinking, stupidly.

'I think you lost this.' His voice was strong, assertive, and she wasn't sure her shiver was completely from the cold. 'Here.'

'Thanks,' she said, taking the paper. Her cold fingers brushed his – he wasn't wearing any gloves – and electric pulses shot up her arm, making her heart race. Swallowing and ignoring the feeling, she tucked the sketch back into her pad – which she closed properly this time. He was still staring at the drawing pad in her arms by the time she was done. 'Do you . . . are you . . . do you draw?' she asked, feeling flustered under his gaze, and unsure of what to say.

He nodded. 'Sometimes. Not much on paper anymore, though. I do freelance graphic design. Alongside the driving,' he added, motioning to the van.

'Oh, really?' she said brightly. 'I bet you could teach me a few things. I'm still brushing up on the digital side.'

'Sure. There's plenty of resources out there.'

The intensity of him was staggering. Or maybe it was just her nerves, the thought of him assessing her work. 'Graphic design sounds impressive. I bet you have a good eye!'

He smiled faintly, and her heart skipped. 'I hope so.'

'What did you think?' She gestured to the pad in her arms. 'It's not really a style everyone likes, but I think it works for animals. I like cutesy styles, especially for drawing cats. It just works somehow. And there are so many adorable art accounts . . .' she chattered.

'Ah.' His lips tipped up at the corners. 'I bet you have one of those adorable accounts too? You look like you might.'

What did *that* mean? Was he calling her adorable too? She paused as the back of her neck became hot and clammy, even in the cold. *Don't get ahead of yourself.* He was likely poking fun at her. He didn't seem like the type to sit at home on his phone, scrolling through cutesy illustration accounts.

'I'd like to see it sometime. Your art account, I mean,' he said.

Now *he* sounded flustered. He was actually taking her seriously after all.

'Of course!' she said, with overly forced cheer to cover her nerves. 'I also follow some people who do incredible pet portraits – sometimes for people who've lost pets . . .' She was turning into Aunt Sylvie and babbling. She snapped her mouth shut to quell the torrent.

His expression turned closed for a moment, and she was sure a shadow passed over his features, but a split second later, the smile was back in place. It seemed a bit strained this time; Emmie wasn't sure why.

'It's a nice thing to do,' he said. 'Have you ever done it? Pet portraits?'

His tone was back to normal; maybe she'd only imagined the shadow. God, being around him was making her feel ditzy.

She shook her head. 'I always thought people would want the realistic style for that. Not . . . cute. Something more grown-up.'

'Your cute style . . . It has character.'

'Really . . . ?'

He looked her straight in the eye, making her knees feel a little weak. 'Really. Probably inspired by animation as well as games and manga, right?'

'Right!' she said, too loudly, but delighted that he'd noticed. 'I love animated movies. Pixar, Ghibli . . . And I take a lot of inspiration from graphic novels, even some of the cuter pixelated art I've seen in indie games . . . Oh God, I'm sorry,' she blurted. Why did she feel like she was going to melt like a puddle of snow under his gaze? And she was going on about all her interests when they both had work to be doing.

'No, it's okay,' he said, flashing his teeth at her as he grinned a broad smile that sent her chest pulsing. 'I dabbled in drawing a comic book once. Until I realised I suck at drawing people. It's the hands.' He wiggled his fingers as if to demonstrate, and she laughed at the movement. 'Now I stick to Photoshop and typography.'

'Well, you must be the chalk to my cheese, because I suck at *those*. I'm getting better at drawing with a tablet, but . . .' Why had she used *that* phrase, like chalk and cheese? Embarrassing. And why was she trying to regulate the way she spoke when she didn't normally care? *Get a grip, Emmie.* 'I'm Sylvie's niece, by the way – Emmie Hartell.'

'She mentioned you at my interview,' he said. 'I'm Jared.'

'Sylvie . . . she told me you were allergic to cats. And here I am, throwing a sketch of one at you.' She forced a laugh, but all the while, she was wondering, why would he work here, if he was allergic? Why not just get a job somewhere else, or stick to graphic design instead?

'I'd better grab the food and litter from the van,' he said, before she could decide on whether or not to ask her questions. He moved away from her and, after rolling open the back of the van, began unloading cat litter bags and boxes of food, dropping them close to the back door. He did it with ease, as if they were featherlight, and she had a ridiculous image of him lifting *her* up to kiss him . . .

'I'll start moving some through to the storeroom,' Emmie said, trying to push the image out of her mind. 'Do you know where it is? I can show you—'

'Oh. I . . . well, my allergies . . .' Jared dropped another massive bag of cat litter close to her feet. There were three of them already, and they looked heavy. He assessed them and scraped a hand over the back of his neck. 'Never mind, I'll be fine bringing them through for you. There are no cats in the storeroom, anyway, right?'

'That'd be great,' she said, beaming. 'There's another takeout delivery for you too.'

He nodded, and grabbed two of the giant bags of litter while Emmie held the door open for him to come through. Aunt Sylvie had mentioned he came into the staffroom for his interview, and he'd apparently been okay with that – close contact with the cats was bad for his allergies, but coming into areas the cats didn't frequent was okay.

'Let me help you carry them,' Emmie offered.

'It's okay, I've got it.'

They manoeuvred down the hallway, Jared dropping the litter off in the storeroom, huffing as he went. He returned to the car park for the rest, and the boxes of food, refusing to let Emmie lift a finger to help, which made her feel a bubbling sense of delight – as if she were being appreciated and looked after. He was both handsome *and* kind. When he was done, there was a sizeable stack of bags and boxes filling the storeroom.

Faye appeared at the top of the hall, her dark pony-tail swinging as she rounded the corner and called to Emmie over the sound of scraping chairs and chatter. 'Hey, Em, when you've finished there, Kitty needs her medication. I've got some orders to sort and Sophie's on nail-trimming duty – can you do the meds?'

'No problem,' said Emmie.

'Thanks!' Faye glanced at Jared and gave him a toothy grin. 'Hey, wait there a sec, Jared, I have that takeout order for you!' Faye waved at him and vanished back into the café.

When Emmie turned back to Jared, he had an odd expression on his face. Was he unwell? He looked pasty.

'Are you okay?' she asked him, automatically reaching for his arm, as she would with any friend or colleague. Even his shoulders had tensed. She pressed her finger-tips to the crook of his arm, something buzzing through her at the simple act of touching him.

Jared stared at the back of her hand, seeming to come back to himself. He cleared his throat. 'I'm okay, thanks.'

'If you're not feeling well, I can bring the takeout order to the van. You can go wait out there. Get some fresh air. It can get stuffy in here with the heating and the drinks machines.'

'I . . . Yeah, that'd be good. Thanks, Emmie,' he replied, looking grateful.

When he'd left via the back door, Emmie tried to ignore how her chest felt at the sound of her name on his lips, at the mutual sense of care they'd just shown each other. Faye soon appeared again, clutching a brown take-out bag between her long, sharp nails.

'Here you go,' she chirped. 'Where'd he go?' She craned her neck towards the back door. 'What do you think?' she asked slyly, poking Emmie in the ribcage with a fingernail. 'He's cute, right? Don't worry though, I have my eye on someone at uni, so he's all yours.'

'Faye, watch those claws of yours!' Emmie said, pretending to be aghast, but she laughed along with her before carrying the takeout bag to the back door, and out into the car park.

Her cheeks were pinched by the cold air, her hair breezing about her shoulders and making icy tendrils run up her neck. Jared was leaning against the van, waiting for her, one leg crossed over the other, arms folded, looking across the street and into the trees. His long grey coat fluttered around his legs, and she had a ridiculous imagining flit across her mind: of Jared pulling open his coat and enclosing her within it to ward off the cold.

Well, it was clear. She had a crush on the *delivery guy*. She had come here to the Lakes to escape her brother, to focus on her art career alongside working at the café, not for romance. Yet Emmie felt winded, the breath knocked out of her, when he glanced in her direction and offered up a faint smile.

She crossed the car park, feeling awkward just from the act of walking – as if she were a waddling duck. Which was also silly, because she was on her feet all day in the café and she was never self-conscious of the way she moved. But with him watching her, her every movement felt clunky, awkward.

He *seriously* needed to stop looking at her like that, with those lovely eyes, or she'd end up kissing him on the spot.

Reaching him, she held out the bag, and he took it from her with a nod.

'Thanks,' he said gruffly.

'No problem.' She hesitated. 'Are you feeling better?'

'Yeah, I'm okay.'

'Good.'

They were both silent for a beat.

'Was there something else?' he asked. A smile curved his mouth. 'Did you want to ask about Photoshop lessons, or something?'

'Well, I'd have to see your credentials first,' she quipped. 'I only accept criticism and lessons from the *finest* sources.'

Fine. Should she have said that? Maybe he'd pick up on the fact that she found him attractive. Maybe she should let him.

His smile grew. 'I'll bring my qualifications next time then.'

'Have you seen a stray black cat, by any chance?' she asked him, changing the subject. It had been on the tip of her tongue to suggest that yes, they *should* have some Photoshop lessons – private ones, in a cosy corner of a restaurant somewhere – but she chickened out. 'We've been leaving food out for it, and trying to find out if it has a home.'

'No,' he said slowly. 'I haven't seen it. I'll keep my eye out for it, though. Did you see it nearby?'

'Yep, near the café. Across the street.'

'You should contact the shelter, if Sylvie hasn't. I know they're inundated this time of year, but still . . . It's cold out here. The little dude should be warm and dry.' A concerned line had wrinkled his brow, and Emmie found herself feeling warm herself at his level of concern for the animal.

'Thanks. I have to get back to work now,' she said. 'It was nice meeting you.'

Turning, Emmie hurried back to the doors. When she turned to wave him off, he was still there, watching her, and rubbed the back of his neck before giving her a slight wave. She awkwardly waved back, and shut the doors after herself, feeling oddly breathless.

When Emmie returned to the main café, customers were dotted about the seating areas, chatting and admiring the cats, and Salem was in pride of place atop the cat tower, his black tail swishing as he observed all the goings-on below.

Faye's words reverberated around Emmie's skull. *He's all yours.* And a tiny sliver of her brain said: *I wouldn't mind him being all mine . . .*

Chapter 3

Jared stepped into Sheila's Cottage – a little café he liked to visit in Ambleside. It was located down a small, hilly side street, and had a stonework façade, colourful flowers either side of the oak door, white-panelled windows, and a homey atmosphere. The only animals were a couple of dogs, resting at the feet of their owners. Jared would sometimes come in here to do his freelance work with a sandwich or copious amounts of coffee. Lately, the more he could get out of the house, the better – but he couldn't afford much in the way of lunch these days. Sheila's was currently decked out for Christmas, with a towering tree sparkling with yellow lights and gold-and-silver baubles. All the festive hits were playing in the background.

He was still thinking about his interaction with Emmie out in the car park earlier, and almost walked into a table as he manoeuvred across the room. The way her nose had turned pink in the cold kept flitting across his brain, like skipping a stone over a lake. The way she'd smiled, her lips pink and shiny. And he'd found himself feeling lighter than he had in *months*, since before he learned Poppy was ill. He'd borderline flirted when he'd realised that not only was she pretty, but shared some of his interests.

The thing was, he knew he wasn't ready for another relationship. Not now. It wasn't the right time.

His brother was sitting in a corner by the window – and to his surprise, his mum was there, too. She beamed up at him, waving. As always, she was dressed eccentrically, with an array of necklaces hanging around her neck and round silver earrings, the tree of life glinting at the centre. Her dyed strawberry-blonde hair was arranged in a wild tangle of curls, half piled on her head, and she wore a long black dress, with a knee-length floral cardigan draped over the top.

'Mum,' said Jared, when he reached their table. He leaned down to kiss her on the cheek, catching the scent of sandalwood on her clothes, and slid into a seat opposite his brother. 'I didn't expect you to be here.'

'I gave your brother a call when he was on the way here and he said I could come with.'

'Ah.' Jared smiled. 'It's good to see you.'

His mum leaned over, gripping his hand. The waitress came over seconds later to ask Jared if he wanted something to drink.

'Just a water,' he said. 'Thanks.'

Shane already had a full cup of flat white in front of him, and a half-eaten scone smeared with a decadent amount of jam and cream. His brother's brown hair, almost the same shade as his own, was slicked back over his ears with gel. People often commented that they looked very similar, with the same set to their jaw and similar noses. Where Jared had brown eyes, though, Shane's were moss-green. Shane was already in his mountain rescue uniform – a bright red-and-black waterproof jacket, the hood bunched up at the back of his neck.

'You didn't waste any time ordering food,' Jared said, quirking a brow.

His brother had always had a sweet tooth; most commonly found with an assortment of cakes or pastries, or baking batches of biscuits. It was probably why, even in his mid-twenties, he always had a toothache. His mother, on the other hand, only had a coffee in front of her.

'What's wrong with scones? I need energy in this job, anyways.' Shane rolled his eyes and grabbed the other half of the scone, stuffing it in his mouth as if to prove a point, and giving a crumb-filled grin. Bits of scone dropped onto the front of his jacket.

'What you don't need is more bills at the dentist,' Jared joked. 'How many fillings was it last year – fifty?'

'He's right. All your teeth will soon be falling out at this rate,' their mother pointed out.

The waitress arrived and deposited a bottle of water and a glass on the table. 'Can I get you anything else?' she asked Jared.

'Is that all you're having? Water?' Shane asked. 'I'll get you a proper coffee.'

'There's no need. I'm fine with this.'

Shane ignored him pointedly, ordering him a flat white. The waitress nodded and scurried away.

'Thanks,' said Jared, slightly embarrassed by the charity, but appreciating it all the same. He was the older brother – admittedly only by a year – so he should be the one looking out for Shane, but lately it had been the other way around.

'I'm sorry about before—' Shane started.

'Forget about it.' Jared waved the comment aside. 'It's forgotten.'

'Forget about what?' his mother asked, drinking some of her coffee and brushing her curls behind her ear.

'It's nothing.'

'I hope you boys aren't fighting—'

'We're not,' Shane cut in. 'You know we don't fight, Mum; we haven't since we were kids! How's work?' he directed at Jared. 'Are you successfully avoiding the cats?'

'Yep.'

'Jared? *Avoiding* cats?' his mother said incredulously. 'That'll be the day.' She brightened. 'Did you accept the job?'

Jared nodded. 'Hey, were you in on this too?'

His mother shot Shane a withering look. 'No. He told me after.'

'Don't look so worried. I'm not angry about it, and I accepted. It's only driving anyway.'

He didn't add the lie he'd told to Sylvie, and his brother had the sense not to mention it either.

'Oh, good!' His mum beamed at him, clasping at one of her necklaces. 'It'll do you good to get out of the house. Meet some new people.'

He couldn't help but think of what had happened with Emmie and her drawing – the little cat with the sparks of magic on the tail. Thoughts of Megan and what she'd done to him put a stopper on any further imaginings. Right now, he didn't want to risk finding out if Emmie was different. He didn't want to get hurt again.

His brother nodded. 'Mum's right. You can't avoid people forever, Jared. You do live on planet Earth with the rest of us, you know.'

'I know,' he said, smiling. 'Such a shame.'

'Now *there's* a statement I wonder about sometimes . . .' said his mum.

'Oi!'

51

She smirked at him and drained her coffee.

Jared's thoughts were still on Emmie. She had been pretty – okay, that was understatement, she was downright beautiful – her short ash-brown hair laced with blonde, skirting her shoulders, the apron she wore accentuating her soft curves. And the way her cheeks had turned red in the cold had made him feel things he hadn't felt in a long time . . . He shook himself, glugging down some more water, hoping to wash the image away. He shouldn't be thinking about her at all. He needed to focus on getting himself back on track.

Shane took a swig of his coffee and lifted an eyebrow. 'What's with that look on your face?'

'Nothing. You didn't ask to see me to talk about work, did you?' Jared said.

His brother had wanted to see him in person – that meant there was something he wanted to say that he'd decided wasn't appropriate for a phone call or a text. And it wasn't about their earlier conversation or Poppy; Shane had made that clear. Jared didn't think he could handle any more bad news. The year had been terrible enough already, what with losing Poppy, and the unpaid bills in the wake of that giving him a mounting sense of anxiety and dread.

Shane set his coffee cup down and sighed, raking a hand through his hair. As he leaned back, the wooden chair creaked beneath him. He drew a breath, as if weighing up how to deliver the news. 'Megan's been in touch with me.'

'What?' Jared's mouth dropped open.

His mother took the news in her stride, as if he'd already told her about it on the way here.

When the waitress returned, depositing his coffee next to him, Jared could barely splutter his thanks. He grabbed two sugar cubes from the little red bowl on the table, dropping them into his drink and stirring it so aggressively the liquid sloshed over the sides onto the saucer.

'What does she want, after all this time?' he said, through gritted teeth. 'I don't have any more of her stuff at the flat. And why do you still have her number?'

'I don't,' Shane replied, shrugging. 'She found me online.'

Jared groaned in disbelief that Megan had gone that far. He'd made sure she was blocked when the relationship was over. He didn't think he'd needed to ask his family to do the same. He'd hoped this would be enough – she didn't live here in Cumbria anyway. When they were together, she was always the one driving here to meet him, from Liverpool. In hindsight, he should have known something was wrong, because there was always some excuse as to why *he* couldn't go and visit her. Still, he'd trusted her, because her reasons had seemed valid at the time, and she'd said she liked the peace and tranquillity of the Lake District.

'She's . . .' Shane continued. 'Well, apparently, she's coming on a trip up here to the Lakes for the holidays, and wanted to see you. She was wanting to know how you and Poppy are.'

'A trip?' Jared echoed, and his heart caught at the mention of Poppy – his brother's words bringing to mind an image of him curled on the sofa with her, half-asleep. 'What's she coming here on a trip for? She doesn't have any family here. She only ever came to see me. And didn't you tell her what happened, with Poppy?'

He shook his head. 'I didn't think it was my place. I know you don't want to talk to her, but it should have been you.'

Jared imagined Megan had probably scoped him out online before contacting his brother, too. He had work-related profiles for his graphic design. That was how they'd met, in fact – she'd wanted someone to help with graphics for her new website, and she'd offered to come and meet him here. He'd been glad not to have to drive to a client – the irony of that now, given she never let him visit her – and they'd hit it off. Pretty soon, they'd kissed, and she ended up becoming more than a client.

But he'd made sure to block Megan's email address from everything, including his website and work email. He'd told her they were over – no going back, no keeping her on his profiles like the ghost from Christmas past. And now she was coming here, so close to Christmas? What was she playing at? If she thought he was going to get all sappy and start believing in the magical healing powers of the season, making him decide to revive their relationship, she was mistaken.

'Now she cares about Jared's wellbeing?' said his mother. Her fringe covered her brows, but he could tell by the way it shifted that she was scowling. 'It's a little late for that.'

'Right,' said Jared. 'She didn't care when she was off with her *fiancé*. I was just a bit on the side. Why's she bothered now?'

'She's split up with him, she said,' Shane replied.

Jared had been taking a sip of coffee to calm himself, and nearly choked on it, erupting into a fit of coughs. 'She wanted to marry him. Even if she has broken up with the guy, why does she think I care or want to talk to her again, after what she did?'

'Because she's an idiot?' his brother suggested lightly.

'You know, because of her, Poppy . . .' Jared trailed off, clenching one of his fists, a pang of pain striking him in the chest.

He remembered the vet's words clearly, as if they'd been etched on the inside of his mind. Jared had been grilling him about what could be wrong with his cat; his local vet had some suspicions after he'd finally got Poppy there for a scan. *Based on what I've seen, I'd say cancer or FIP, but she needs a specialist.* And the cost would have been thousands upon thousands of pounds for testing and further treatment – four to eight grand, on top of the few thousand he'd already paid for blood tests, scans, and special food. He couldn't afford anything else.

Jared needed to know if they could do anything, if they could fix it, make it all go away with what little resources he had. Poppy had been burrowing her furry face into his elbow, frightened, on the vet's cold table, and Jared had been fighting back his emotions, fighting the hard stone lodged in his throat. *It's hard to say,* the vet had explained. *If it is cancer and we'd caught it early enough in the scan, it's possible we could have treated it, but I obviously can't say for certain. And if it's FIP? There's nothing we can do. Her symptoms really don't point to anything good right now – she's severely ill.*

He'd asked what his options were, and they were grim. Stump up four to eight grand for additional tests – with the outcome looking bad, anyway – and buy her some time, maybe another year, or give her palliative care until the end. He'd chosen the latter; he hadn't been able to afford the former. And it nearly broke him all over again, nearly put him back into that dark place in his mind he never wanted to go back to. He still felt like he was fighting that every day – like trying to swim upstream during a storm.

He shook himself. He had to stop going over this in his head, wondering if there was something he could have done differently. *Stop thinking.* The guilt was hot in his chest.

'You still blame Megan?' his mother said softly, cradling her mug between her hands. 'I know she hurt you and did a terrible thing, but she doesn't even know what happened to Poppy.'

'I know,' Jared said, pressing his fist onto the tabletop and almost upending his coffee. 'But she was supposed to drop Poppy off at the vet for a scan. The only time I couldn't go, and she forgot, because she was too busy in bed with her fiancé.' If Poppy had been at the vet's that day, maybe they'd have caught things in time; maybe his cat would have had a chance to survive.

'Why didn't you ever tell her before?' asked Shane.

'I'd only get angry with her, we'd have an argument, and she can't fix it. It's too late.'

Shane nodded, finishing the last few chunks of his scone and dusting his hands on a napkin. 'Are you holding up okay?' he asked.

His brother sounded casual, keeping his eyes on his napkin, but Jared noticed how his eyes briefly flickered upwards, in that awkward way people did when they were skirting around a difficult topic and didn't want to ask about it directly. His family had always had a hard time coming out and saying what they really meant, tackling emotions head-on. His brother wouldn't say, *How's the depression going? Still got a black dog at your feet? Are you getting out of bed okay in the morning?* In the past, Jared wouldn't have even told them when he was struggling – but after what happened last time, he knew he couldn't be like that anymore. That was why, even though his brother hadn't understood about Poppy, he had made it clear that this was a regular reaction to a life stressor and not depression.

Jared glugged some coffee, unsure of how to respond. He'd come a long way from where he'd been before he met Megan, when he was at his lowest, but her cheating on him – well, technically cheating on her fiancé *with* him – and losing Poppy had thrown him slightly off course. Still, he was soldiering on, wasn't he?

'I'm doing fine,' he said eventually. 'No worse.'

'You cancelled family takeaway night, love,' said his mum.

'I know. But that was more because I was trying to save money.' When she opened her mouth to reply, he went on: 'And I didn't want you to pay for me, Mum. You should keep your money for you.'

'Well, when you're on your feet with the new job, we can rearrange,' she said kindly.

Shane settled back into his seat. 'You should know that I told Megan to sod off, but if she's coming here for a trip, she could turn up at your flat. Or, God forbid, at family takeaway night.' He gave an overly theatrical shudder.

'I appreciate the warning,' Jared said, and gulped down some of his hot coffee, trying to stamp down the uneasy thoughts that were collecting like dust. 'But it's been six months and I'm done with her. With relationships in general. She won't get anything from me.'

'Good boy.' His mum's eyes twinkled.

Shane nodded. 'I knew you'd say that. But you know what she's like. It took her months to stop contacting you in the first place.'

'Let her try contacting me,' said Jared, offering his brother a wry grin. 'I'm damn good at not being interested.'

'Hey, being interested is a good thing – with the right woman, I mean—'

'There isn't going to be one,' Jared insisted, clutching his coffee cup. He didn't need to tell his brother he'd almost flirted with someone earlier. 'It's just me and . . .'

He caught himself on the brink of mentioning Poppy. It was no longer just him and Poppy. Instead, he'd been left with the emptiness, the hollow shell his flat had become, the aching sense of loss. He'd anticipated it, known it was coming, and it still wasn't any easier. Poppy wasn't here to help him with the darkness now. He felt like a lost lifeboat, drifting, without destination, and that was a dangerous feeling for him.

'It's just me and good old coffee, and my work,' he said, lifting his coffee cup in a *cheers* gesture before taking another swig.

'Fair enough,' said Shane.

'And you have us, love – you always do. Oh, I *do* hope you find a nice woman, though, you deserve it after all you've been through . . .' his mum put in.

They didn't talk about Megan or Poppy again, shifting instead to Shane's wife Danni and what they were both getting up to, Shane's mountain rescue work, and his mum's – sometimes outlandish – clients. She did palm and tarot readings for a living, so her clientele could be quite eccentric and interesting.

After they finally parted ways, Shane heading off to drop their mum home, then to work at the Mountain Rescue Centre, Jared paused at his work van – he'd come here right after his recent delivery – to fire off a text to his mother. He still felt bad about the family takeaway night; it was a regular thing, and they all looked forward to it. By the time he'd climbed into the vehicle and clipped in his seatbelt, she'd replied, her status showing as *online*.

> *Jared:* Sorry about family takeaway night. We can rearrange it and have another one soon. My treat when I get paid x
>
> *Mum:* It's fine. Are you really okay? Your brother told me he upset you and I understand why xxxx
>
> *Jared:* I'm okay, promise
>
> *Mum:* I know you miss Poppy and she meant a lot, but she wouldn't want you to be upset. You can give another cat love when you're ready . . . you'll be ready for another little fur baby in time and it will help you heal xx

Jared couldn't even contemplate getting another cat right now. Eventually, when he was ready, but not now. Her heart was in the right place though.

> *Jared:* Thanks, Mum xx

He clicked off his phone, stashing it in the glove compartment and driving through the streets of Ambleside and the hodgepodge rooftops and brickwork buildings, back to his flat near the Stock Ghyll Force waterfall.

He parked the work van in the vacant spot next to his own car; luckily, he had a kindly neighbour who had agreed to let him use her parking space, since she was getting along in age now and didn't drive anymore. The trees were swaying in the wild wind, leaves scattering into the air and swirling over rooftops like dancers, and the steady rush of the waterfall was like an exhaling breath in the background. It was quiet here, the only sounds birdsong.

When he arrived at the block of flats where he lived, and unlocked the door, the emptiness struck him like a physical blow as soon as he crossed the threshold into the small hallway that opened onto his living room. The TV stand and his games console were off to the left, and on the rug below them, there was a scattering of cat toys – fluffy mice and ducks – and shoelaces. Weeks later, he still hadn't cleaned them up. He couldn't make himself do it.

At the back of the living room was his kitchen, a counter separating the dark cupboards, oven, and refrigerator from the rest of the space. There were still reminders about Poppy's medication, and his vet's business card, pinned to the fridge. He could see them from here as he flipped on the lights, the white papers a glaring, stark reminder.

He hadn't decorated for Christmas. Hadn't even felt like it.

He was a few paces into the living room when his eyes slid to Poppy's ashes, sitting in a tube on a bookshelf next to his sofa, along with a framed photo of her, perched on his desk. The ghost of her was everywhere: on the back of the sofa, one of her favourite places to sleep; in the toys on the floor; the food bowl and dish of water in the kitchen. And all she'd been reduced to now was a cardboard tube and a bunch of ashes. It was surreal, after he'd spent fourteen years with her, always close by.

The realisation was almost physically painful, a blow to his windpipe. And Jared saw what lay ahead of him tonight. A night of cooking for himself, sitting alone on the sofa, streaming shows or playing a video game aimlessly, absorbing the storyline as if it could make him forget the empty spaces and the joy he should be feeling at this time of year.

No, not tonight. He wouldn't allow himself to be mired in the sadness. If he got stuck too deep again, he might never get out. He had to fight it.

Jared thought of going to his mum's, but sometimes she had last-minute evening clients, so he dismissed the idea. He'd go back out to Sheila's or one of the other restaurants for a bit. If he had to nurse a glass of water and breadsticks for three hours because it was cheapest, he would. He'd drive round the Lakes until it got dark, maybe take a walk.

Still, he thought, as he snatched up his laptop bag and car keys and switched the lights off, it wouldn't prevent him from coming home to another night going to sleep on his own.

*

Emmie adjusted the phone in front of her – it was balanced on a pop-up breakfast tray, and her parents' smiling faces were waving at her from the screen. 'Hi,' she said, and waved her coloured pencil at them. 'Hope you don't mind me doing two things at once.' She was working on portraits of the café's cats, and she'd been using photos on her phone as references to get the sketches down. After her conversation with Jared, she'd decided to do them in her trademark cute style, rather than serious and realistic. Now she was adding colour, testing to see what she liked and disliked before doing the final, more polished versions on nicer, higher-quality paper. Her favourite so far was Kitty – the Bengal's colours and markings had turned out beautifully with a set of sparkling, oversized eyes – with Salem a close second, his big green eyes standing out against void-black fur.

'That's my girl, a little grafter,' said her dad proudly. 'Nice to see you still working on the art.'

'How have you been, love?' her mum asked.

Her parents were sitting at their kitchen table, against a backdrop of terracotta tiles and a splash of Spanish sunshine, bathed in a yellowy glow. Her dad was wearing his trademark striped shirt, his reading glasses hooked over his neck on a chain, and her mum wore a white dress that showed off her tan. Her hair was freshly highlighted with blonde and skirting her collarbone. They'd caught up a few times since Emmie moved here and it had become a bit of a weekly check-in, although she was growing tired of them asking her about Dustin.

'Not too bad,' said Emmie. 'Sylvie wanted to chat but she's still cleaning up downstairs. We had a birthday group in today.'

'I'm sure we'll catch her next time,' said her dad, his blue eyes crinkling as he smiled at her.

'Sylvie said she hired a driver who looks like an actor!' her mum said, leaning closer to the screen, the dainty gold necklace at her throat gleaming in the sunlight. 'Have you met him yet?'

Emmie rolled her eyes, adding a dash of orange to one of the cat sketches; Baron's mixture of colours were the most tricky to get right. Trust Sylvie to tell her mum about *that*, though. 'Yes, I've met him. He doesn't come inside because of allergies, though.' She didn't say anything more, while her brain whispered that he was absolutely her type, because he was gorgeous and rugged and she'd like to run her fingers over that jawline and through his hair—

'You should put yourself out there, love, go on some dates while you're there! It'd be good for you,' said her mum.

'Okay, I really don't want to talk about going on dates!' Emmie said, trying her best not to squirm so she didn't mess up her drawing. 'Can we change the subject? We've been feeding a stray out—'

'Have you heard from Dustin?' her mum interrupted.

Emmie moved on to highlighting Baron's eyes and adding shading. 'From dates to my brother! Watched any good movies lately? Netflix shows? I know you love your Christmas Hallmark movies, Mum—'

'We just worry about you, Em,' said her mum, her eyebrows knitting together. 'With us not being there to look out for you, and Dustin . . .' She trailed off.

'I know you do. But I promise I'm okay.'

They'd moved to Spain years ago, and she'd encouraged them to go for it – after all, it was their dream, and she was an adult; she could take care of herself. Unfortunately, Dustin had taken a turn for the worse once they were settled in Spain. Emmie sorely regretted agreeing to move in with him, and she'd let it go on for far too long, spending years putting up with him – until recently. She'd chosen not to tell them about the incident with the wall.

'I've been trying to talk some sense into him all this time, you know?' she said. 'He phoned me at work, and he was too drunk to remember the conversation we had when I left, so . . . I don't think I can get through to him anymore.'

Both of her parents looked perturbed at this. Her dad shook his head in disbelief.

'I can't believe he's still drinking like that,' said her mum, fiddling with the necklace at her throat, tugging it back and forth along the chain, a nervous habit she had.

'What did you expect?' her dad said, but he sounded more resigned than angry. 'He never learns.' Her dad scowled into the camera. 'Do you want us to talk to him? Because we will, if you—'

'No, leave it,' said Emmie quickly. She didn't want them getting embroiled in her brother's mess again. 'You cut him off for a reason. We've all tried our best to help, but ultimately, he can only help himself. We aren't at fault for that.'

Her father nodded; beside him, her mother was biting her lip and looking worried.

'Maybe we should speak with him . . .' said her mum slowly.

'We've tried,' said her dad, exasperated. 'Over and over again. We gave him seven bloody grand to do that training course so he could learn to code, and what did he do with it? Gambling, I expect. Booze.'

Alcohol and online gambling were two of her brother's favourite pastimes now, although they hadn't been in the past. It hadn't always been like this. And she didn't know what had happened to prompt the change in her brother.

'We can't keep helping him, love,' said her dad, taking her mum's hand. 'Not like that. Emmie's right.'

Her mum bobbed her head, like a miniature figurine on a car dashboard. Emmie could tell she wasn't really listening, lost in her thoughts.

'Your room looks nice,' said her dad, changing the subject and peering into the camera. 'Have you been reorganising?'

Emmie cast her eyes around the bedroom. Sylvie had allowed her to do as she pleased with the flat, and she'd added some touches of her own, changing things around on a day-to-day basis until she was happy. She'd hung a rose-gold wire board on the wall, pinned with her favourite art prints: cute cats and lazy sloths hanging from branches; dragons coiling through cotton clouds; a couple embracing against a backdrop of swirling galaxies. She'd brought her video games, books, and sketchpads with her, and added a mini Christmas tree to her desk. Even her collection of plush toys were arranged on the bed nearby: characters from her favourite video games, rabbits in Christmas outfits, Pokémon. She couldn't help but think of Dustin, the things he'd said at their old flat after getting too drunk one night and stumbling into the wrong bedroom. *God, how old are you, Emmie, five? Toys? No wonder your ex-boyfriend dumped you. You need to grow up!*

'I've been making the place my own,' said Emmie, clawing her way out of the memory. She didn't need her brother's approval; she was her own person. And if these things made her happy, who was anyone else to judge? It was *her* life. 'I'm glad I came here. I love the café, and Sylvie's been good to me.'

'We'll have to treat her to a Spanish holiday when she gets five minutes to relax,' her mum suggested.

'Maybe once you get promoted to manager and she can leave you in charge,' her dad added, winking and tapping his nose.

Emmie smiled. 'I don't know about that. Manager's not my style.'

This was only ever meant to be temporary, a place to stay and a job while she figured out what to do next. A management role didn't feel like *her*, and although she was really enjoying the work at the café, she didn't want to work as a barista forever, not really.

'I'll be on my own in the café soon, at least for a day or two,' she told them. 'Sylvie's going to pick up Gran and Grandad.'

'They'll love spending Christmas there,' her mum said. 'They've been meaning to visit since she opened the place.'

'You'll do a grand job, love,' said her dad. 'Sylvie obviously trusts you to take care of things while she's gone.'

'I'm going to the winter fair for her this weekend too,' said Emmie. 'She has a stall there, and she said I could try to sell some art pieces along with some of Clem's baked goods. Fundraise for the shelter.'

'Oh, is that this weekend? That's wonderful, love!' Her mum clapped her hands together, her face radiating as brightly as the sunshine behind her.

Emmie glanced at her desk, where she'd printed out some of her *The Cat and the Cauldron* illustrations to fit into frames. They were her best work, and given that she no longer had a picture book contract, she didn't want them to go to waste. At least they could be useful in raising money for the shelter while she perfected her portraits of Sylvie's cats. She'd turned a few into stickers using her sticker machine, too. She'd tried to choose the least Halloween-y designs, with it being closer to Christmas, picking cats in piles of leaves and curled in autumnal trees instead.

'The fair will be good for you, but try to enjoy yourself while you're there, Emmie,' said her mum, giving her a pointed look. 'You work too hard sometimes.'

Emmie smiled. 'So everyone tells me. Don't worry, I will.'

They talked for a while longer, her parents giving her some updates on how the English school was getting along – they'd hired more teachers – and their home in the mountains, where they had a growing collection of cats, some of them rescues. Emmie was so envious of them, having the means to jet off and buy a big house in the mountains with the money they'd made selling the family home. She couldn't imagine buying a home on her retail wage, let alone as an artist, even though she dreamed of a sprawling place with her own art studio and a nice garden, with plenty of room for pets, of course.

'We'd best go,' said her dad, after they'd chatted for another fifteen minutes. 'We have some evening classes to teach tonight. Same time next week, if you're not too busy?' he added, with a wink.

'Yep,' said Emmie. 'Next week.'

They said their goodbyes, and when she'd disconnected from the video call, she found herself thinking of Jared, the soft curve of his mouth, the way he'd looked at her drawing.

She wanted to know what was going on behind those eyes of his, what had created those minute expressions on his face, what he was thinking when he looked at her illustration.

And why his lips looked so perfectly *kissable*.

Chapter 4

Sylvie had an instruction for Jared's weekend shift, not long before Christmas Day, that made it extra difficult to avoid thinking about Emmie – and he couldn't exactly say no unless he wanted to jeopardise his job.

'Emmie's heading off to the winter fair for me,' Sylvie had explained at the back door of the café, as a chill wind blustered around them. 'It's one of the fundraisers we do every year at Crescent Wood Country House – just a small stall, selling some baked goods, promoting the café. I'd like you to drive her down there with the supplies and help her out. She'll be selling some of her art pieces, too. I was going to go with her myself, but something came up with the café, and I have to reshuffle things.'

Jared had felt sick. Crescent Wood Country House? That was where Megan had been planning to marry her fiancé, Ethan. He knew he shouldn't let it affect him, not when it had been six months since they split, but being here made those sharp, stinging memories rise up. That day, when he'd found the text message on her phone: *Mum wants to take you to see Crescent Wood Country House next week . . . I know it's your dream wedding venue. Can't wait to properly make you mine as my wife.* He'd only looked at her phone because she'd ordered them a takeaway, it was late arriving, and she was still soaking in his bath.

Did a betrayal like that leave a permanent mark, he wondered, colouring his world view in tinges of grey? They'd only been seeing each other for about nine months, but he'd naively thought they had a future. He still couldn't grasp how someone could be so deceitful to someone they claimed to care about, to love.

He swallowed a hard stone in his throat. It didn't mean anything that he would have to go to the country house – it was just a place. Megan was in the past, and it wasn't like he was going to bump into her there.

That was how he'd found himself sitting here today, the weekend before Christmas, with Emmie in the passenger seat of his van. All her gear was loaded in the back – her art, Clem's baked goods, a display table and banner – and they were on the way to the venue, winding their way through the narrow streets of Oakside, which were quiet and crisp with a layer of sparkling frost this early in the morning. It was a cloudy, gloomy day, the sky a watercolour mixture of greys splashed across a canvas. And Emmie looked extra pretty, in a light cream-coloured coat that hugged her waist, a chunky knit scarf, and a dusting of glittery eyeshadow on her lids.

'We avoided the school rush,' he said, stupidly. Not the most interesting conversation starter he'd ever used, but still. 'Ten minutes earlier, and it'd be a nightmare on these roads. It always is.'

'Good thing we missed it, then!' she said brightly. She was gazing out of the window at the passing tourist shops and pubs, her brown eyes wide as she soaked it all in. He couldn't help but notice their unusual, almost beautiful, hue – like milky tea.

'Is this your first time doing a stall?' he asked her.

69

'I've done car-boot sales with my parents and brother before, ages ago – but I wasn't trying to sell my art, just pieces of junk and old clothes.' Her voice kicked up a notch. 'It's pretty exciting. I've always wanted to do a stall, with all the trimmings. One day it'll be even better – I'll do keychains and stationery, calendars, have post-cards and maybe business cards . . . I've always wanted to do a colouring book!'

'Sounds fun,' he said. Her enthusiasm was infectious, making him feel light and airy, too. 'Have you sold your art anywhere before? Online?'

'I've sold a few bits on social media. Not too seriously, though. I was going to open a proper web shop. But then I had . . .' She hitched in a sharp breath. 'Never mind, it doesn't matter.'

Huh. Her expression looked significantly dimmed and he wasn't sure why. An urge to fix it, to make her feel better, reared up inside him. 'I could help,' he offered, 'if you ever wanted to set up a website. I did my graphic design site myself.'

'Oh . . . thanks,' she said, breaking into another lovely, genuine smile and adjusting her scarf. His stomach per-formed a twist and he glued his eyes back on the road. 'I'd like that.'

'It should get warmer in here soon,' he said, hitching up the heating a notch.

She nodded. 'I hope there'll be *tons* of cat lovers at the hall,' she announced. 'People with fur babies to go home to. Makes them more likely to buy something, doesn't it?'

Her words made Poppy resurface in his memory, made him think of how much she'd meant to him. He could feel it swelling inside him. He'd never expected it to feel this way, so intense. As if the world around him were spinning with a piece missing, and everyone else was oblivious to it. Everything seemed off, sometimes, like he was walking through a painting. It felt worse than when he'd lost his grandfather – but he'd hardly known the man, as he hadn't really got along with the rest of the family. And his grandfather hadn't saved his life when he needed saving the most, not like Poppy.

Jared turned the radio on, catching the end of a weather update . . . *it's difficult to predict this far ahead in a ten-day trend but we do anticipate some unsettled weather on the horizon, with high winds and the possibility of a white Christmas . . .*

'A white Christmas!' Emmie repeated, clapping her gloved hands together. 'I haven't seen snow here yet. Sylvie used to send me pictures!'

'It can be nice,' he said, 'especially over near the big lakes.' He nearly added that people often came here for Christmas weddings, but an image of Megan and her fiancé surfaced, making him swallow back the words with a sour taste in his mouth. His fist tightened on the wheel.

'I bet it's so magical,' said Emmie. 'Like a postcard.'

A dreamy, wistful look settled over her face, and she returned her gaze to the window beside her, as if imagining the landscape thick with snow. In spite of himself, his lips tilted.

By the time they arrived at the venue, it was getting on for nine thirty. His mum must be up because she'd already sent him a message to be careful in case it got increasingly windy today. Crescent Wood Country House was tucked away down a gravelly country road on a private patch of land, surrounded by frosty grass and shrubs. It was smaller than the grand name suggested, all grey brickwork and creeping plants, with white-panelled windows and a large tree standing proudly outside, which had been strung up with dim Christmas lights. Someone had arranged tasteful decorations outside, the bushes adorned with silky bows and ribbons. There was a rustic charm to it, with red flowers in vases in every window, and creeping leaves running up latticed wood at the side of the building. Shiny garlands interspersed with pale baubles hung over the doors and windows.

Had Megan and her fiancé Ethan come here for viewings while she was seeing both of them at the same time? He no longer had any interest in Megan – that was the past – but standing here, it was like a slap to the face, a fist dragging him back by the scruff of the neck.

'Wow,' said Emmie, at Jared's side. She whistled. 'Nice place. Imagine living *here*.'

'Yeah. Bet the mortgage is a fortune, though,' he quipped, to cover up what he was truly thinking. 'Not in reach of us lesser mortals.'

'Probably owned by a baron or something,' Emmie added. She yanked out her phone and snapped a photo, tapping away at her phone screen. 'For the cat café socials,' she explained. 'Sylvie asked me to post about the fair. Wow, it comes out nice in pictures.' She held up the phone to show him an Instagram draft.

Already, people were milling about the area: another van was parked nearby and a man was having a cigarette break over by the stone wall lining the road. They were guided inside by a rosy-faced attendant with a name badge pinned to her chest, who led them into a large hall with a gleaming wooden floor at the back of the property. Two sets of huge floor-to-ceiling windows looked out upon another endless stretch of field and trimmed hedges, with white-painted metal tables lined up on a quaint patio.

'You can get set up in here,' she told them, waving around at the room. Other stallholders were setting up, splaying tablecloths onto their stands and unpacking their wares from boxes. 'Toilets are over there, through that corridor and on your right. There's a bar near the front entrance on the left, if you need any food or drinks while you're here, but we have some complimentary water bottles in the storeroom for stallholders.' She motioned to a door across the room, marked *private*.

'Thanks,' Emmie said. 'We appreciate it.'

Together, they brought all their things through into the hall. It didn't take too long to get themselves set up, and Emmie snapped more photos for Catpurrcino's social media pages when they were done. There were fewer decorations in here, but the ceiling was filled with more garlands and hanging red ribbons, miniature potted trees in the windows dusted with fake snow.

When the doors opened at ten, their table was covered in plates of cat-shaped doughnuts and pastries, paw-shaped cookies, cat cupcakes, and illustrations of Emmie's, most of which were in shiny gold and silver frames. Sylvie had also given them a roller banner that Jared had managed to set up beside them, with the Catpurrcino logo and address on.

By this point, Emmie was also bouncing on the heels of her feet with excitement. 'I want a roller banner too,' she said. 'For my art accounts.'

'And your website, when you get one,' he said.

'Yes! I can take it to all the conventions. Sadly, I won't always have a chauffeur to drive me around . . .' she added, giving him an amused look.

He bowed. 'Jeeves is only too happy to help.'

Her laugh came out slightly strangled. 'Sylvie should have made that your job title. Oh my God, I could do a drawing based on that – a cat butler! It'd make a really cute sticker! I can give it a bow tie and a suit and everything.'

He couldn't help but laugh at her delight and the way her eyes sparkled at the thought. God, when was the last time he'd laughed like this? He'd never known anyone to be so infectiously . . . joyful.

There weren't many visitors to the market in the first hour – mainly elderly people, who were more interested in the stalls selling homemade lotions, ornaments for the holidays, and soaps claiming to have the benefits of relaxation and stress relief. One couple only briefly passed Emmie's stall, seeming uninterested, their eyes roving over the wares as they drifted away. He glanced at Emmie.

'Not to worry,' she said, shrugging it off. 'I'm sure more people will come along soon.'

It didn't get much better than that for the rest of the day. Despite there being around fifteen to twenty stalls set up in the hall, very few people passed through the doors, and those who did browse the Catpurrcino table only seemed interested in the festive snack food.

'How about an illustration to go with your doughnut?' Emmie asked one of the women, who had just settled on a white doughnut with cat ears and an iced white face. The nose had been made to resemble a carrot, like a cross between a snowman and a cat.

'Oh, I have enough things in frames all over the house, lovely as they are,' said the woman, looking apologetic as she clutched her brown paper bag to her chest.

'Of course, but they'd make lovely gifts, don't you think?'

Her eyes squeezed together. 'It's not Halloween? Bit far away now.'

Emmie's cheeks turned pink, although she forced a smile. Jared had noticed that most of her work had a distinctly Halloween edge: cats stirring cauldrons, wearing orange and black scarves, jumping in autumn leaves, riding broomsticks or wandering through autumnal forests. The artwork definitely was out-of-season. Why was that? She was talented; he imagined she could draw illustrations for any season she chose.

'Thanks, love. This'll hit the spot nicely.' The woman clasped her doughnut bag and turned away to follow the man she was with, heading for the lotion stall.

'Thank you!' Emmie called after her.

Jared felt a strong desire to reach out and squeeze Emmie's shoulder – hell, even to hug her. He settled for an awkward pat instead.

'It's just a tough crowd,' she told him, standing up straighter.

'True,' he said. 'How about we head off for lunch, take a break? Come back refreshed?'

'We might get a lunchtime rush,' she pointed out. 'I don't want to miss it. You can go, though.'

'Nah. I'm good. I'll stay and help.'

Jared had to admire her perseverance, how she didn't let *any* sign of dismay show. Every time someone bought an iced cookie or a doughnut – which wasn't very often, granted – she offered them an illustration, suggested their grandkids might like it. Nobody seemed interested. What was the matter with these people? Could they not see how hard she was working, how talented she was?

At close to three o'clock, hardly anyone had been into the hall for hours. A few stalls had already packed up as the wintry sunshine dwindled outside the tall windows, sinking behind a copse of trees. It seemed odd for a winter fair to be so quiet.

'Let's go,' Emmie said, handing him some empty plates from the table, sounding put out now. All of the food was gone; only her illustrations remained, their shiny frames duller in the fading light. There wasn't long left before the hall would be closing.

The woman who had ushered them inside earlier in the day appeared in the hall. Discreetly, Jared pulled her to one side and said, 'Any reason it was so quiet today?'

The woman looked crestfallen. 'Oh, I'm so sorry if you didn't have a positive experience,' she said, shaking her head. 'It's usually so busy, the winter fair, but it did clash with that big Christmas music event over in Kendal, the one with the ice rink? It's why we were charging less for you to have a stall here this time.'

'Oh, I see,' said Jared. How frustrating for Emmie. And on top of clashing with another big event, her items had been distinctly seasonal. The wrong season, to be exact. He wondered again why that was.

He returned to their table as another stallholder approached the woman from the country house with questions. Jared was just in time to see Emmie shift around the side of her table, reaching for more items to collect; the stall beside them was also packing up. She moved at the same time as the man close to her, and, as he was carrying a large box and could barely see her over it, he bumped into her, likely harder than she'd been expecting. The man cried out in surprise.

Emmie slipped, stumbling forward, her hand skimming the table edge and catching on one of the framed illustrations. It tumbled to the wooden floor with a smash, glass spilling everywhere. Emmie floundered, but she fell, too – swerving to dodge the shattered glass and throwing out her hand to brace herself.

Jared hurtled around the table, heart in his throat, and hurried over as she landed hard on her side, arm outstretched. Emmie gasped, tears in her eyes now.

'Watch where you're going, you daft bloody girl!' the man cried, struggling with his box and peering over the top.

'Hey!' Jared snapped at him, glaring. 'You're the one who should be watching where you're going! That box was practically covering your eyes!'

The man spluttered something incomprehensible, jostling the box into his abandoned seat. His cheeks were red, as if he knew he was in the wrong, but was determined not to be. 'If she wasn't so ruddy close to me—'

'It wasn't her fault!' Jared hissed. He knelt beside Emmie. Why was his heart pounding so much? She'd only had a slight fall; it was nothing life-threatening. And yet after the day she'd had . . . 'Watch the glass.' He held out his hands, as if that would provide a physical barrier between her and the shards. 'Did you get cut?'

'N-No, but – my wrist.' She lifted it tenderly, wincing. 'Ouch. I landed on my hand and my wrist hurts.'

'Hey,' Jared fired at the man, who was still blabbering out his excuses with gusto. 'Go get someone who works here – it's the least you could do!'

77

'It's okay,' said Emmie breathlessly, cradling her injured wrist. 'It wasn't intentional.'

'It's not okay!'

The woman who had first led them inside the hall rushed over; she must have returned to the hall. Her eyes were wide as she crouched down next to Emmie. 'I know first aid. Let's take a look,' she offered.

She assessed Emmie's wrist. Jared waited, glad she hadn't been cut by any of the glass, at least. The man had vanished along with his box – Jared couldn't decide whether he was an arsehole, a coward, or both. While Emmie was being checked out, Jared turned slightly, glass crunching beneath his shoes, and dusted the shards off the illustration carefully. His heart thumped harder in his chest. How hadn't he noticed what this depicted, all day? It was a black cat holding an open bottle marked *summoning*, and another ghostly cat – drawn as a hazy outline, and much smaller, as if it were a kitten – was pouring from the bottle. The first cat looked awed, its sparkling eyes glistening with tears.

An adult cat summoning the ghost of a kitten. A lost child, maybe?

His throat hurt looking at it: the expressions, the detail, the emotion. How did she manage to bring out things that were so deep, so raw, and convey them through cartoonish animals? His family could barely even bring themselves to talk about feelings much. And yet she'd poured them into this image, infused them in every line and shaded section.

He tucked it in his pocket for safekeeping.

Jared told himself that maybe she'd want to reframe it later. Really, he didn't want it to end up in the bin when the glass was swept away.

Chapter 5

Jared had driven her to A&E, which Emmie had been touched by, as she'd offered to get herself a taxi if he took their work things back to the café. The woman at the fair's hall who was familiar with first aid had suspected she'd fractured her wrist, but it needed to be confirmed on an X-ray at the hospital. Emmie now found herself sitting on a plastic chair in the A&E department waiting room, her wrist still throbbing with spikes of pain, and her chest heavy. The fair hadn't gone as she'd wanted it to and she hadn't sold any illustrations.

'Thanks for bringing me here,' Emmie said. 'At least it wasn't my dominant hand . . .' She could still draw, thank goodness.

'It was no trouble,' Jared said.

'And for . . . defending me,' she said. That man with his box hadn't intended to do her any harm – but Jared's reaction, his care for her, had been tender, and so appreciated, given how the fair had gone. In fact, it had made her throat feel thick with emotion. In all the chaos of living with Dustin these past few years, she couldn't remember the last time someone who wasn't her Aunt Sylvie had looked after her like that. 'I guess my next illustration should be a cat knight, instead of a butler?' she added lightly.

He shook his head, a wry smile playing on his face. 'I just did what anyone would do. And that guy was out of order. He didn't even stick around to see if you were okay.'

They were both clutching plastic cups of coffee that he'd got them from a vending machine and had insisted on paying for. It didn't taste the best – too watery – but she'd dumped in extra sugar. There was an array of sparkly tinsel strung around the waiting room and a slightly right-leaning Christmas tree, covered in snow-flakes and red baubles, squatting in the corner next to a stack of health and wellness magazines.

'It's fine,' said Emmie. 'He was probably embarrassed. I don't think he meant anything by it.'

Jared lifted an eyebrow. 'You give people a lot of credit.'

'I like to assume people have good intentions when I can.'

For a minute, Jared was silent, then he said, 'I'm sorry you didn't sell any illustrations. The woman at the hall said there was a music event in Kendal, a big one with an ice rink.'

'Well, that explains things. I'll just have to try again – I think Sylvie said there's a spring arts and crafts fair. I can have more seasonally appropriate things by then.'

'You did have a lot of autumn-related things. I mean . . .' he said hurriedly, glancing up from his cup. 'You draw well. I'm sure you could tackle Christmas and wintry scenes. They'd match your style. I'm surprised you didn't have anything like that already.'

'Well . . . It's just . . .' She fumbled with her words. He'd seen the illustrations back at the hall, and he was right; they weren't seasonally appropriate. Sadly, she hadn't had anything remotely festive as she'd worked so hard on the book illustrations before the picture book contract was cancelled. She hadn't really had time for much else. 'They were left over from a contract I had. It fell through. I was proud of them and wanted to do something with them, and I figured if I mostly picked the least Halloween-y ones, it'd work.' She snorted, let a smile slip onto her lips. 'It didn't work. There's always next time, though!'

'Good. All those old couples will have missed out on first dibs on a local celebrity.' He sipped his coffee, wiggling his eyebrows at her, which was funny and made her laugh, yet equally, it did something to her insides, twisting them like tangled Christmas lights.

'I have an idea,' Jared said, yanking out his wallet from his coat pocket with one hand. He hesitated.

'An idea . . . ?' she prompted.

Jared shoved aside some flaps in his wallet, and looked up at her, uncertainty in his face. 'Well, I was going to say I'd buy a picture, but I spent my last pennies on these coffees and I'm guessing you can't take card payments.'

Emmie felt her cheeks heat with surprise. 'No, don't be silly. You don't have to buy anything from me!'

'I want to. But you'll have to sign it too.'

'Why? So you can get rich off me, when I'm famous?' she joked.

'Exactly.'

Oh, she loved the way his face lit up like that when he smiled. She wanted to tell him he should do it more often, but that might sound rude.

A silence stretched between them, filled only by the screeching of a toddler who had just entered the waiting room, and the low conversation of the receptionists over by the door. Emmie had noticed Jared scraping change from his wallet to buy them a coffee each, avoiding using a bank card. He was shaping up to be good-looking *and* nice.

'You know,' she said eventually, 'I really thought you didn't like my artwork at first.'

'What?' he said, glancing at her, shoving his wallet away.

'When I first met you, I don't know . . . You seemed like you didn't like my sketch. Maybe because of your allergies. Like, you're not a cat person. Which is fine,' she added quickly. 'But you work at a cat café, so I didn't understand. And now you want to buy my art. I don't get it, I guess. Do you like animals?'

'I do like cats. And I like your art. I was just surprised. It's not every day you catch a girl's drawing out of thin air outside a cat café, is it?'

She snorted. 'I guess not. It was a good catch, though.'

'And it's not every day that girl is *clearly* talented,' he added.

'You can stop trying to make me feel better now,' she said, tempted to playfully bat him with her good hand, but wanting to avoid any unnecessary movement until she got her wrist looked at. 'They'll have to treat me for extreme embarrassment if you carry on.'

Looking amused, he went back to his coffee. They both fell silent again. Emmie focused on the TV opposite them, mounted on the wall and displaying a stream of news headlines that soon switched over to the weather forecast, where they were still promising snow to come.

'Emmie Hartell?' called a nurse who had just emerged from down the corridor.

'I'll wait here,' Jared said, sipping at his coffee and settling back in the plastic seat.

Emmie stood up, nodding, and followed the nurse through to get her wrist examined.

*

It turned out that Emmie had fractured her wrist – when she returned to the waiting room and Jared caught sight of her, she was wearing a splint, her coat placed awkwardly over it. He walked through the exit alongside her, chucking his empty coffee cup in a bin on the way. When they were outside in the cold air, misty breaths coming in clouds, he said, 'How long do you have to wear that?'

'Six to twelve weeks.'

He whistled and shook his head as they crossed the road, heading for the car park. 'That's a lot, for an artist and a barista. Frustrating.'

'It'll be fine,' she said brightly. Her face was already turning pink in the cold and he couldn't help but think how pretty it made her look. 'I'll manage. I can decorate it with stickers or something, brighten it up.'

'Can you still work?' he asked. Sylvie was going to stay with family for a few days before bringing them back to the Lakes for the holidays. Emmie and Faye would be taking the reins until she returned – the staff were going to have a meeting about it, and he'd be looped in via email.

'They said yes, but to pace myself,' she replied. 'Either do a phased return, or adjusted duties, where I gradually increase what I do over time. I might just have to do the admin stuff until the splint is off. Could be fun, though – I love the stuff in the gift shop, so it'll be a change.'

When they reached the van, he grabbed the door for her, and she clambered inside, her arm wedged awkwardly across her lap. He was about to close it again when she looked up at him uncertainly, her eyes rounded.

'Um . . .' She began. 'The seatbelt . . . Could you . . .'

He'd completely forgotten about that. Of course she wouldn't be able to do it herself. Not easily, anyway.

His mouth was robbed of all moisture – he'd have to lean in, close to her, to snap it into place. That . . . would be awkward. Not entirely *bad*, but . . .

He pulled the seatbelt down from its position by her shoulder and leaned into the van, across her. Jared could almost feel her tension and stiffness, the way she was ramrod straight against the seat. Was she holding her breath, like he was? She smelt like perfume – sweet and floral – and as he clipped the belt into place, he caught a fruity, banana-shampoo scent. His arm brushed hers, and he was incredibly conscious of how close he was to her face, risking a glance over to find her staring at him – to see the freckles scattered like cocoa dust across her nose and cheeks. He could see flecks of hazel in her eyes, like the inside of a marble, her long eyelashes—

He drew back immediately, banging his head painfully on the roof as he went. It hurt more than he let on, but he didn't swear and curse until he'd slammed the door shut, rubbing the painful spot as he moved to the driver's side.

When he was around her, the simplest interaction almost unravelled his senses, and that wasn't something he'd been prepared for.

*

Emmie was seated with her auntie, Faye, Clem, their receptionist Kaitlyn, and Sophie and Miles, their cat caretakers. They were sitting in the staffroom; they'd just been briefed on what to do while Sylvie was away, visiting Emmie's grandparents. She'd agreed to help them with some painting and decorating since Emmie's grandfather had recently had cataract surgery. When that was done, she was bringing them back here to celebrate Christmas together. She would be away over the last days that the café would be open, before it shut for Christmas. Emmie and Faye would be taking on a bit more responsibility while she was gone.

They'd decided that Emmie wouldn't do any of the barista and waiting tasks, like making coffee and bringing drinks to customers. Instead, she'd take payments in the gift shop and reception, which she could do, albeit slowly, one-handed, answer phone calls, and do some of the other admin. Kaitlyn would help out with drinks.

'So, you all know what you're doing?' Sylvie asked, leaning forward onto the table with her elbows.

There was a series of nods.

'Emmie and Faye will be in charge of things, so raise any questions with them,' Sylvie reminded them all. 'And Jared's been sent an email explaining all this to him. It'll only be a couple of days, so I'm confident you can all manage until I get back.'

'We'll be just fine, Sylvie,' Faye reassured her. She grinned. 'Don't worry. We won't host any wild parties with the cats while you're gone.'

That drew a round of chuckles from the rest of the team. Sylvie smiled, too, and rose to her feet. 'Great. And make sure you leave some food out for that stray. The shelter got back to me – no cats matching his description have been reported missing. They say they'll come out to see if he's microchipped when they can.'

The team murmured their agreements.

'Thanks, all of you, for coming in. Oh, and one more thing, before I leave this afternoon, I'm getting a tourist settled into one of the flats above the café,' Sylvie explained. 'She knows I'll be away for a bit, but I've assured her that she can come to you, Emmie and Faye, if she needs anything.'

'How long is she staying?' Emmie asked. Sylvie often rented that flat out to tourists for short stays. There was back-door access to both that flat and Emmie's, and the flats were separated from the café floors via another locked door.

'She'll be here over the Christmas period. The dates are in the staffroom,' said Sylvie. 'I don't think she'll need much attention as she'll be out, or working, most of the time – she works remotely. It's just in case she needs anything.' When everyone nodded, she clapped her hands together. 'Okay, great stuff. I need to get off.'

They all filtered out of the staffroom. Sylvie hugged Emmie briefly when only Faye lingered in the doorway, and Emmie caught the scent of the coffee she'd been chugging during the meeting.

'Are you sure you'll be okay, Emmie?' said Sylvie, drawing back and giving her a toothy smile.

'Of course! Don't look so worried, Sylvie. I know I'm all . . . splinted up, but I'll handle it. I can't wait for Gran and Grandad to see this place.'

'I have complete faith in you,' said Sylvie. 'It's your inability to take breaks that worries me! Remember to rest, love.'

Emmie smiled. 'Thanks. I will.'

She gave Emmie another quick hug, and followed the others out the door.

★

Sylvie left to see to the new tenant before driving to Manchester, and Emmie and Faye got cracking on working their final shifts at the café before Christmas.

They got a range of customers at Catpurrcino: tourists, people who had found them on social media, locals who worked in the area and came in regularly, elderly couples, young couples, students. They had a limit on how many customers they admitted at one time – so the cats didn't become overwhelmed. And there wouldn't ever be toddlers charging round to deal with; the café only admitted children over the age of eleven. It was always, strictly, to be kept as calming an environment as possible.

Emmie took over reception duty for the coming days in the cloakroom-style entrance to the building, which also housed their gift shop. The entrance was the only place that had been decorated with a full-on Christmas tree with all the silvery and white trimmings, standing proudly in the window by the front door, lights ablaze in the dull, grey day. Clem popped in on her last day at work before the holidays to buy a dainty rose-gold cat necklace on a delicate chain.

Emmie so rarely got the chance to talk to Clem, since Clem was always baking away in the kitchen. They'd all gone out for a group meal when Emmie arrived at Catpurrcino – Sylvie's way of introducing Emmie to everyone and helping her get settled in – but Clem hadn't

87

been there. Emmie thought they'd get along well, though, since they both had a creative streak. Her baked goods sometimes reminded Emmie of the sweet styles of illustration she loved so much.

'Is it for anyone special?' Emmie asked kindly, taking the necklace from Clem over the counter.

Clem's cheeks flushed, and she tucked a strand of black hair behind her ear. 'For my mum, for Christmas.'

'I'm sure she'll love it – I've always thought these are so dainty and pretty.' Emmie proceeded to place the necklace in a small black box for her. 'Do you have any nice Christmas plans?'

'Just dinner at home, and some family visiting.'

Once Clem had paid with her card, Emmie smiled at her. 'You know, I've been thinking of doing some cat illustrations inspired by the things you make in the kitchen. Doughnut cats and cupcakes like yours.'

Clem's eyes widened, her cheeks turning a more vibrant shade of red. 'Really?'

'Really! You're so talented. Would it be okay, if I did that?'

'Of course! You don't have to ask.'

'Great. I'll have to show you them, when I get around to it. Have a nice Christmas, Clem.'

Clem beamed at her. 'You too.'

On Emmie's last shift before the café closed – the day before Christmas Eve – Jared dinged the intercom. Emmie was on her break in the main café room, finishing off a coffee and sandwich Faye had made her, the process of trying to eat with one hand messier than she'd expected it to be. Faye had already taken a tray up to some customers on the café's second floor, so she figured she'd go and answer it herself.

When she got there, she pulled the back door open with her good hand. A gust of cold air met her, winding around her neck and making her shiver. It was drizzling out – and blowing a gale – with her wrist the way it was, she couldn't even cross her arms over her chest to block it out. She settled for clutching her bad arm with her good one, and waved her good fingers at Jared.

Jared was standing at the kerb, and waved back. His appearance made her stomach flip over; he'd been wearing his Catpurrcino T-shirt when he accompanied her to the winter fair, but he was dressed more casually today, in his woollen coat with a grey T-shirt underneath, and loose-fitting jeans. His shoulder-length hair was streaming in the wind, whipping about his ears. Why did he have to look like he'd stepped right out of a fashion Instagram page for nomadic wanderers?

He glanced down at her arms, and for a split second she wondered why he was staring at her splint.

'The orders?' he called.

'Oh!' she burst out. Faye must have left them on the counter and she'd – perhaps in her eagerness to see Jared – forgotten them. 'One moment.'

'Maybe Faye should get it . . .' he began.

'No, it's okay. I can do it!'

Emmie hastened through to the café, banging her way through the door – awkwardly, since she was one-handed – to see an older man hovering near the counter uncertainly, by the cake displays.

'Love,' he said, gesturing over the counter. 'Are some of these vegan?'

'Yes, there's a list of today's vegan cake right there.' She pointed at the cards set out to the right, smiling brightly.

Faye wasn't here. 'I'll be with you in a second,' she called, snatching up Jared's delivery order – two bags, which she grasped between her fingers – and hurrying out back, hoping the man wouldn't think she was rude for leaving.

When she burst out of the back door again, slightly awkwardly since she was holding a bag and struggling with her splint, Jared was still standing on the kerb, waiting. She made to hand him the bags, and one of them slipped out of her grasp, crashing to the ground, the bag bursting open, coffee and slices of cake splattering the pavement with cream and liquid.

'Oh!' Emmie cried, clutching the remaining bag more tightly, not that it would make much difference now. Her lip quirked. What a *day*, running around one-armed and then splattering the pavement with cake cream. It was like a scene ripped out of a funny graphic novel. 'Shit. Sorry.'

'It's okay,' he said, and he was clearly trying not to laugh too.

A wave of amusement rolled over her, too, and then they were both laughing. She lifted up her foot, where the front of her shoes had been flecked with a cream-and-coffee mix, and glanced at her splint. 'This better be my superhero origin story or it's not even worth it.'

He looked bemused, but his smile was still in place. 'What?'

'You know, she hurt her wrist, got cake all over herself . . . and then got superhuman powers involving cake, or something.'

'You're so weird,' he said, but it sounded like a compliment.

'Thank you.' She took a half-bow. 'I can ask Faye to redo that. Just give me five minutes.'

There was a slight flush to Jared's cheeks – either from the cold or his laughter – giving them a pinkish hue that made him look even more gorgeous, as if he'd spent time in the sun. 'I did arrive early, so there's no rush. I'll wait in the van.' He jerked his thumb over his shoulder. 'Bring it out when you're ready, Cakewoman. Take your time.' He flashed her a faint, encouraging smile, and her heart did a somersault in her chest.

'Cakewoman? Original.'

When he turned his back, she made her way back inside, not sure if the pounding in her chest was because of his smile, and how silly she felt around him, or something else.

Faye was behind the counter now, plating up some cake. The older man had gone to sit down, and Baron had just swanned over and dropped a toy mouse at the man's feet, demanding play.

'We just need to redo an order for Jared,' Emmie explained. 'Sorry. I dropped the bag all over the pavement. Wasted one of the cakes Clem made before she left . . .'

'No, I'm sorry, Em,' said Faye, giving her an apologetic look as she added a napkin to a tray and set the cake on top. 'I *really* had to go to the bathroom. I'll get on it.'

'It's okay, really.'

Emmie hesitated, an idea striking. She would add the money to the till for it later, from her own pocket, but she wanted to say thank you to Jared properly, not just for taking her to A&E but for being patient with her now. She grabbed one of the cat doughnuts – her favourite one, covered in brown and white icing, with ears poking up, two iced blobs for eyes, a curving mouth and whiskers either side. Shoving it into another brown paper bag

– with some help from Faye – she made her way out to the back with the fixed order and the doughnut. They had plenty, since Clem had made a big batch of almost everything before she left for Christmas.

Jared was sitting in his van, as promised, eyes down as he studied his phone, his hair a curtain of golden-brown around his eyes. She crossed the car park, moving carefully over the frost-covered gravel – she certainly didn't need to break or fracture a leg on top of her wrist – and tapped on his window with her nails. He wound down the pane. The radio was playing a folksy rock song that poured from the speakers, and she had the ridiculous thought that he'd look right at home in an indie folk band like Iron & Wine himself. She had a ridiculous urge to draw him like that.

'Here you go,' she said, handing him the order and the second bag – carefully – which he took and placed on the seat beside him.

'There're two bags?' he pointed out.

'The second one is for you.'

'For me? I didn't order anything.'

'No, ah . . .' She fumbled over her words, feeling stupidly nervous now. 'I put something in there for you. You know, to say thanks for the other day. For taking me to the hospital.'

'You didn't have to do that,' he said, but his eyes were gleaming with something like joy. It lit up his entire face, creasing the light stubble around his mouth, and her heart fluttered in her chest. 'Thanks.'

'No problem.'

There was an awkward silence, and the song in the van shifted to the latest news headlines. *Now, the weather. Yellow warnings for wind are still in place in some areas throughout the night, with the possibility of some snow moving across parts of the country into the early hours of tomorrow.*

'I hope that doesn't affect Sylvie's journey,' said Emmie. 'Hopefully it's all blown over before she comes back.'

She was thinking about the stray too – the skinny black cat. Could the shelter come and collect it to be scanned for a microchip before the snow hit? She hoped so. She hated to think of the thin little guy out there in the snow with nowhere to keep warm and cosy. He could freeze to death. She doubted she'd be able to coax him into the café; he'd been so wary of her before. But then, the other cats might not take to him, and she hadn't seen him since anyway. Sylvie had said the food she'd been leaving had been disappearing steadily – but they couldn't prove that was the doing of the stray, or if it was some other creature.

'Will you be okay, with your aunt being away?' Jared asked her. 'She sent me an email about everything – and you being in charge.' His brown eyes were full of concern; the same concern she'd seen when she'd been failing to sell her illustrations at the market. Her heart skittered and stalled in her ribcage.

'It's fine, Faye'll be helping me too. There's a tourist staying in the other flat upstairs from today, but she should have everything she needs in her room,' said Emmie. 'I'd better get back,' she added. 'No rest for Cakewoman. Enjoy your doughnut. And Merry Christmas!'

She picked her way carefully back towards the café, trying to still the thrumming of her heart, which was raging a fierce beat in her chest.

*

When she returned to the café, customers were sipping at their froth-topped drinks and stroking the cats who weaved between their legs, and Faye was setting out a fresh batch of cat doughnuts and star-shaped cookies. A young couple left their table and said goodbye, waving enthusiastically as they left through the latched gate, heading back out into the reception area and gift shop. Emmie still had ten minutes left of her lunch break, so she hovered around the counter, chatting to Faye. A few moments later, a woman pushed her way into the café and through the latched gate.

The newcomer was beautiful, with long dark hair arranged in movie-star waves. Her eyes were a greenish grey, emphasised by smoky black eye pencil and thick mascara. She wore a long camel-coloured coat over a white jumper, with a cashmere scarf around her neck, and made a beeline for the counter.

'Hello!' she said, sounding out of breath. Her lips were tinted with red stain, and up close, her make-up was even more immaculate – she must have skills to rival a make-up artist on a film set, because she looked positively airbrushed. Maybe she was a beautician. 'I've paid for half an hour,' she explained.

'Great. What can I get you?' Faye asked, gesturing to the chalkboard menu on the wall to her right. 'I'm sure Kaitlyn on reception explained, but drinks are free and unlimited. You only need to pay extra if you want food.'

'Yes, she told me,' she said, glancing over at the menu and adjusting the tan handbag that was hooked over her arm. 'I'm Megan. I'm actually staying in the flat upstairs, but I wanted to check out the café as well before it closed for Christmas!'

'Oh! You're the one who's staying!' Emmie said, beaming at her. 'Sylvie mentioned you. Nice to meet you. I'm her niece, Emmie – I live in the other flat.'

'Let us know if you need anything while you're here,' Faye added. 'Sylvie said to look after you.'

'Thanks,' Megan answered. 'I will.'

'I *love* your nails,' said Faye, who must have noticed Megan's French manicure – which was decorated with swirly pastel designs and tiny flowers.

'Thanks.' Megan grinned, turning to look at the cat-shaped baked goods and cookies on display. 'There's so much to choose from! I love cats, so I just had to stay here while I'm in the Lakes! I got a ragdoll about six months ago.'

'Oh, ragdolls are beautiful, we have one here. Duchess,' said Emmie. She hadn't had a cat since she lived with her parents during university. She was sure Sylvie wouldn't mind if she got one, but she'd wait until she was more settled; she wasn't sure how long she was staying here, in any case.

'That's a beautiful name for a ragdoll! My girl's called Sassy.' Megan smiled and spent a moment tapping her nails against the handle of her bag and *hmm*ing. 'I'll take a flat white – and one of the cat doughnuts, please,' she finally decided. 'The strawberry one.'

'Good choice,' said Faye. 'I'll bring it to your table if you let me know the number.'

Megan nodded, glancing over her shoulder. 'I'll sit there. Table two.' She headed off to the table, where Thomas was sitting on one of the chairs, paws stretching over the edge. When Faye was done with the flat white, she brought it, along with the doughnut, across to

Megan's table, carefully dodging around Eric – who was wandering over to a feeder with his tail high in the air. She set everything down in front of Megan.

'There we go,' she said.

'Wow!' Megan said. Faye had dusted some cocoa powder on top of the flat white, creating a waving cat paw. 'That's so adorable! And even your *napkins* have cats on them. So cute.'

'Of course,' said Emmie, laughing at the look of delight on her face.

'My latte art isn't as good as Emmie's,' Faye told Megan, 'but she's out of action.'

'Oh.' Megan shot Emmie a sympathetic look when she noticed the splint. 'What happened?'

'Ah, you know, the dangers of falling over and slamming your hand into the floor to catch yourself.'

Megan pulled a face. 'Ouch.'

'I'm just upstairs from your flat while you're here, so you can give me a knock if you need anything while you're staying,' she told Megan. 'I've picked up on a few of the best tourist spots since I've been working here.'

'That'd be great.' Megan smiled at her, then shook her head and laughed, as Faye returned to the counter, where another customer was studying the menu. 'I'm not really here as a tourist, I guess . . .' added Megan.

'Oh,' said Emmie. 'Do you have family here?' This was the final day that the café was open, and Christmas Eve was tomorrow – it had come around so quickly. She'd assumed Megan was here to see family for the holiday season.

'Not exactly. You'll probably think it's ridiculous, but . . . I'm here because of my ex-boyfriend. I made some stupid mistakes, and . . .' Megan sucked in a breath. Her shoulders sank towards her coffee cup and, since she'd removed her coat, she looked small and frail, her thin hands clasping the handle of the mug. 'I just hope he can forgive me.'

Emmie's heart warmed. That was probably the sweetest thing she'd heard from a customer – and she'd heard some of the elderly say some pretty adorable things on her shifts. Just the other day, an old man had held the latched gate open for his partner and said, 'After you, beautiful.'

'I'm sure he'll come around,' Emmie said, as Thomas hopped up beside Megan, prompting her to tickle his chin and croon sweetly.

'I really hope so,' said Megan. 'Maybe it's the right time of year for forgiveness?'

Emmie nodded, but her only thought was of her brother, and how she'd just cut him out of her life completely. She wondered if she'd done the right thing after all.

Chapter 6

The next day, on Christmas Eve, snow had begun to fall, coating the landscape in thick layers of white, making the hills look like buns dusted with icing. It looked like Emmie would get her white Christmas after all. The temperature had dropped significantly, making Oakside feel like part of the Arctic rather than Cumbria, the chill as sharp as teeth biting against skin. Jared was about to leave for the café – bundled in as many layers as he could manage – and had just locked up his flat, when his phone buzzed in his pocket. He tugged it out. The screen flashed with the word *MUM*. He still had plenty of time to get to the café – he'd decided to leave early since it was snowing – so he picked up.

'Hi, Mum,' he said, lingering in the quiet, narrow hallway outside the flat, watching the soft snowfall through the window at the far end.

'Hi, love,' she answered.

'You okay?'

'I'm fine, it's just . . . Have you seen the weather this morning? The forecast?'

'No . . . ?' The truth was, he'd tried to rise fairly early this morning to get some life admin done, and had struggled with that heavy, overbearing feeling he sometimes got when his phone alarm buzzed him awake. As if he were swimming in treacle and couldn't surface to face the day, his motivation lost somewhere he couldn't reach. So, he'd spent another few hours in bed, only rising when absolutely necessary to get ready for work.

'They've been talking about Storm Marie,' she told him. 'They named it this morning. It's going to last for days, they're saying. I was worried – you know they only do that when it's serious, don't they? And it's Christmas Day tomorrow! What a time for it . . .'

'When's it hitting us?' he asked.

'The worst will be tomorrow! There's a yellow warning. Have a look. Are you working?'

'Just going to drop something off now, but it's my last drop-off before the new year.'

'Good. Maybe you should come here tonight, stay over. You might not be able to get here for dinner tomorrow. Your brother's coming with Danni before it gets any worse.'

'Probably a good idea. Thanks, Mum. Do you need anything? I can swing by the supermarket?'

'No, love. Just get yourself here safely.'

'Are you sure?'

'I'm alright, son. I had a delivery and stocked up on things last week.' She chuckled. 'Just make sure you get here! I can't cook a dinner without you – you know I'm useless at a turkey.'

'I'll be there. See you in a bit.'

'Okay, love. You take care.'

He swiped to end the call and left the building, de-icing the work van thoroughly and clambering inside the freezing-cold interior, flicking the heat on full blast. He made sure he drove slowly – and carefully – as he pulled the van away from the parking space. Flakes were

99

dappling his windscreen with wet flecks, the wipers moving swiftly to clear them.

He navigated the winding, topsy-turvy roads of the Lakes; he'd been driving since he was eighteen, but he didn't especially like doing so in these conditions, if he could help it. There were no home or business deliveries to do today, at least, with it being Christmas Eve, but he needed to drop off a load of cat litter he'd picked up yesterday before closing time – then he could go to his mum's and spend the holidays there, hunkered down. The tall trees lining the roadside were already collecting lines of solid white along their branches, some of the lakes glistening coldly, like polished glass.

It was only four, but already the roads were darkening on his way into Oakside, the hills around him falling into shadow. He was hunched forward over the wheel, listening to the wind whistling across the landscape like a yowling toddler.

As he accelerated up the hill leading to the café, he thought he felt a vibration run through the van – had he scraped over something on the road? A pothole, or some loose stones? Or was the van just struggling with the hill because of the cold weather? He'd have to tell Emmie at the café, and get it checked out.

Rounding the corner to the cat café, he saw the telltale triangular lamp posts standing sentinel nearby, lit up in hazy yellow, snowflakes falling softly around them. He made his way up the wide stretch of road in front of the building, made to pull into the car park – and skidded.

Ice? He cursed. Crying out, surprised by the sudden shift in the vehicle, he tried to correct the motion, and heard roaring vibrations and a strange collection of sputtering, bumping and clunking noises somewhere inside the van. The wheels *thunk*ed onto the kerb and he was jostled in his seat as he brought the van to a screeching halt, diagonally and across the entrance to the car park.

He stayed where he was, sucking in a sharp breath and breathing heavily, adrenaline rushing through him. He'd blocked the way into the car park, but it was empty anyway, save for a blanket of untouched snow.

'What the hell?' he grumbled. Something was obviously wrong with the van.

He zipped up his coat, stuffed on his beanie and gloves, and climbed out into the frigid air, circling the van to assess the damage. The wheel near the kerb looked . . . wrong. It was sticking out at a strange angle, like it hadn't been attached properly in the first place. Oily grease was spilling onto the snowy road like chip fat. That wasn't good. Even if he could start the vehicle back up, driving around with it like this in the snow would be nothing short of stupid. And he couldn't exactly walk back to Ambleside to his flat to pick up his own car, either – that would take *many* hours and would be incredibly stupid with a severe weather warning in place.

He crossed the car park to knock on the back doors of Catpurrcino. He'd drop off the litter delivery first, then see about getting someone out to fix the van.

Emmie opened the door to him, as usual. Somehow, seeing her lifted his spirits: she was dressed in a bright yellow turtleneck jumper, and there were two golden hairclips shaped like cat faces holding sections of her hair back from her face. There was a cat-shaped sticker on her splint.

'Hi! Come bring the litter into the storeroom,' she said. 'Thanks so much.'

'I actually have a problem.'

'A problem? Are you okay? I almost told you not to come out, because of the weather . . .' She tilted her head, and something surged inside him – why did she look so cute when she did that, and when she was concerned for him, too? Her nose had scrunched up like crinkled paper and it was adorable.

'The van . . .' He scratched his head, making his beanie shift around on his scalp. 'There's something wrong with it. I skidded on some ice, bumped the kerb – but it's been making weird noises anyway. I'll let Sylvie know, text her, but I'm going to see if someone can come out and sort it.'

'That doesn't sound good,' she said. Puffs of white air were billowing from her mouth in the cold. She rubbed one of her arms vigorously. 'Do you want to wait inside? In the staffroom where your allergies won't bother you?'

How could he reveal that he'd lied about being allergic to the animals *now*? What would she think of him then? He never normally lied, and now he'd got himself all tangled up in his own mess. And . . . he liked her. The more time he spent with her, the guiltier he felt, especially when she was struggling to work while her wrist was wrapped in a splint and he could be coming inside more often and actually helping. He felt like a royal ass.

'I'll bring the litter into the storeroom,' Jared said. 'I'll see about getting a breakdown service out, and I'll stay in the van in case they can come out.'

'Do you think anyone will be able to come out, in this weather?' Emmie continued, glancing around the deserted car park.

Good question. With the snowfall and the quiet that had fallen over the surrounding trees and hills, they could be the only two people in the world. The cat café was situated partway up a hill, and there wasn't much else here, except a row of office buildings on the other side of the road, mostly concealed by trees. Most of the other shops and restaurants were at the bottom of the hill; yet still, people walked up here just to visit the café.

'I can only give it a try,' he said.

'Okay,' she replied, and glanced around the car park again.

'Are you okay? Have you heard from Sylvie – wasn't she coming back today?'

'Oh, yes . . . It's just . . .' She shook her head. 'We've been texting all day and it's too dangerous, really, for them all to drive back with the warnings in place and the snow. So she'll stay with my grandparents in Manchester until the storm's over.'

Jared frowned. 'The storm could last days though. Where does that leave you? I mean, what will you do about Christmas?'

'Oh. I'll be fine,' she said, although her tone said otherwise – she sounded crestfallen and he didn't blame her. 'We'd all planned to have dinner here together, but if it's safer for them to stay put, then that's what we'll have to do. The cats can keep me company!'

Her smile seemed somewhat strained. He had the wild, reckless idea to invite her to his mum's if he could get the van sorted. It was on the tip of his tongue.

'Is there anyone else here with you? Other family?'

'Nope, just me, and the tenant upstairs. Sophie and Miles went home ages ago to hunker down. Let me know if you need anything. I'll put some coffee on for you, just in case you're stuck here for a bit.'

He was stunned by how generous she was being, and how she was taking the possibility of spending Christmas alone in her stride. With losing Poppy, he hadn't been able to face the prospect of being alone in his flat and had planned to spend a few days at his mum's. He wondered if the tenant had plans for the season – probably visiting family.

'Thanks, Em.' The nickname had slipped out. God, why had he *said* that? They were barely friends and he was giving her affectionate nicknames? Had swerving the van jostled his brain around too, scattering all the pieces like tossed dominoes, until he was incoherent? 'Shit, I mean . . . Emmie. I don't know if you like it shortened . . . Sorry.'

'You can call me Em,' she said, her voice rising in pitch, as if she was happy with his choice. 'Most of my friends do!'

Jared nodded, turning back to the van, still feeling as though parts of his brain were in the wrong place. And feeling awful that she was spending Christmas by herself. Maybe he should invite her to his mum's after all. He'd see about the van first, then suggest it.

*

'What do you mean, no one can come out today?' Jared said, exasperated. He had the heat blasting in the van, but he still felt freezing, and was rubbing his hands together as he talked to the breakdown service he was subscribed to, phone nestled between his ear and shoulder. 'If it's a broken axle, like you said, I can't even change the tyre, right?' He'd spent the last few hours first on hold, then explaining the situation and doing a variety of checks to try to establish the issue, and finally, learning that no, they couldn't get anyone out to help.

He glanced up. Emmie had emerged from the doors at the back of the café with a coat wrapped around her, and thick gloves and woollen boots. He could just see the splint poking out beneath her gloves. A pink bobble hat was yanked over her ears. She weaved her way around the front of the building, holding a box of cat biscuits, which she was shaking vigorously as she walked with her good hand. What was she doing, out in the snow? Looking for the stray she'd mentioned before? She rounded the side of the building, where he couldn't see her.

'That's right,' said the woman on the other end of the line. 'I know it's frustrating. But we've checked, and there's no one available in the vicinity this evening – not even from our Christmas Reindeer Rescue Service. This sometimes happens with smaller, more remote areas, and I imagine the weather has hindered things. I can have someone call you back tomorrow with an update, but there're no guarantees we can get anyone with it being Christmas Day then. We can sort a taxi for you to get home in the meantime, or to somewhere nearby where you could stay, until we're able to come out to the van.'

Jared pressed his fingers to his forehead, working to control his frustration. It wasn't her fault; this was just a shitty situation. He nearly laughed, insanely, at the idea of a reindeer rescue service pulling up with a magical sleigh to rescue him – but of course that was just the name of their emergency Christmas cover. 'No, it's okay, I can sort all that out myself. But you'll phone me in the morning?'

'Yes, we'll have staff on for emergencies so we can call you, but I'm not sure when we'll be able to get to your van, what with Storm Marie expected too. We'll keep you updated though. Call back if you decide you need help arranging a local taxi, okay?'

'Sure. Thanks for the help.'

Jared jabbed his finger onto the red button to end the call. He called the local taxi service at once, glancing around again for Emmie, but she hadn't returned.

There was an automated message to greet him on the end of the line. *Services are currently suspended due to Storm Marie. We apologise for the inconvenience.*

He let out a breathy laugh of disbelief. No way.

He tried some other taxi firms, including one in Ambleside and another in Grasmere. They all saw him listening to the tell-tale *beep-beep* noise meaning the company was already engaged on the phone. Or they were suspended, like the service here in Oakside. Even if he called the woman from the breakdown service, they'd only encounter the same issue with the local taxis, wouldn't they? All they could do was phone on his behalf. They couldn't force them to send out drivers.

What was he going to do now? Even the Uber app got stuck in the *searching for a driver* stage, implying there was nobody around – or there was too much demand – and eventually, he cancelled the request. He thought longingly of his own car, all the way back home in Ambleside – completely out of reach.

Finally, he called his brother.

'Not the best time, big bro,' said Shane a few minutes later. Jared could hear Danni saying something in the background.

'What's up? Are you at Mum's yet?'

'We just got here. Danni asked if we could nip out to the supermarket quickly – Mum always forgets she can't have regular milk – but now the car won't start.'

'You're *kidding*.'

'Nope. Probably a battery problem with the cold temperatures. Why, where are you?'

'I was hoping you could give me a lift . . .' He quickly explained what had happened, and where he was, and his brother let out a low whistle.

'Well, I don't think you'll be getting a lift from me anytime soon,' said Shane. 'Who knows when this car'll start, and the storm's meant to get worse. Can you hunker down at work? Is anyone there?'

'Uh . . .' Jared hesitated.

'What?'

'Emmie's inside – you know, Sylvie's niece.'

'*Ah.*' There was something suggestive in Shane's tone – and Jared could swear he heard a smirk in his brother's voice. 'Well,' he continued, 'that's not so bad. She lives there now, doesn't she? I'm sure she wouldn't mind letting you in for a bit.'

'It'll be longer than *a bit*. I can't get hold of a taxi, a breakdown service . . . Nothing,' he explained. 'And my car's at home. Mum'll be disappointed.'

'She'll understand. I'll tell her what happened. I'm sure she'd rather you holed up somewhere and didn't get smacked in the windshield by a tree, or something.'

They said their goodbyes, Jared firing off a quick text to his mum to apologise anyway. He was debating what his next move would be when Emmie appeared again, bright as a tiny sun in her jumper and coat. She shook the pink treat box in his direction with her good hand.

He left the van, hunching his back in the cold as he made his way towards her through the sheet of white. The snow was falling faster now, the wind howling around the roof-tops further down the hill, his boots crunching beneath him. The layers of snow in the car park and beyond were building. It felt like it had got significantly colder.

'It's freezing out here. You should go inside!' he told her.

'I was looking for the stray!' The tip of her nose had turned luminous red, the colour spreading over her freck-led cheeks. Her eyes were sheened with tears and she was gripping the box of treats so tightly the cardboard was dented. 'I called the shelter and they weren't able to find him before the snow started, and . . .' She trailed off, looking around, as if expecting to see him.

His heart twisted at her kindness, her care. She looked so genuinely devastated that she hadn't been able to find the stray. He almost wanted to go trekking off into the distant snow just to find it for her.

'You did your best,' he told her. 'I'm sure he'll have found somewhere to shelter until the weather gets better. What did he look like?'

'Black, with a white mark like a beard on his chest.'

'Well, we can keep an eye out. If he's a stray and used to being outside, he'll be smart enough to take shelter. Maybe someone else took him in, or he's hiding in a shed some-where.'

She nodded slowly, but she was biting her lip, still scanning the area for any sign of the cat. 'You should come inside too. You can sit in the staffroom. It's far too cold and it'll be dark soon.'

*

Emmie was acutely aware of her proximity to Jared in the narrow corridor leading through past the kitchen. Her heart sank when she thought about that stray cat. She hadn't been able to find him. Hopefully Jared was right and he'd found somewhere safe and warm to shelter.

'This way,' said Emmie, leading Jared towards the staffroom and beckoning with her non-splinted hand. 'Do you want a coffee? There's some in the pot now.'

'Coffee would be good,' he said, following her into the staffroom and over to the little kitchenette. 'Here, I'll do it.' He reached into the cupboard for a spare mug, pouring himself some coffee, and she was grateful not to have to struggle with her splint again.

'The milk's over there in the fridge,' she told him.

Jared wandered over, adding a dash of milk and grabbing some sugar cubes from a cat-shaped pot on the countertop.

'Did you have any luck with the van?' she asked him, pouring herself a coffee, too, clunkily, since she was doing it one-handed.

He shook his head. 'No luck. And my car's back in Ambleside, outside my flat.'

'I'd have offered to drive you home myself, but I don't have a car. What happened to the van?'

'Broken axle, most likely – it's what rotates the wheels. No one can come out. They said it could be tomorrow – or not, because of the storm and Christmas. They offered to get me a taxi. That didn't work out, either.'

'I imagine everyone's trying to get back from somewhere all at once, before the worst of the weather hits – and before Christmas Day in the morning . . .' Emmie said, taking the milk from him when he offered it to her, pouring some into her mug. 'I was watching the news upstairs. They've upgraded the weather warnings to red now – danger to life.'

'Already? That was fast.'

'I know. They're telling people to avoid travel. Could be the worst storm in a decade. I wouldn't be surprised if most taxis aren't running.'

Jared sighed, taking a sip of his coffee.

Emmie sat down at one of the nearby tables, cradling her coffee in one hand. He couldn't get home; that much was clear. He couldn't drive his van, or get a taxi. There wasn't anything else for it – he had to stay here. Even if the thought made her insides squirm, and her hands feel clammy. She was acutely aware that she hadn't spent the night under the same roof as a man – her brother didn't count – for several years. At the same time, there was a bright feeling underscoring all of that, that she didn't have to spend Christmas on her own.

'You can stay here,' she said. 'I'm sure Sylvie wouldn't mind. Let me shoot her a message.' She slid her phone towards her from where she'd left it on the table, and tapped out a message to her aunt. At least sending messages wasn't too difficult with the splint.

'Thanks,' he said.

When she set the phone aside again and looked up, Jared was studying the photos of the various cats on the walls. How were they going to handle his allergies, if he had to spend the night? And what was Christmas Day going to be like? One unlike any other, that was for sure.

'I know the allergies are a concern,' Emmie said, thinking aloud, 'but there are places the cats don't really go, like here in the staffroom, and the storeroom. Only, there's no bed down here. I can scrounge up some blankets and pillows to make somewhere for you to sleep, and I'm sure we have antihistamines, just in case. Or I have a sofa in my flat—'

She stopped abruptly, wondering if she should have mentioned her flat, her insides coiling at the very thought of him joining her up there. *Stupid, stupid,* she scolded herself, wishing she could retract the invitation. Jared was shaking his head, his eyes on the ceiling.

'Emmie,' he said, setting his mug down on the table.

'What?' she said, her heart hammering at the base of her throat. 'Is the allergy worse than I thought?' Maybe the allergy was life-threatening if he came into contact with a cat? She knew someone with a serious allergy whose throat could close up if they made contact with the allergen – maybe he could die if he inhaled a cat hair? Was that even possible? 'I can give wherever you sleep a once-over with disinfectant to be safe,' she offered. 'I'll clean the whole room, maybe hoover as well, and—'

'Please, stop. You don't have to do any of that.' He heaved a great sigh and avoided looking at her. 'I'm not allergic to cats.'

'You . . . what?'

'I'm not allergic.' He was looking anywhere but at her, his attention now on the pink, paw-shaped magnets stuck to the fridge, arranged in a heart shape. He tapped his fingernails on the side of his mug and gave a hollow, bark of a laugh. 'I know I told Sylvie I was, but I'm not.'

'Why would you . . .' Emmie laughed, then when she realised he was serious, she felt heat rising up the back of her neck. She'd been sitting here, fussing, wondering about how she'd cater to his needs if he had an allergy, and he'd been lying all along? 'Why would you lie about something like that?' she said, sitting ramrod straight in her chair. 'Sylvie's been so accommodating, and—'

'I know,' he said quietly. 'I'm sorry.'

'Then why?'

'I didn't . . .' He finally looked her in the eye, and she almost softened at the sadness in his face. Almost. 'I didn't mean for anyone to find out. And I didn't want to deceive anyone, really.'

What kind of an excuse was that? Her face was blisteringly hot. She was thinking of Dustin, how she sometimes didn't know whether he twisted situations intentionally, whether it was just who he was at his core, or if it was the gambling, the alcohol, the state he'd been in.

She felt so stupid, and let down. Then again, she hardly knew Jared, did she?

'But . . . why did you lie about that?'

'It's . . . It sounds silly.'

'Try me?'

'I . . .' He trailed off.

'Well, you really should tell Sylvie the truth at least,' Emmie said. Why was he dodging the question? If it was really so silly, why not just say? 'She'll find out if you're staying here anyway, but it's better if it comes from you. I'll go fetch some blankets and pillows. You can sleep where you like if you aren't allergic – in here, or in the Cat Lounge.'

'Emmie—'

She didn't let him finish – she was feeling far too prickly to deal with this right now. 'I have things to sort out.'

★

She'd brought down some blankets and pillows, enough to make a reasonably comfortable bed, and Jared had arranged them against the wall in the staffroom without a word. Equal parts hurt and frustrated with him, Emmie had moved off into the Cat Lounge with some of the cats, watching the snow flurry down through the windows – Binx was attempting to catch it with his paws and hitting the glass instead. Emmie found it hard not to think about the poor, skinny animal out there somewhere in the freezing cold, lost and alone if it hadn't found somewhere to stay.

She'd decided she would only talk to Jared if absolutely necessary. Knowing he'd lied, but hadn't yet told her aunt, made her feel awkward – like she was in on the secret – and she hadn't asked for that. There was enough space here – two café floors, her flat, the staffroom and storeroom – that she could keep a wide berth from him. She couldn't shake the sense that she truly didn't know him after all, no matter how kind and considerate he'd been. People could act like that, and then show another, meaner side of themselves later, just like her brother did.

She wandered around the café, topping up the cat feeders and water dispensers – Baron immediately ran, skidding along the floors with his claws, when she poured fresh water inside, vanishing into a cat flap, and she smiled faintly. He hated the possibility of being splashed.

Finally, she went into a small room on the second floor, which was locked and accessible only to staff and the cats via a built-in cat flap. The walls were plain, a pale cream shade, but Sylvie had stuck giant stickers all over the place – paw prints, colourful humming-birds, and giant cherry trees. There were shelves and cat beds nailed to all of the walls, and a frosted-glass window with a seat beneath it. Emmie cleaned out the litter trays lined up against the far wall and sprinkled in some freshening powder. Everything took longer than usual because she was doing it all one-handed.

Salem was in here, and he came across to her to investigate what she was doing as she scrunched up the top of the litter bag – she couldn't tie it anymore, so scrunching was the best she could do. But he moved glacially, and even when he clambered into the tray, he seemed lethargic, slowed down. That was unusual – he normally hopped inside, lithe and bouncy as a lamb. Sylvie had warned her that lethargy in cats was a sign that something was wrong.

'What's the matter, little guy?' said Emmie. She watched him rooting around in the tray. She'd have to keep an eye on his eating habits; she hadn't seen him use any of the feeders today, either.

When he was done in the tray, she scooped him into her arms, being careful of her splint, and brought him downstairs to the Cat Lounge, depositing him on the rug, where she could keep an eye on him. Salem lumbered over to the water dispenser and took a long drink, then lowered himself down onto his front paws on the rug, settling into the fuzzy surface. His movements were slow. He stared at the cat feeder nearby, but didn't make any move to eat.

Emmie frowned. The food was a flavour he usually scoffed down with vigour. Maybe he just had a hairball that needed to be coughed up? That must be it. He was a sweet, shy little thing, but he'd taken to curling in her lap sometimes when she lingered in the Cat Lounge in the evenings. She'd even let him sleep on her bed a few times, curled near her feet. She was only hoping he'd be back to his usual self tomorrow.

Taking her eyes off the cat, she scrolled through the news on her phone. The internet was awash with alerts and warnings about the storm.

'We'd better prepare, eh, Salem?' she said, rising to her feet. 'I'm sure Aunt Sylvie has some candles in case there's a power cut later.'

She wandered around the café and dug out everything they might need in the event of a power cut: hot water bottles, flasks, warm socks and clothes, blankets, mittens, hats. Kitty sat watching her in fascination in the main room, until she grew bored and began to wash her paws. They'd make do with what Emmie could find, and she could use some of the spare items and clothes from lost property if she needed to. Stowed away in the staffroom was a power bank. Emmie set that to charge – it was already half full, but in the event of a power cut, it wouldn't hurt to have a full battery.

She was filling up flasks from the café's hot water dispenser, her wrist throbbing steadily, when Jared appeared in the doorway, still wearing his coat.

'Hey . . . It's gone really cold, hasn't it?' he said quietly. He noticed what she was doing. He seemed apprehensive, lingering there in the doorway. Probably because he knew he'd done wrong in lying to everyone. 'Can I help with anything?'

'The heating's on, but it's always colder in the staffroom – I think there's a draught,' she told him curtly. 'And no, I'm fine.'

'You shouldn't be doing so much with your wrist like that. You need to rest it.'

'I took some painkillers a minute ago. I'm fine.'

She didn't want his help. Whenever she looked at him now, she felt awkward, which made her even more prickly, like a porcupine bristling under a breeze. Jared moved closer to her, leaning over and observing the flasks – she'd already filled two. She'd stacked the hot water bottles on a customer table nearby, sheathed in their furry coverings. Jared was so close, she could smell the aftershave lingering on his skin, a strong, heady mix of pine and woodsmoke that made her head spin. A shiver ran up her neck and she shifted an inch away from him, even more annoyed that he was having this effect on her when she was already mad at him.

'What?' she said.

'That's a smart idea,' Jared replied, and her cheeks warmed. 'We should check for blankets, gloves, maybe a power supply . . .'

'I've done all that,' she said. 'I have a power bank charging in the Cat Lounge.'

'You seem prepared. But your accent . . . I take it you aren't from Cumbria originally. Where are you from?'

'Manchester,' she said, and began filling another flask from the dispenser.

'Ah, a Mancunian girl.' She looked up to see him flashing her a grin, and the way he looked when he smiled startled her so much that she stopped paying attention, dribbling a trickle of hot water down her hand.

She cursed as her hand seared and stung. She left the flask under the dispenser, hurrying over to the sink behind her – she needed to run her hand under the cold tap.

'Are you okay?' Jared asked urgently, following her. 'Here, quickly.'

'I'm *fine*—' She wanted to tell him to leave her to deal with it, but he somehow got to the sink before her and turned on the cold-water tap. Before she could argue, he was taking her gently by the hands and guiding her scalded fingers under the freezing water.

Emmie found herself unable to say anything at first, too choked by his touch, even while her hand smarted.

'Keep it under there for a few minutes,' he advised, his breath warm against the side of her ear. He was still holding on to the side of her hand, the pad of his thumb touching her palm. She could barely feel it thanks to the cold water, but his closeness to her made her brain almost as numb as her hand. His brown eyes were full of genuine concern.

'I'm fine,' she managed, as repetitive as a robot that was glitching, breaking her hand away from his and turning off the tap. 'It was only a few droplets.'

Moving away from him, she searched for some kitchen towel to mop up the mess she'd made, ignoring her smarting hand.

'Does Sylvie have a first-aid kit?' he asked her. 'It might be a good idea to know where that is, too.'

'It's under the sink.'

'And candles?'

'That's . . .' She sighed. 'Actually, that's the only thing I couldn't find, at least, not down here in the café.'

When she'd moved here to live with Aunt Sylvie, she'd wanted to keep her belongings to a minimum for the journey, so she'd left her own candles behind, and she hadn't been able to find any here. She could ask Megan, but she was here on a trip and Emmie didn't want to intrude. Then again, maybe she *should* be checking on her. Sylvie had told her to look out for Megan while she was here, and she must be worried about the coming storm. Emmie hadn't spoken to her since they'd first met in the café. And it was a good excuse to get away from this swirling discomfort she was feeling in Jared's presence.

'I'll check again upstairs,' she told him. 'We have a tenant in the flat and I need to check on her anyway. She might have some.'

He scratched the back of his head. 'I'll finish up filling your flasks,' he offered.

She retreated from the room. This was something her brother would do: lie about how much he'd been drinking, or say something cruel, then try to make up for it afterwards by being nice to her. A perpetual cycle – she'd escaped that once. Did she really want to repeat it with Jared? Maybe she just sent out all the wrong signals and attracted men just like Dustin. They'd all gone out of their way to accommodate Jared and his 'allergies', which hadn't even been real.

And yet . . . he'd been so kind and considerate towards her, even before today, and she couldn't forget about that side of him. She felt as stirred up as milk swirling in a teacup, the proximity of him only having intensified her feelings.

Chapter 7

Emmie rapped on the door to the flat where Megan was staying. She didn't answer right away. Emmie hoped she was alright. If Jared had ended up stuck here, Megan could be stuck somewhere else, or broken down on a road somewhere, if she'd decided to go out. Her worries weren't necessary, though, as a few minutes later, Megan pulled opened the door.

Megan was slightly more unpolished than the first time they'd met, but she still managed to look stunning, even bare-faced – as if she were about to be primed for a walk down the catwalk. Emmie usually felt like a gremlin in her sweatpants and comfy clothes on a weekend. Megan, on the other hand, managed to look like she was modelling her clothes for a perfectly homely social media post, dressed in lilac yoga pants and an oversized T-shirt, with a thick headband scraping her hair away from her face. She must have eyelash extensions, because there was no way anyone had eyelashes that dark and long naturally. Her skin looked like she'd run it through a beauty filter.

'Emmie, hi!' said Megan, smiling at her, a tiny dimple appearing in her left cheek.

'I'm so glad you're here,' Emmie said. 'I thought you might have ended up stuck on a mountaintop or something in this weather. Are you okay? I meant to check on you before but—'

Megan interrupted her, waving her concerns to one side with a manicured hand: 'No, it's fine. I decided it was probably best not to drive anywhere because of the storm.'

'Do you need anything?' Emmie asked. 'I'm down in the café with the cats. And our delivery driver broke down outside and can't get home, so he's spending the night down there as well. I actually came to see if you have any candles in case there's a power cut. I can't find any.'

'Oh!' Megan said. 'Yes, there were some in the bathroom – Sylvie mentioned them. Come in. I'll get them.' She held the door open so Emmie could step inside the narrow hallway, where Megan's coat was hooked onto the wall with an umbrella and her handbag. She could hear water running, and the bathroom door was open a crack.

'If there's a power cut, you can always come downstairs,' said Emmie. 'I can build up a fire in the Cat Lounge. I've sorted a power bank, some hot water bottles, flasks . . . Were you planning on going anywhere, for Christmas?' she added, remembering what Megan had told her when she'd arrived, about the boyfriend she wanted to make amends with. Perhaps they'd managed to make plans for the day?

'Yes, but I guess I'm not going anywhere now! It'll just have to wait.' Megan smiled at her again and led the way down the hall.

Aunt Sylvie had showed Emmie this flat when she first arrived, and Emmie was floored by how polished and pretty it was. The hallway opened out onto a beautiful bright kitchen, with wooden floors and an oak-topped kitchen island, the cupboards all painted a smart, modern grey. The living area, opposite the kitchen, held two squashy-looking grey sofas. A sloping wall with three windows overlooked the trees, which were blowing around in a frenzy in the snow flurries. There were only very subtle Christmas decorations in place: a mini LED tree on the table, which Megan had flicked on so it sparkled, and a throw blanket decorated with a snowscape and reindeer-drawn sleigh strewn across the sofa.

Sylvie had added cat café touches to the flat, too: the walls were decorated with artsy, watercolour pet portraits, and there were cat-shaped handles and magnets in the kitchen. Emmie found herself smiling – she loved the cat-like touches Sylvie brushed over everything, like an artist with paints.

'Hold on, I'll grab the candles,' said Megan, padding away across the wooden floor.

When Megan returned from the bathroom, she was holding three large glass-encased candles, and Emmie caught the faint scent of berries. 'There are only three,' said Megan. 'Better than nothing though.'

'That's perfect.'

Megan handed over the candles, and Emmie balanced them in her arms, keeping the weight on her uninjured arm. They both paused, and Emmie felt slightly awkward, as if she should be doing more to make Megan feel accommodated.

'Are you sure you'll be okay up here on your own?' she asked her.

'I'll be fine. I'm just catching up on some work – I'm running a bath to shoot some brand photos, so I might as well soak in it afterwards. I do beauty content online,' she added, when Emmie lifted a questioning eyebrow. 'And photography for brands – make-up, haircare products, skincare. That kind of thing.'

'Oh! That sounds amazing. You're working over Christmas?'

'Yeah. It's a busy time. And freelancers never really stop, do they?' she added. 'I don't mind – I love it all. I was going to take tomorrow off.'

One of Emmie's friends worked online, too, designing costumes inspired by movies and TV, and sharing elaborate make-up creations with her audience. She admired both her friend and Megan's abilities to carve out a career with their creativity, and to have that succeed. She hoped that would be her, someday.

'You'll have to give me some tips when you're not busy,' Emmie said. 'I do art and have a few accounts, but I can never seem to grow them much.'

'Sure,' said Megan. 'I'd love to. And I know what you mean. I have a love–hate relationship with the whole thing. But y'know, a girl's gotta eat. It can be tough to get noticed when you're starting out though.' Megan glanced over her shoulder; the bath was still running. 'I better get back to it.'

'Let me know if you need anything else,' Emmie said. 'And I'm sure we can knock together some Christmas cheer for tomorrow, too, between the three of us!'

'That sounds like fun,' Megan agreed.

★

Jared decided he'd sleep in the staffroom, rather than joining Emmie in the Cat Lounge. She'd been looking at him strangely ever since she found out he wasn't allergic to cats after all, and he couldn't really blame her, especially when he'd felt too pathetic to share the real reason. Leaving her alone was probably best right now until he could work out what to say.

His mum had been buzzing him – as had his brother. *Looks like you got your wish to force this place upon me,* he rattled off to his brother, adding a smile to show that he was kidding. *Sorry I can't see you both today,* he added to the group chat.

His mum sent back a slew of sad faces and wrote back: *Lockdown all over again, lol. We'll see you AS SOON as this blows over.*

It wasn't long before he bitterly regretted his choice to sleep in the staffroom. It was cold, even though he was bundled in his clothes, hat, gloves, and layers of blankets. There were radiators in here, but they were on a low heat; maybe Emmie thought it best not to have them on full blast at night, so she didn't run up high bills for the café while Sylvie was away. The goosebumps on his arms made him think of that stray cat Emmie had been trying to find. Poor blighter. He hoped it was a tough little thing and could take care of itself.

His night was fitful – he spent it tossing and turning, his hat making his head itch; but it was too cold to sleep without it. When daylight finally came he felt groggy, almost drunk, through lack of sleep, and for a split second, he expected to be at home in bed, with Poppy wedged between his feet. But when he looked up, he remembered where he was, and that she was gone, and felt that familiar crushing disappointment, and that heavy reluctance to begin the day. It was Christmas morning, he realised slowly.

He hauled himself upright, out of the cocoon of blankets he was wrapped in. He wanted to check on the weather, and see if the worst of the storm had hit. The first thing he did was roll up the blind at the back of the staffroom, which looked out over part of the car park and some trees on the other side.

What he saw made him reel back. It was like he'd woken up on another planet; he'd seen plenty of snow here in the Lakes, but this was something else. Everything was covered in even more layers of snow, and it was coming down in droves, creating a churning blizzard that obscured the hills and rooftops from view, as if the sky had been put through a blender and shaken out. The pavements and pathways were invisible beneath a covering of white, and he could barely see across the street, the air a thick haze.

He shoved on his coat and gloves – they'd fallen off at some point in the night – rubbing his hands together. It didn't look like he'd be going anywhere today, or getting the van sorted.

A phone call from the breakdown service not five minutes later confirmed that. By the time the woman had finished explaining everything, his head felt muzzy, and he let a curse slip through his lips.

'No one can come out at all?' he tried, even knowing it was hopeless.

'I'm sorry, we just can't get anyone out to your van right now. The road connecting County Durham and Cumbria is closed. With the red warning in place and the government advising people not to travel, and it being Christmas Day, we—'

'I understand.' Jared sighed.

'You have somewhere to stay, which is the main thing,' the woman said – that had been the first thing she wanted to establish. 'We'll have someone out to the van as soon as is reasonably possible.'

'Alright, thanks.'

'We'll be in touch.'

He cut the call. He rubbed the space between his eyebrows, where it felt like someone had been pressing on his skin. He *really* needed a coffee. In the group chat with his mum and his brother, he quipped, *Merry Christmas! Still stuck in Cat Land.*

His brother sent back a stream of cat emojis and Santas, but his mother's reply was *Merry Christmas, darling. Send photos of the cats, please! We miss you. Your presents are here waiting! xxxx*

He left the staffroom; the rest of the building was heating up, too, the radiators cranking into life. A few of the cats had chosen spots directly where they could find warmth – beds hanging over radiators, and even directly underneath them. Jared cracked open the door to the Cat Lounge and found Emmie, a portable games console in her lap chiming out a twinkling soundtrack. A black cat was nestled on her knee, nose between her knees, and his heart sank like a stone at the memory of Poppy, sitting on his knee in the evenings while he played video games or watched movies.

Two more cats were curled on a leather sofa nearby, one huge and ginger and the other one a ragdoll with beautiful blue eyes and smoky wisps around her face. Emmie was bundled in a thick, woollen jumper dotted with stars, a blanket, leggings, and what looked like two pairs of socks, as well as stripy fingerless gloves – in spite of the central heating. On the table nearby, Emmie had propped up a laptop, playing some sort of Christmas chill playlist, a cosy scene displayed on the screen of a log cabin interior, with a huge sparkling tree, a stack of presents, and a roaring fireplace.

'Morning,' said Jared. 'Merry Christmas.'

'Oh, hi.' Emmie glanced up from her game, but her greeting wasn't quite as warm as it usually was, and her smile didn't reach her eyes. Was she still upset with him about the allergy lie? He really did owe her an explanation, but every time he tried, it was like his tongue became glued to the roof of his mouth. His explanation made him sound so weak, and he didn't want to seem that way, not to her.

'Are you okay?' he asked.

Emmie gave a half-shrug. 'I was hoping we could clear the air before today, but . . . Well, I can't make you talk to me, can I?'

She doesn't trust me, he realised. 'I really am sorry,' he said. His throat was claggy, like he'd swallowed a bunch of rocks.

'It's Christmas Day, and I don't want it to be weird,' she answered. 'I just don't understand you at all.'

There was a long pause, as if she was giving him an opportunity – again – to open up. And fool that he was, he couldn't make the words come. How could he word it, so he didn't sound like a total screw-up?

'There's a pot of coffee in the café, behind the counter,' she said, when the silence stretched on for too long.

'Thanks. Have you seen outside?'

She nodded. 'Yes. I always imagined Cumbria would get snow, but not like this.'

'This isn't anything like what we usually get – way more than we're used to. You were right to prep so much yesterday.'

Emmie sank back into the armchair. 'I pulled out some spare things from lost property – hats, gloves,' she offered. 'They're in the staffroom. If you want to change, there are some hoodies and spare T-shirts. They're clean and about your size.'

Jared nodded. 'Do you want a coffee?' he asked her. There was a stained, empty mug on the table, and it must be annoying for her to have to do everything with her splint on. He wondered if the injury still hurt.

She blew out a breath of air, looking relieved that he'd offered. 'Yes, thanks.'

'I don't know how you can play that thing, with that splint on,' he said, as he crossed the room and grabbed her mug. From here, he could see what was on the console screen: an illustrated library filled with old books, and an old man wearing a lopsided hat, a text box stretching across the screen reading *WIZENED LIBRARIAN*.

'It's totally fine,' she said. 'All story-based, so I can do it one-handed.'

'What other games are you into?'

'I like a lot of the cosy ones, you know, like *Bear and Breakfast*, *Cozy Grove*, *Stardew Valley* . . . I love the art and the storylines.'

'*Stardew Valley* . . . there's a throwback. I used to spend too many hours planting shit when I should have been working. I couldn't be arsed with it now. Give me an open-world grind instead. Much more refreshing.'

Emmie smiled faintly, and he felt a surge of pride. He could tell she still felt weird around him – the smile was slightly strained – but it was a start.

'Do you take milk and sugar?'

'Yeah, two sugars please.'

He headed off to get the coffee. One of the cats followed him – the one with the splodge that looked suspiciously like Poppy. Jared grabbed the coffee jug, wondering if he could rustle up some kind of Christmas dinner for everyone with what they had in stock. He'd suggest it to Emmie and they could invite the tenant down too. They might be stuck here, but he could at least make sure everyone had a proper Christmas meal.

Once he'd made the drinks, he thought he might glance out of the back door briefly – see how his van had fared overnight. He hadn't been able to see it from the staffroom window. He shoved through the door behind the counter and made his way to the back of the building.

The door wouldn't budge. He shoved his shoulder into it. Nothing.

No way.

He hurried back through to the gloomy café. The two steaming coffee mugs sat abandoned on the side of the counter. He made his way through the latched gate and through the reception area. In the small entrance, he tugged open the main doors that led out onto the street – and he was met with a wall of solid snow.

Jared gaped. The outline of the door – the edges of the window and the handle – was imprinted in the thick block of snow. The cold that hit him from outside was intense, making him breathe heavily, the air fogging before him thickly. This must be why the back doors weren't opening.

They were snowed in.

He swallowed. Bad weather was one thing, but this, he hadn't expected. How long were they going to be stuck here? He shoved the door shut, and made his way back through to the latched gate, into the café. The door to the Cat Lounge was open a crack.

'Emmie,' he called. 'Emmie!'

Her voice floated back to him: 'What?'

'Come here and look at this. It's important.'

He could just tell her, but it seemed important that she see the situation for herself.

A few moments later, she appeared at his side.

'What?' she said again.

'This way.' He led her out to the small entryway, where she stood beneath the giant poster of the café rules, shivering in the cold. Like a magician unveiling a magic trick, he opened the door, a frown on his face. 'Look at this.'

Emmie stared, her mouth hanging open. She took a step closer, reaching out to prod the indent made by the doorknob. 'That . . . I . . . That . . .' she spluttered, shivering again, and drawing her hand back. 'I've never seen anything like that! We're snowed in?' Her voice rose in pitch with every word. She turned to him, looking horrified.

'I tried the back doors. They're the same.'

She didn't say anything for a long minute. Then she glared at him and said: 'Well, it's a good job you aren't deathly allergic to cats, isn't it?'

He sighed, rubbing the spot between his eyes. 'You said you didn't want things to be weird on Christmas Day.'

Emmie studied him for a long moment, then exhaled, her breath visible in the chilly air. 'It's too late for that – I mean, look!' She gestured at the block of snow. 'You told a stupid lie you won't explain to me, and now we're snowed in, so it's already weird!' She huffed out a frustrated-sounding breath. 'I should check the other door – the exit from the flats. Maybe that's not as bad.'

She vanished back into the café before he could reply. After five minutes, he followed her, meeting her in the main café space, by the counter. She stood behind the empty cake display, shaking her head, lifting her coffee cup to her lips with a perturbed look on her face.

'It's the same!' she said. 'I even checked the fire escapes, but I can't open them!'

'There's plenty of food, right?'

Emmie nodded, taking a swig from her coffee. 'Between the café, my flat, and probably hers, yes, there's plenty. I'll have to go and talk to her, tell her we're most likely stuck here for now.'

'But we have food. Warmth. You've prepared for a power cut. The café has first-aid kits. We'll be fine. I'll see if I can rustle up some sort of Christmas dinner for us all.'

'You will?' she said, eyeing him suspiciously.

'Of course. I used to be a chef,' he added. Why was she looking at him like that? 'I'm not going to let you all go without your Christmas dinner.'

'I'm not sure there's much you can make a Christmas dinner *with*,' said Emmie. 'I can see what I have in my fridge-freezer—'

'I've whipped up things with random ingredients before – you'd be surprised. You can let the tenant know, in case she wants to join us. No pressure though.'

Her eyebrows knitted together, as if she were trying to determine whether he had an ulterior motive for cooking up a Christmas dinner. Eventually, she said, 'Okay . . . Well, thanks, Jared.'

Jared's insides tumbled at the sound of his name on her lips, even though she didn't sound as warm and upbeat as she usually did when talking to him. He tried to ignore all of this, to focus on other things.

He was curious about the tenant upstairs, and what type of person would book a stay here, at a cat café, especially over Christmas. He was imagining a sweet old lady who wore fuzzy but itchy jumpers and baked batches of cinnamon cookies; the kind of person to soothe any kind of tension. It seemed like that was what they needed right now.

'I'll call Sylvie.' Emmie hesitated. 'Maybe you should call Sylvie yourself and explain why you're sleeping here. And tell her about your non-existent cat allergy?' she added, sounding icy.

'I will tell her,' he promised. 'When she's back. In person. I just think it's better that way, face to face.'

She frowned. Maybe she thought he was trying to wriggle away from the truth. But this wasn't a conversation to have on the phone, not when he needed Sylvie to understand his reasoning fully. And he needed time to think about how to explain. *My cat died, I was in a financial mess, I was worried about getting depressed again, and I really needed this job. I didn't want to be around cats so I panicked and made up an excuse.* That sounded pathetic, even to him, so it'd probably sound ten times worse to Sylvie. No, he needed to reason it out, explain more carefully, so he didn't sound like such a sap. How could he possibly explain?

Emmie lifted her chin. 'What's the point in waiting? You don't want to tell her the truth, do you?'

'That's not true,' he said. 'I want to talk to her in person, that's all. I like having important conversations face to face.'

'Are you trying to get out of talking to her—'

'No! I told you I'll tell her, and I will, when she's home. You're not the most important person here, even though she put you in charge for now, so just let me handle this, okay? I promise you, I'll tell her.'

What he meant by 'you're not the most important person here' was that Sylvie was the one who would judge him for what he'd done, and make a decision about what to do with him. Sylvie was his manager. But he knew as soon as he spoke that the words had come out sounding all wrong – probably the lack of sleep and the lack of caffeine in his bloodstream. He functioned better after at least two coffees – and after ten o'clock in the morning, ideally.

Emmie's eyes widened, and the hurt that crossed her face was unmistakable. She disappeared down the hall without another word.

Jared stood shuffling his feet, feeling horribly guilty. He hadn't meant to hurt her feelings; he really was going to explain to Sylvie in person. He heaved a sigh. Maybe staying here was going to be more complicated than he'd thought.

Chapter 8

You're not the most important person here.

The words rang around Emmie's head. They sounded just like something Dustin would have said, when he got drunk. All Emmie had to do was something simple – like taking a long bath with a face mask on after a long day at work – and Dustin would come in, trashed from a night at the pub, scoff and say, *God, Emmie, you're not that important! Who do you think you are, the queen of England?* Jared wasn't even drunk and he'd still thrown similar words at her.

Emmie fired off a message to her Aunt Sylvie as she climbed the stairs to Megan's flat. *We're stuck in the café, snowed in,* she explained. *Jared's here. The van broke down outside. Megan's upstairs. We'll be fine but just wanted to let you know.* Even though she was upset, she held back on explaining Jared's lie – that was up to him. She wondered if he'd even keep his word and talk to her aunt.

And yet, the way he'd defended her at the winter fair; took her to A&E; bought her coffee and offered to purchase her artwork when he was clearly skint; and his offer to make them Christmas dinner while they were stuck here . . . He seemed kind, thoughtful, genuine. Like a good person. All of this only confused her. She couldn't pin him down and it was exhausting her.

She hovered her finger over the send button, biting her lip. Should she tell Sylvie about Salem? She didn't want to worry her if it was only a hairball. And there was nothing she could do right this second anyway. Sophie and Miles wouldn't even be able to come back and check on him in this storm, and although they had cat care training and behavioural knowledge, they weren't veterinarians. In the end, she tapped send, leaving Salem out for the time being.

Sylvie had buzzed Emmie back by the time she'd reached Megan's door.

Sylvie: Feel awful for not being there, pet. I'd come back early but not safe and some roads into north closed.

Emmie: Don't feel bad. We'll be fine. The shelter couldn't get to the lil stray guy in time though ☹

Sylvie: Oh no, he's out in this weather!

Emmie: I know. I tried shaking biscuits before we got stuck here – no sign of him. Fingers crossed he's just in a shed or hiding out somewhere.

Sylvie: Here's hoping he's okay. Take care, love.

Emmie pocketed her phone and knocked on the door of Megan's flat. Shortly after, Megan swung it open. Not for the first time, Emmie found herself doing a double take at how beautiful she managed to look without a speck of make-up, even first thing in the morning. Her skin was flawlessly smooth, and it looked like her hair had been styled for the perfect morning-after scene in a movie. *How* did she not even have bags under her eyes? Emmie should probably take eye-cream recommendations from her.

'Hey,' said Emmie. 'Merry Christmas!'

'Back at you,' said Megan, tugging the door open wider. 'I've not been up long! Feels weird to wake up here on Christmas morning.'

'Well, I don't want to worry you – we have plenty of food and supplies here, but . . . We might be stuck here for a few days.'

Megan raised her perfectly groomed and plucked eyebrows. 'What do you mean?'

'We're snowed in – all the doors,' Emmie explained. 'We've checked.'

'*What?* Are you serious?'

'Yep.'

Megan swore. 'Damn. I didn't expect that.'

'I'm sorry you're stuck here with us, but we're thinking about sorting out a Christmas dinner, if you'd like to join us?' she offered. 'We can make the most of it.'

'That's good of you, thanks.' She glanced down, where she was wearing fuzzy lilac slippers over a pair of purple socks, and silken pyjamas. 'I'll join you later? I should probably get dressed. And I promised I'd video-call my gran. We do it every year.'

'Sure. Join us whenever you want.'

*

Salem was sitting on the squashy armchair when Emmie pushed the door to the Cat Lounge shut behind herself. The lounge was toasty, the warmth from the central heating tingling through her body, and she pulled off her gloves and hat, careful not to yank her bad arm too hard in the process. She tried to tempt the unmoving cat with the food dispenser by clinking some biscuits out, but he simply stared listlessly, his greenish-yellow eyes shining. All she did was cause Jess to come trotting over for some snacks, which she dug greedily into. Most of the other cats were snoozing by the radiators or on the sofa, but they'd all eaten properly and were sleeping off their full bellies, completely flat-out. She was starting to worry about Salem. Why wasn't he eating anything? Was it really a hairball, or something else?

She sat on the floor in front of the armchair, not wanting to disturb Salem. She wanted to be close to him, to keep an eye on him and let him know she wasn't going anywhere. He was sleeping with his head tucked into his tail, his fur sticking up, slightly spiky along the ridge of his back. She set up her laptop, streaming some news footage about the storm, and picked up her drawing tablet. Jared, as promised, was digging through the cat café's food stores to see what they had available. Emmie had also laid out some random things from her fridge in the café – mostly veg – that he might be able to use for a dinner.

Emmie had thought that injuring her non-dominant hand would mean she'd still be able to get work done. Yet it was awkward and clunky to hold her tablet this way.

I'll just have to work extra slowly.

A good while later – maybe an hour or two – there was a gentle tapping on the door that had several of the cats sitting upright with their ears tipped back. Thomas, who was always skittish, darted into a hidden alcove in one of the cat towers and out of sight.

Jared pushed the door open with a creak. Emmie's laptop was now showing footage of the sea near the coastline – grey waves rolling treacherously in the extreme winds and splashing up onto walkways. It soon switched to a newsreader explaining that the wind in some areas was reaching ninety miles per hour, causing huge, sturdy trees to topple onto power lines and buildings. Someone's house by the coast had been completely crushed, and the old man it belonged to was close to tears as he was interviewed outside, the destroyed home in the background. What an awful thing to happen on Christmas morning.

'Christmas dinner is *on*!' Jared declared.

Emmie looked up from her tablet.

Jared had changed clothes – he wore the same jeans, but he'd clearly been rummaging through the lost-and-found clothes she'd offered him too, and was wearing a thick grey cable-knit jumper and a black scarf looped around his neck multiple times. Despite the jumper looking like something Emmie's grandfather might have worn, he still managed to look attractive, like he was advertising clothes for the old and wise at heart. He was holding a hot chocolate overflowing with whipped cream, marshmallows, and chocolate sprinkles. It was in a cat-shaped mug, the handle a curving black tail. In his other hand, he held a plain mug, steaming, and she caught the aroma of brewed coffee.

'What's that?'

'I made you this too,' he said. 'Consider it the starter. Where's the tenant? I made her one too. It's on the counter.'

'Thanks,' she said, gesturing to the table. He was doing all of these nice things for her again, and she couldn't decide whether it was the guilt he was experiencing over his lie, or if it was genuine. But she wasn't going to say anything this time; she just wanted a peaceful Christmas, even in these bizarre circumstances. 'She said she'll be down when she's ready. She was getting dressed, calling her gran.'

He gave her a tentative smile and set the mug down on the round table by the armchair. 'It's nice and warm in here.'

Three of the cats – Jess, Binx, and Eric – were sharing the furry rug, sprawled out together, jostling for space, even though the wood burner wasn't going yet, just the central heat. Kitty was almost lying on Eric's face, and she had her head angled back, looking grumpy, her tail twitching, but refusing to move. It was a real shame the stray hadn't been able to come in here, share this warmth and comfort and wait things out.

'I can't believe you managed to rustle up something for dinner,' said Emmie, shaking her head. 'I'd be clueless.'

'It'll be a hodgepodge,' he pointed out, 'but hopefully it'll be festive enough. And you have a good kitchen here.'

Jared glanced at the cats. She couldn't help – *again* – but think that his lips looked perfectly kissable, wondering how the light stubble would feel against her mouth. It had been *years* since she'd kissed someone. When she moved in with Dustin, she'd had a boyfriend, but that hadn't lasted long – he'd taken one look at some of her cartoonish sketches and dropped several hints that she was immature and needed to think about getting a 'proper job', never mind the fact that she'd been working nine-to-five in admin to pay her rent and squeezing her art in on the sidelines.

There was a long silence, filled only by the news report on Emmie's laptop switching over to a weatherman in front of a map of the country.

Storm Marie has brought exceptionally strong winds and snow, with the Met Office predicting that this will be the worst storm since Arwen, with power outages expected across the country. We're not out of the woods yet, with Storm Marie set to continue into tomorrow, and . . .

Tomorrow. So they could be stuck here tomorrow, too?

'I put some hot water bottles under a few of the cat beds out in the café,' said Jared. 'And boiled some more hot water.'

'You really don't have to do all this,' said Emmie, leaning forward to pick up her hot chocolate.

She took a drink, sipping away some of the cream before the hot liquid reached her mouth. It tasted rich and velvety, with a hint of caramel and cinnamon. 'That's delicious,' she said, surprised, leaning back, careful not to disturb Salem as she pressed her spine into the armchair.

He grinned at her, making her heart leap unexpectedly. 'When I was a chef, I sometimes did the desserts too,' he explained. 'Worked in a few Michelin-star restaurants where everything was *extra* fancy.'

'Not a bad skill to pick up,' she said, taking a longer swig at the risk of burning her mouth – but it really was deliciously creamy. 'How come you aren't doing that now?'

'I just always wanted to do something more creative. So I started freelancing.'

'Well, you can make me one of these drinks any time if you want to keep your skills up to date,' she said lightly.

He drank his coffee, the hint of a smile on his face. 'Listen, I'm sorry about what I said before. I really didn't mean to hurt your feelings. It all came out wrong. I didn't mean you weren't important. Just that Sylvie's my boss and I'll talk to her when she's back.'

Emmie opened her mouth and closed it again. That was unexpected. She'd anticipated some sort of excuse – *you just weren't listening to me*, or worse still, a non-apology like *well I'm sorry if you feel I hurt your feelings, but . . .* Dustin always twisted situations like that, after a drink, until it was mangled and she couldn't even unpick her own words enough to know if she was still being accurate.

'It's okay,' she said. 'We're in a stressful situation. I understand.'

Jared relaxed into the sofa cushions, a frown line on his forehead smoothing out. 'I don't want this to be awkward or uncomfortable for either of us.' He gestured at the laptop. 'It doesn't look like this is a brief thing.'

One of the other cats – Lilian – padded into the room through the cat flap in the door, and hopped up onto the sofa. To Emmie's surprise, she made her way over to Jared, looking up at him with her big green eyes, assessing his lap. Jared looked like he might shoo her away, his arm rising, eyes widening, but when she leaped onto his lap and circled, readying herself to get comfortable, he froze. He was holding his coffee mug out awkwardly, to one side, as if the cat were a dangerous wild animal.

'Don't look so worried,' Emmie said, biting back a laugh. 'She's an affectionate girl and she won't bite. Are you . . . afraid of cats?' Maybe she had him all wrong, and that was why he'd lied, and he was just embarrassed to say so, although she still couldn't understand why he'd choose to work here, if that were true.

'No.' His voice was strained, as if he were holding back a series of emotions, but Emmie couldn't decipher what they were. Lilian settled on his lap, her paws tucked underneath her, in the perfect loaf position. Her green eyes blinked slowly shut.

'Why did you lie about being allergic to cats, if you aren't afraid of them, then?'

Jared sighed, raising his mug to his lips and taking a swig, his attention fixed on the wall to his left. 'If we're stuck here, you might as well know, even if it does make me feel stupid.' He paused, swirling his coffee in the mug, as if contemplating how to frame his words. That crease was back on his forehead. 'I just thought it sounded so . . . ridiculous. Didn't really want anyone to pity me, least of all you, so I didn't want to explain.'

Emmie waited.

'My cat, Poppy, she . . . She passed away. It wasn't long before I started working here. A few weeks before.'

'Oh,' Emmie said softly. A creeping warmth moved up her neck. She'd been so stupid. That wasn't long ago at all, and right in the lead-up to the holiday season. The pain he must be feeling – it was so fresh, so recent. And yet she'd been sitting here comparing him to her brother, jumping to all sorts of conclusions. 'I'm so sorry.'

'She was unwell for months – I knew it was coming, but . . . Anyway, my ex-girlfriend was supposed to take her to the vet for me once, and then I found out she was cheating on me, so . . .' He trailed off.

To lose his girlfriend as well as his cat, and in that way? How awful. Emmie felt guilty, the feeling rising inside her. 'You don't have to talk about it,' she said quickly. 'I just—'

'No, I get it. You thought I was a liar. And I was . . . I am. I did lie. But I wasn't trying to be a bastard, or to trick anyone. I want you to know that. Things have just been . . . weird for me lately.'

'All that happened . . . and you still came to work here?'

'I needed the work, and I couldn't find anything else. The graphic design has been slow lately.'

Emmie now felt like an utter fool. He *was* a genuine person, kind and caring and generous. She shook her head. She hadn't realised living with Dustin had made her this way – so willing to give people the benefit of the doubt, to see the best in them, but quick to be suspicious when they put a foot wrong. Seeing Jared sitting there with Lilian, looking vulnerable, made her edges soften.

'You're not a bastard,' she said, then added lightly, 'I don't think a bastard would bring me such a delicious drink, anyway. Can bastards even *make* drinks this good? I think not.'

He smiled.

'I was harsh on you. I'm sorry, too. I didn't mean to be. I . . .' She drank some of her chocolate to give herself time to think. She barely knew him, yes, but she felt she'd been unfair, and he'd opened up to her, so she'd give him something in return, at the very least. 'Before I came here, I had a difficult living situation. I guess when you lied, I thought . . .'

'You didn't trust me. That's fair enough. Trust has to be earned.'

'Right.'

'Is that why you came here, to live with your aunt?' he asked her. 'Because of your living situation?'

'Yes, sort of,' she said. 'I was living with my brother, and he's not the best person to be around. And then . . .' She sighed. 'Trying to be an artist isn't easy. I graduated with my art degree six years ago. Since then, it's been really tough to land a creative job. To get any kind of traction. Aunt Sylvie offered me this job, and the other flat upstairs, when my brother got to be too much.'

'I get that. It was like that for me, with graphic design. I fell into kitchen work, but I'm a self-taught designer. It was what I really wanted to do.'

'Wow. And you still managed to get freelance work? That's amazing.'

He looked sheepish, a pink flush pooling over his cheeks. 'I'm no good at drawing – the digital stuff is my forte. I'd actually thought of getting an illustration or sketch done of Poppy, but . . .' He shrugged, and – rather tentatively, it seemed to Emmie – stroked Lilian's back. 'I just haven't yet.'

'That's understandable,' Emmie replied.

A silence fell over them like fresh snowfall. She wouldn't push him to open up further unless he wanted to. Emmie hadn't lost a cat – her parents still had the two calicos they'd got when Emmie was fourteen. But she understood what it was like to love a pet, and she'd been heartbroken when she moved out and her parents eventually went to Spain, taking the cats with them. Living with her brother had been unbearably lonely, and she'd missed them curled near her feet or nestled in her lap.

They sat together in companionable silence, and she was unnerved by the strange tangle of feelings inside her, because now that she didn't feel uncertain about Jared and his reasons for fibbing, she felt something else – something she couldn't pin down.

*

Jared was in and out of the staff kitchen, rustling up some food. The cats couldn't get in here, since it was carefully sectioned off, past the gate leading behind the café's main counter. The few times he popped back into the café, though, the cats were clearly aware something food-related and delicious was going on, as very few of them were napping now. Several of them were prowling the area, or sitting on tables sniffing the air, and he almost trampled on a huge black-and-white cat with green eyes who was hovering right behind the gateway.

When dinner was nearly ready, the scent of chicken, herbs, and spices filling the air and wafting into the various café rooms, Emmie agreed to fetch the tenant from upstairs. She hadn't been down yet, but his prepared dinner would be done soon, and he needed to know how many people to serve food for. He left some of the food warming in trays – the roast potatoes needed more time in the oven – and took a coffee break in the main room, ready to say hello to whoever was joining them. Cats circled his ankles, mewling for food, and he couldn't help himself. He bent down to scratch a soot-grey cat along the spine, its tail curling around his arm, and smiled. It wasn't so bad here after all.

Emmie had pushed some tables together, and even dug out a Christmas tablecloth covered in reindeer to drape over them. She'd set the table with cutlery and glasses and her laptop was plugged in, playing a soft Christmas playlist. She'd set a few Christmas ornaments around the table, too – some festive wreaths and deer ornaments in the centre.

When Emmie returned from upstairs, Jared was at one of the tables around the edge of the room, draining his coffee cup. A ragdoll with serene blue eyes was sprawled on one of the seats nearby, dozing, paws reaching out.

'Sorry I took so long!' a strangely familiar voice said. The ragdoll's ears pricked up and her blue eyes opened wide. 'I wanted to dress up a bit since it's Christmas, and I was on the video call with Gran for ages . . .'

The voice trailed off, sounding surprised. Jared's heart skittered when he set his mug down, and he nearly upended it when he saw who was standing there.

Was he part of some cosmic joke? He felt like he'd been slapped in the face.

Megan – his ex-girlfriend Megan – was standing by the café's counter. She was wearing a bright red jumper, run through with sparkles, and her make-up looked fit for a magazine spread – matching red lipstick and huge eyelashes.

The air was slicing through his lungs like kitchen knives. All the blood had rushed to his brain, making him dizzy. *How?* How had this happened? How was she *here*? His brother had mentioned she might come to the Lakes, but with Storm Marie happening . . . ? How long had she been here, building up to coming to see him? Why was she at the café?

She looked exactly as he remembered her. Tumbling, dark chocolate hair – artfully arranged – green eyes, a pointed chin and elven features. There was something vulnerable about her. Maybe it was the way she shrank back and paled when she spotted him, her smile vanishing like smoke.

'What are you doing here?' Jared choked out. He sounded like an aged record player sputtering. Time didn't seem to be working right, the moment stretching on. He laughed then, the sound bubbling up and bordering on hysterical. 'You have to be kidding me. What kind of scheming is this?'

'S-Scheme?' Megan choked out. Next to her, Emmie was looking baffled. She opened her mouth to speak, but closed it again when Megan continued: 'I didn't set up any scheme!'

'You knew I was working here – you must have. Did you stay here on purpose?' he demanded. 'You already pestered my brother, and when he failed to give you the response you wanted, you turned up at my workplace! What kind of game is that?'

'What? I didn't stay here because of you!' Her cheeks were flushed pink, with rage or humiliation, he wasn't sure. 'Yes, I came to the Lakes to see you, to talk to you – but I stayed here because it looked cute and interesting, and I like cats. I didn't even know you were working here when—'

'Of course you didn't.'

She had to have known. Otherwise, his life had just sailed past satire and landed squarely in Cloud Cuckoo Land. Maybe he needed to stop drinking so much caffeine. It must be making him hallucinate. He blinked, but she was still there. The ragdoll was watching them all with interest. The big black-and-white cat was still on the prowl for food; she'd emptied one of the dispensers completely.

'Um . . . you two know each other?' said Emmie tentatively. She glanced at Megan. Was Jared imagining it, or was there a slight slump to Emmie's shoulders? He felt a stab of something unpleasant – guilt? 'Is he . . . the boyfriend you wanted to win back?' Emmie continued.

Megan gave a barely perceptible nod.

Jared gaped at her. 'That's why you wanted to come here?' He barked out another laugh. 'To *win* me back? You should go back to your fiancé.'

'We . . . aren't together anymore,' said Megan. Her eyes were glassy and she swallowed thickly. 'I . . .'

Tears, really? He didn't want to shout or be angry with a crying woman, but what did she expect him to say? He'd been the man on the side. She'd had a fiancé, lied to him. All the clues had been there, from not letting him visit her in Liverpool, to the moment he'd first called her his girlfriend – a slip of the tongue since they hadn't even discussed *what* they were – and she'd shifted uncomfortably, a flicker of something in her face before she'd agreed. He'd thought she was being shy – had thought it was *cute* – not that there was someone else.

He'd moved on. He wanted nothing to do with her – and most of all, no drama. All of a sudden, the air seemed to be too heavy, weighing him down.

Jared addressed Emmie, his voice weary. 'I'll finish up dinner and get it plated up. But I'm really not sure I can eat with you. I'm sorry.'

'But, Jared—' Emmie began.

He barely heard the rest of her sentence. He just wanted to be away from Megan, away from that pleading, tearful expression.

He pushed his chair back with a scrape, startling the ragdoll, and stepped through the middle of the two stunned-looking women, retreating into the kitchen.

Chapter 9

Emmie was rooted to the spot, unable to move, her fingers tight and her nails cutting tiny crescents into her palms – making her bad wrist throb with pain. She relaxed, breathing through the stabbing pain. Megan was on the verge of tears, but Emmie had no idea what to say. She'd found herself not only snowed in with Jared, someone she was very clearly attracted to . . . but also his ex, and she was now playing piggy-in-the-middle. This situation was so ridiculous she almost laughed, but she held back because Megan was clearly upset. And so was Jared.

'Let's go into the Cat Lounge,' she told Megan, who was stroking the ragdoll's soft head.

Megan nodded mechanically. Could this situation get any more awkward? Emmie almost wished she was snowed in by herself.

They headed into the Cat Lounge, and Emmie set to work building up the fire. It was soon crackling, turning the walls orange and throwing a soft light across the furniture and the cats curled around the room, illuminating Kitty's lovely Bengal colouring and Baron's brown and orange hues. The dancing light flickered off the windowpanes, making Binx sit up to watch, tail lashing. Thomas's eyes glowed from the darkened alcove in the cat tower. It seemed the cats had grown bored of waiting for scraps of pre-cooked Christmas dinner.

'I wonder how many other people are snowed in?' Emmie mused, for something to say. Megan had hardly said a word. 'I've never been snowed in before. Have you?'

Megan shook her head. 'No, I haven't.'

'I always wanted more snow. Manchester always seemed to get everyone else's dregs.' She knelt down beside the armchair, stroking Salem's head. 'Are you okay, little guy?' she said softly. The cat opened its eyes and blinked at her slowly. Emmie stroked the white diamond-shaped patch of fur on his forehead, then gave it a kiss. 'He's been off-colour,' she told Megan.

'Oh no,' said Megan, moving closer to them and leaning over to peer at Salem. 'I hope he's okay.'

'Me too. I hope the stray is too . . .' When Megan looked at her curiously, she explained about the cat they'd been feeding, and that she'd been trying to coax inside.

'Poor cat,' said Megan.

There was a long pause. Binx wandered over to them and brushed up against Megan's legs; she stroked along the ridge of his back.

'I'm sorry if I've made things awkward,' Megan said. She straightened up and crossed to the sofa, taking a seat in the middle and hooking her legs up onto the edge. Binx followed, hopping up beside her. 'I honestly didn't know he worked here.' She drew in a shuddering breath and shook her head, looking at her hands, interlinked in her lap. 'I know why he thinks I'd be that vindictive, though. I hurt him. I made a huge mistake. Maybe I shouldn't have come here, not at Christmas.'

Emmie had heard every word. *You should go back to your fiancé,* Jared had said. And earlier, he'd said his ex-girlfriend had cheated on him. Her stomach twisted. Why was she feeling so iffy on his behalf?

'You really don't have to explain yourself to me,' she said diplomatically, trying not to take sides. Megan was technically a customer, a tenant, after all. And it was really none of her business, what had gone on between them.

'I know, but . . .' Megan whispered, so quietly Emmie barely heard her. She gave a breathy laugh. 'You heard him. I was already engaged when I met Jared.' Her hands crept up her arms, hugging herself.

Turning away from Salem, Emmie joined Megan on the sofa. Emmie could never understand why someone would cheat – when she was with someone, she was committed, no matter what, and if she wasn't happy, they worked it out, or she moved on. She didn't understand how Megan had got into this situation, and she also felt deeply sorry for Jared, who had been dealing with the loss of his cat as well. But she wasn't going to vocalise all that to Sylvie's tenant.

'I didn't mean for it to happen,' Megan whispered, as Binx settled beside her and curled into a ball.

'You really don't have to explain yourself to me,' said Emmie.

'I feel like I do,' she insisted, with a shrug. 'You're stuck here with both of us on Christmas Day, of all times, and that's partly my fault for coming here.'

'Well . . .' Emmie didn't know what to say. She trailed off.

'My fiancé, Ethan – he was so . . . controlling. I know it's no excuse.' The words came out hurried, as though Megan were stumbling over her own thoughts. It sounded like she'd been holding all this in for a long time. Maybe

151

she'd had no one to talk to, or had been too ashamed to share it with anyone close to her. 'I wanted to leave, call it off, but whenever I tried, he guilt-tripped me into staying. He was so toxic. I met Jared when I hired him for a graphics job and I really liked him, started coming here a lot to see him. One thing led to another . . . I always meant to sort things out, to tell Jared the truth. But eventually, he saw a text from Ethan and it was too late.'

Emmie shook her head and sighed. 'I do know what it's like,' she said. 'To live with someone toxic.'

Megan glanced up, hitching in a surprised breath. 'Really?'

'My brother. It isn't easy.'

'No, it's not.' Megan leaned back against the brown leather sofa cushions, picking at a loose spool of thread on her jumper sleeve, her eyes sheened with tears. 'It took me a while to pluck up the courage to leave. Of course, Jared had scrubbed me out of his life by then, so I came here hoping Jared would understand, forgive me, if I explained in person. I was an idiot . . . I shouldn't have come. And now we're all stuck here. I'm sorry.'

'Don't be. There's not much we can do about that,' said Emmie. Megan looked so dejected and upset, her lip wobbling, that Emmie, naturally, wanted to make her feel better. Being snowed in was a hard enough situation to be in without all this drama on top of it. 'Except . . . we can make *full* use of the facilities. Hot chocolates galore, cookies, doughnuts . . . we have it all.' Emmie nudged Megan's leg with her foot. 'And we have a chef making us Christmas dinner, even if he is your ex. It isn't all bad!'

Finally, Megan gave a watery smile. 'I don't know why you're being so nice to me.'

'Do you want me to be horrible instead? That wouldn't be very festive.'

'No!' Megan laughed. 'No, I just . . .' The brightness in her expression faded. 'I don't deserve it.'

Emmie got to her feet, thinking of Dustin. He'd scared off the one decent boyfriend she'd had whilst she was living with him – they'd drunk together and Dustin had said some mean things. And Emmie's friendships hadn't exactly flourished back in Manchester, because she'd always been so caught up in *working* and striving, giving every spare moment to her art career, or to working unrelated jobs to fund her art. Every moment she wasn't working towards something felt like a missed chance. She wondered if that was wrong, or if that was what you had to do, if you were chasing a dream and doing what you loved. She didn't know the answer.

'We all make mistakes, Megan,' she said. 'And anyway, what happened between you and Jared is between *you*. Why would I hold it against you, when we've only just met?'

Megan was quiet for a long moment, then she nodded. 'Thank you.'

'I'll talk to Jared. I don't think any of us should be alone on Christmas, do you?'

Slowly, Megan shook her head, looking down at Binx's soft belly rising and falling. 'That's why I came here in the first place,' she said quietly, turning to look at Emmie in earnest. 'I thought he'd agree to spend it with me.'

*

Jared tried to ignore the wrenching sensation that was tugging at his stomach as he checked the oven. Megan was *here* and his mind was crackling with irritation and confusion. Surely, she had to have known where he worked. He fired off a text to his brother, which, thanks to his data, managed to get through: *Did you tell Megan about my job at the café?* His brother didn't answer, and he growled at the screen, before a message from his mum popped up. When he replied, she was still online.

> *Mum:* How are you, love? We've just had dinner. It wasn't the same without you. Danni did the turkey, she's a life-saver
>
> *Jared:* Not bad, rustling up some dinner for us too
>
> *Jared:* Pretty sure I'm cursed at this point, tbf
>
> *Mum:* What? Why??
>
> *Jared:* Wait, check the group chat

She sent him an animated image of a dog waggling a pair of oversized, bushy eyebrows and he snorted out a laugh. Wait until she read the group chat. *Megan is here,* he'd sent. *Snowed in with us. Shane was totally right, she turned up unannounced and was renting the flat upstairs!!*

Truth be told, he wanted to pretend this wasn't happening, and he preferred it when they were chatty and jokey, not serious. So, he added, *Shouldn't you have predicted this wild turn of events, Mystic Ma?*

She took forever to type a simple response: *OMG*

His brother sent a series of mind-blown little faces, following it up with: *Are you JOKING?! And no, of course I didn't tell Megan where you work!*

Jared shook his head and set down his phone. He tugged the potatoes out of the oven – finally done – and started to plate up the food. He remembered when he'd discovered Megan's fiancée existed . . . She'd missed Poppy's crucial vet appointment, and it had come out that it was because she was too busy with *him*.

It felt like someone was squeezing his insides with a clamp. He breathed out slowly.

He could hear them both talking, their voices muted.

While he was still plating up, Emmie stepped inside the kitchen. 'Hey,' she said gently, lingering in the doorway.

'Hey.'

'Um . . .' she began. 'I know this is awkward. But I don't want you to eat on your own, especially not after you went to all this trouble. Can we all eat together?'

He huffed out a laugh. 'With my ex?'

'I know. But do you really want to go sit in the cold staffroom and eat alone? On Christmas Day?'

No, he didn't. He really didn't – the very idea was bleak. He had never wanted to spend Christmas alone, certainly not this year. Suddenly, a bolt of determination shot through him. Why *should* he? She was the one who had come here and thrown a spanner in everything. Even though he hadn't asked for her company over the holidays, why should he spend it alone because of her? She'd put him through enough.

'Alright,' he said, steel in his voice. 'I'll be civil but it doesn't mean I'm going to start having fun with her.'

'Of course,' said Emmie. She grinned and bounced on the balls of her feet. 'Can I help with anything?'

He attempted a smile, even though the prospect of eating with Megan nearby was making his insides swirl. 'No,

I've got it. You rest that wrist. I'll bring out the food in a minute, if you both want to sit down.'

Emmie nodded and hurried from the kitchen.

*

'It looks amazing, Jared,' said Emmie, once they were all gathered together at the table to eat. The cats were circling like vultures waiting to pick over a carcass – she had to stifle a laugh, because Eric kept rearing up like a meerkat to sniff the air. 'I can't believe you managed to get all this together. Thank you.'

'It was no trouble. Eat up before it gets cold,' he replied, smiling back at her.

If they were eating, she noted, there was less room for conversation – and she knew he likely wanted as few interactions with Megan as possible. But really, the food *did* look incredible. He'd heated up some of the pre-packaged soup they had in stock to sell to customers, mainly butternut squash and carrot and coriander, and the middle of the table was absolutely loaded with bowls for them to cherry-pick their own unique Christmas dinner. Roast potatoes with chicken strips and stuffing, along with a jug of gravy and various mixed veg (Emmie had supplied those from her flat); turkey and cranberry sandwiches (opened from packets – another customer staple); mini pot pies; 'festive' mini sausages and sausage rolls. And according to Jared, he'd even rustled up a pudding from scratch that was big enough for all three of them – an apple crumble currently baking in the oven. Along with some of the leftover Christmassy cat cookies, shortbreads, and doughnuts Clem had baked in bulk, they weren't going to be low on food. This feast could last for days.

Megan mumbled her thanks, too, and they all tucked in, in silence, finishing their soup. Emmie could practically feel the awkwardness radiating off them both, each averting their gaze from the other as they spooned food onto their plates and poured gravy. Emmie was struggling with the dish of potatoes and trying to get them onto her plate one-handed; the splint made it a challenge.

'Here, let me help,' said Jared, getting up and hurrying around the table. A row of cats followed, expecting something from him, like he was the Pied Piper, and she snorted. She battled Jess away, who looked like she was about to attempt to leap up onto their plates like a furry circus act.

Her cheeks flushed when Jared leaned over her to get to the potato dish; she could smell his aftershave mingling in with the scents of the food. She forgot all about greedy cats.

'Sorry, I probably should've plated that up for you, instead of having you help yourself,' said Jared.

'I guess this is what Christmas is all about. Awkward family dinners, am I right?' said Emmie, trying to lighten the mood, as Jared dumped food onto her plate. She popped a festive mini sausage into her mouth, Jess watching at her ankles with wide green eyes. 'Where would you two usually spend Christmas?'

'I'd planned to be at my mum's,' said Jared, returning to his seat with Thomas trailing behind him and giving a short meow. 'With my brother and his wife Danni. They know I'm here, though.'

'What about you, Megan?' Emmie wondered if this was the way dinner would have to go – with her keeping a separate conversation going, with each of them.

She gave a one-shouldered shrug. 'Nowhere, really. My dad left when I was a kid and I don't get on with my mum. Gran's in a care home, now.'

A twang of sympathy pinged Emmie's chest. Was this why she'd chosen to come here instead, hoping to rekindle her relationship with Jared? The thought made her feel strange – kind of twisty inside, like the way pigs in blankets were wrapped. One of the food items she was *sorely* missing today. 'I'm sorry to hear that. Is she okay?'

Megan nodded, tucking her hair behind her to keep it out of the way of her food. 'She seemed okay this morning. They're doing dinner and some games for the residents so she has plenty to look forward to today. I'll visit when I get home.'

They lapsed into further silence. The Christmas music Emmie had put on wasn't doing much to ease the atmosphere, but it was better than nothing.

'Well,' she said. 'It could be worse. We could be with drunken and aggressive family members instead.' She'd been trying to pluck out a positive and hold it up to them, like a pearl, but perhaps that was a silly thing to say, so she hurried on, 'All I'm saying is, there are worse places to be at Christmas.'

'I don't mind it here, with the cats,' Megan said slowly, her eyes skimming over the cats sitting nearby, then the table, and landing on Jared. 'The food's good, too. Thanks, Jared.'

He looked up, their eyes locking. Emmie's mouth went dry despite the gravy flooding her plate. Her appetite was suddenly waning. Some people said Christmas worked miracles. And it might bring out the worst in some people – but in others, it brought out the best. The joy and the appreciation and the holiday spirit. Maybe they'd decide they still loved each other, after all? She wouldn't blame Jared – despite her mistakes, Megan was so beautiful, talented, business-minded, a freelancer like he was. They had things in common, and they had a history together. Somehow, the thought made her feel nauseous.

But then the moment was gone and Jared merely nodded and looked away from Megan.

Soon they'd finished their main meal and Jared was dishing up dessert. The audience of cats remained – except for Salem, who was still squirrelled away in the Cat Lounge. They tucked into Jared's homemade apple crumble, which was *delicious*.

'I need someone to make food for me like this *every day*,' said Emmie, leaning back in her chair with a satisfied groan as she polished off the last of the dessert. She was so full now, her stomach felt like a balloon. From the floor, Jess and Thomas were watching her longingly. 'Sorry, you two. How much would it cost me, to have you as my personal chef all the time?' she added to Jared.

His eyes twinkled at her from across the table. 'What have you got to offer?'

Well. That sounded flirtatious. Emmie's neck prickled with pleasure, and she cast a self-conscious look at Megan, feeling guilty for the delight that had run through her.

Megan had clearly noticed whatever had passed between them. She didn't comment and instead changed the subject, the words coming out hurriedly: 'Emmie, how did you end up falling and hurting your wrist? You never told me, exactly.'

'Oh . . .' Emmie glanced at Jared again. 'Well, we went to the winter fair together. Sylvie has a stall there for the café – it's over at Crescent Wood Country House, if you know it?'

'Crescent Wood,' Megan said stiffly, and Jared flinched. 'Yes?'

'I . . . see.'

What was with this strange atmosphere? Jared was concentrating on spooning up the barely perceptible cake crumbs left in his bowl, rather than taking part in the conversation.

Bemused, Emmie decided the best thing to do was carry on. 'Yes. Anyway, as we were packing up, someone bumped into me and I fell. He wasn't really watching where he was going. Jared took me to A&E after.' She smiled at him. 'And he gave that guy a stern talking-to.'

He returned the smile, looking a little happier now.

'Did he?' said Megan. She sounded flat – disappointed. 'Well, thanks for the food but I'm going to take some hot water bottles up to the flat and hunker down there.'

'Are you sure?' said Emmie.

'Yes. I think we've all probably had enough awkwardness for one day. But I appreciate you trying to make Christmas special for us while we're stuck here.'

Emmie nodded as she rose to her feet and moved off, pausing briefly to scratch the top of Thomas's ginger head, between the ears. Jess took the opportunity to leap up onto the empty chair and almost got her face in the leftovers until Emmie cried out and shooed her away. She noticed that Megan had carefully avoided talking to Jared directly before leaving, as if mentioning his name might spark some heated argument or confrontation, or make them both start flirting in front of her. Emmie shuffled uncomfortably.

'Why don't you get comfortable in the Cat Lounge?' Jared suggested, when Megan had gone. 'I'll clear up here.'

'Oh, you should let me help! You've done so much already—'

'No, it's okay.' He laughed. 'What was it you said earlier? That you like keeping busy? Me too. It'll help me blow off the awkwardness of . . . that.' He motioned into the air, and at the table.

Emmie chuckled. 'Okay, if that's what you need.' She got to her feet, snatching up a Christmas cat doughnut from the centre of the table. When he raised his eyebrow, she said, 'There's always room for more dessert! Besides, there's only one of these left, and it's a custard one.'

He burst into laughter, and she couldn't help thinking how much she loved that bright expression on his face, so much more than how troubled he'd looked when Megan had been sitting here. She returned to the Cat Lounge with a smile playing at the edges of her mouth, and a lightness to her step. It might have been awkward for those two, but she'd enjoyed it far more than spending her Christmas alone here.

Chapter 10

When Jared was finished with the clean-up and headed into the Cat Lounge, Emmie was curled in a corner of the sofa with a blanket over her knees and a steaming cup of tea on the table nearby. A black cat was sitting on the armchair opposite, paws curled in front of it. Jared shut the door behind him, locking in the warmth. It was like stepping into a heated oven; the fire was blazing brightly. A cluster of other cats were sprawled on the rug, their fur silky and shiny in the light.

'Hey,' said Emmie. There was a sketchpad in her lap, a pencil clutched in her fingers. She was still drawing, in spite of the splint. He had to admire her stubbornness.

'Hey,' he said. He took a seat opposite her. 'I never got the chance to say that I'm sorry about all this – about Megan being here, and all.'

'You weren't to know. It was worse for you than me.'

Jared found himself yawning widely in the warm room, moisture springing to his eyes. All that cooking and cleaning up had worn him out, and that heavy Christmas fullness was slowly crawling over him. 'She shouldn't have come here,' he said sleepily.

'I think she just wanted to clear the air with you.'

'Clear the air? She already had a fiancé. I was the other guy. I don't think there's any clearing the air to be done.' He leaned back into the leather sofa, enjoying the warmth radiating off his left side from the fire, and trying not to think about Megan. He just wanted to forget she was here.

'Do you still love her?' Emmie asked quietly.

Why was she asking him that? Both of his eyebrows shot towards his hairline. 'No,' he said honestly. 'I don't.'

He'd had plenty of time to think about it and he'd realised that even without the fiancé, they just hadn't meshed, their goals shooting off in different directions like opposing lines on a constellation chart. At the time, he'd barely noticed it, too preoccupied with the laughs they shared and the physical spark jolting between them; he'd convinced himself it could be long-term, serious. In hindsight, it never would have worked. She wanted a bunch of kids; he didn't, because he'd prefer to have a furry family. She wanted a huge TV-worthy wedding – he'd prefer a quiet beach or mountaintop retreat. He'd be happy with having less in order to enjoy his life – working freelance, and at jobs that fulfilled him. Hiking on the weekends. Camping. She wanted the big house, the influencer-worthy holidays, to raise her kids alongside a husband who worked a serious job and could provide all of that for her. A picture-perfect life.

'If she came back here to convince me to start seeing her again, she'll be disappointed,' he continued.

'That's fair enough,' said Emmie. 'But as we're stuck here, maybe you could hear her out. I'm not saying change your mind,' she added quickly when he opened his mouth to retort. 'Put your foot down, if you must.' She shrugged. 'Let her say what she needs to say and be firm. Sometimes that's what people need. Sometimes, you have to tell them very specifically how you feel, and that you don't want to see them again. Not after what they put you through.'

'Maybe,' he said, thinking of Poppy and the festering resentment he'd been holding on to. 'Sounds like you're speaking from experience.'

'I am. My brother.'

'Ah. Drunk and aggressive?' he guessed. He remembered what she'd said around the table, about preferring this whole situation to drunk and aggressive family members.

Emmie nodded, watching Eric and Baron washing each other by the fire, Eric holding Baron's neck with his paws. 'He never used to be. I tried to help him. We weren't getting anywhere and I just had to put my foot down, in the end. I was living with him, so it was a bit of a nightmare. It's why I came here.'

'That sounds tough.'

'It was. It is.' She frowned now, looking upset, and he immediately wanted to make the expression go away, to replace it with something happier. 'It's my first Christmas away from him. Not that it was much of a Christmas last year . . . He got drunk, we argued and he fell asleep on the couch. So, you can see how this is an upgrade.'

'I'm glad me and my ex are an upgrade,' said Jared, with a snort, and they both laughed.

'Thanks for today,' she said. 'I really did enjoy it. Your food and everything.'

He felt suddenly sheepish. She was looking at him like he'd won an Olympic medal, or climbed a mountain, and he didn't know how to respond. 'What are you drawing?' he said instead.

'Oh, this? I struggle with buildings so I'm trying to draw the cat café in the snow,' she said, holding up a rough sketch, so faint it was almost invisible on the paper. She tapped it with her pencil. 'It's kind of hard with the splint. Not the best time to refine my skills.'

'It's better than I could do. Give me a laptop and I'm fine. If I draw anything on paper, it ends up looking like a murder scene.'

Emmie laughed, and something in his chest squeezed with pride. He liked making her laugh, liked that sparkling delight in her eyes.

They sat in a companionable silence for a while, Emmie continuing to add sketched lines to her paper, frowning and pressing her pencil to her cheeks when she was thinking, Jared watching the cats, their bellies rising and falling as they breathed. She checked the news on her laptop again at some point.

The news reports rolled on, the monotone lulling him. His phone was digging into his leg in his side pocket, so he took it out and set it on the table. Soon, he was drifting off to sleep, the warmth making him melt into the sofa, his head sinking into the back of the couch.

*

When he woke sometime later, he was sideways on the couch, a blanket tugged over him. It was dark, and two candles were lit, glowing orange pinpricks of light. The fire still roared, and Emmie was sitting on the floor, her legs drawn up to her chest. A black cat was on the armchair behind her, snoozing. Emmie's sketchpad rested on her legs, and she was studying it intently, occasionally bringing up a pencil and making an adjustment by the light of the fire. The ragdoll cat was sleeping near her other side, pressed against her thigh. She glanced up at Jared, and her eyes widened. He couldn't help but notice how the firelight danced in her eyes, making them look like they contained the sun, and how the small freckles on her face burst to life in the glow. She looked almost ethereal, as if she should be wearing a circlet or a crown. He shook himself; he'd probably been dreaming of some fantastical world and he wasn't thinking right.

'You're awake,' she said.

He yawned, blinking at her. He needed to shake off this dream state. 'I didn't mean to fall asleep. How long was I out?'

'An hour or so. But ah . . . We've had a power cut.'

'What?' He sat up as the muzzy dream state began to fade.

'We should be fine – the place has been warming up with the central heating on all day until now. I've put candles around here and I took one up to Megan, too, with some hot water bottles. She'll be okay, she has plenty of bedding up there. But we'll need to be careful how much wood we use here in the burner, just in case the power's out for a while.'

He rose to his feet, checking the wicker basket by the burner; there wasn't enough wood in there, by his estimation, not if they were going to be stuck here for a couple of days – and all the news reports suggested the storm wasn't done with them yet.

'I made sure to get supplies when I went out before the storm hit,' Emmie told him. 'Food, things for the cats. I even got medical supplies, but I didn't even think to get extra wood!' She tutted. 'I've never had a wood burner or a real fire until I came here, so I didn't think.'

'We won't be able to get outside to collect more,' Jared pointed out. 'Not in these conditions. We should see if there's anything we can burn here in case we run out of wood. Anything with coloured print might have toxic fumes – the same goes for cardboard. It might have ink or wax on it. We have to be careful what we use. No magazines, wrapping paper, or cardboard.'

Emmie frowned. 'What can we use, aside from the wood, if we don't want to end up gassing ourselves, then?'

'Plain paper, old newspaper. If we're resourceful with the wood, we can use the fire to heat food in a saucepan as well.'

'Okay, I'll take a look upstairs in my flat. You look down here.'

They separated, and Jared scoured the rooms of the café to search for paper. The café itself didn't have much they could use – Sylvie was on top of her recycling. But he found some newspaper through a staff door with a cat flap, which led into a basement room. The room housed rows of cat litter trays, visible in the blue-white torchlight from his phone. Sylvie must use the newspaper to line the trays when she ran out of proper litter bags. There wasn't much here, but it'd do.

He hesitated before he left the room, gripped by a sudden image of Poppy, looking up at him and opening her tiny mouth, giving a mewl, before padding over to her litter tray and struggling to do anything, before repeating the cycle an hour or so later. A wash of guilt so strong it threatened to bowl him over consumed him. The medication had helped her, near the end. But he'd felt like he'd been letting her down every day. He hadn't been able to fix it, to help her. He hadn't done enough. The worst part was, animals didn't speak Human, so he'd never been able to communicate to her how desperately he'd tried to help, how all the medication was because he loved her and wanted to keep her with him. It wasn't meant to make her unhappy. He'd wanted to save her – just as she'd saved him. And in the end, he hadn't been able to.

His throat closing up, Jared took a deep breath and left the room, newspaper clutched in hand. Even as he shut the door behind him, he couldn't shift the ache in his chest.

*

When they'd gathered up enough materials to burn, Jared returned to the Cat Lounge with Emmie, where it was still pleasantly warm and the cats were snoozing happily. Jared thought guiltily of Megan upstairs, without a roaring fire to keep her company, but Emmie had said she wouldn't come down, and had insisted on staying where she was. Emmie had left her sketchpad on the table in here, face up, but it didn't look like a drawing of a building. Odd, since she mentioned she'd been drawing the café in the snow.

'Are you still drawing the café?' he asked her, gesturing at the pad.

'I . . . Not exactly . . .' She looked sheepish, and snatched up the pad and clutched it to her chest.

'Hey, if you were drawing me as I slept earlier, you could at least show me the finished result,' he said, giving her a poke in the good arm.

'Okay, I'll show you, but it's still rough and it's not as good because of the splint!' Her laptop had been closed and put aside, he noticed, probably to conserve power, but there was enough light for him to see by from the fire and the candlelight. 'And you have to promise not to laugh!'

'Why would I laugh?' he said. 'You know I like your art, Em.'

Emmie didn't reply, just shuffled over to him and thrust the pad into his hands. He took a seat on the sofa, and looked down at the sketch.

It was as though a snowplough had struck his chest. He couldn't speak, couldn't find any words even if he wanted to. She'd drawn him in his reclined position, only he was awake, and Poppy was in his lap. The markings were unmistakable. The cat was facing forwards, nestled in his arms like a child, and he looked to be fussing over her, one hand patting her head and the other held out to her side. The style was cute, like something from a children's book or an animated movie, so he and Poppy both had large, over-emphasised eyes, and she'd drawn hearts on the cat's cheeks in place of whiskers. It only added to the charm.

He was so floored, he opened his mouth, then closed it again. His fingers tightened on the edges of the pad.

'I've upset you,' Emmie said, sounding panicked. She sat down beside him and tried to take the pad from his grip. 'I'm sorry, I was just practising, and I thought you might like it, after what you told me about your cat. Your phone flashed with a notification earlier, and I saw the photo on your background. I didn't mean—'

'Emmie,' he said, cutting her off. 'Don't be sorry. I love it.'

The walls he'd built up since Megan left, since she'd cheated – well, technically she'd cheated on someone else *with* him, but whatever – seemed to be having problems remaining standing. Here in this room, with the coppery light splashed over everything, and a homey, comfortable warmth despite the violent storm outside, he suddenly didn't understand why he'd been fighting so hard to maintain his shield all that time, when he could have opened himself up to someone like Emmie. This kind gesture, this thoughtfulness, this . . . understanding. He couldn't remember the last time he'd felt that, from anyone.

She was holding the side of the sketchbook, but froze when she realised he wasn't letting her take it. Jared pressed his hand on top of hers, and she relaxed her grip, glancing up at him and biting her lower lip. He'd never wanted to kiss her more than in this moment, but underlying everything was Megan, still upstairs, like a shadow hanging over him.

'Thank you,' he said hoarsely, squeezing her hand, fighting off even more urges he didn't want to give in to. He couldn't let this situation go to his head and it wouldn't be right, not now. 'Can I keep it?'

'It's just a rough sketch,' she said quietly.

'It's perfect,' he told her.

She hesitated, then smiled faintly, and even the smallest of smiles made her entire face a thousand times prettier than she already was. 'You can keep it, then,' she told him. 'It was for you, anyway. Now you don't have to buy anything from me.'

He released her hand, and she leaned back as he gently tore the page free of the sketchpad, which he handed back to her. 'Thank you,' he said. He folded the drawing carefully, tucking it into his jeans pocket as though it were a precious treasure.

Chapter 11

'I was going to sleep in here tonight,' Emmie said. She was feeling warm, too warm, the sensation intensified by Jared touching her hand and the softness of his brown eyes as he took her drawing. 'I can bring more blankets down from upstairs. If you want to sleep here too, by the fire . . .' Her neck felt warm and it had nothing to do with the fire. She hurried on, 'It might be best if we all sleep in here, Megan included. I've been thinking and I don't want us getting hypothermia. They were talking about it on the news – the temperature drops might be extreme into the early hours of the morning.'

She knew Jared wouldn't be thrilled with the idea of Megan sleeping in the same room as him, and she wondered what he'd say. She certainly wouldn't like to sleep in the same room as *her* ex-boyfriend. But it would be a crappy thing to do, to leave Megan upstairs in a freezing cold flat while they enjoyed a fire.

He didn't disagree. 'You're right,' he said. 'No matter what's happened between me and Megan, I don't want her to freeze. I feel bad, her being up there like that, while we hog the fire.'

She found herself smiling like an idiot, because she really hadn't expected that kind of mature and reasoned response – not in this scenario.

'What?'

'Are you always so noble?' she said, turning her odd mixture of feelings into a joke.

He offered her a mock-bow, extending his arm toward the corner of the sofa. 'I can be.' He raised himself up and smirked. 'When I'm not conning people into thinking I'm allergic to cats.'

'Too soon,' she said light-heartedly. 'I'll go get Megan.'

He nodded and didn't say anything else.

She left the warmth of the lounge, the cold of the rest of the café hitting her like a gust of wind to the face. Emmie shivered as she made her way up to the flats, her mind back downstairs in the lounge with Jared.

She'd always found him attractive but now, the more she learned about him, and the more time she spent with him, the more she liked him. This whole situation was probably getting to her, though. Who wouldn't feel like this, trapped with a cute guy during a storm? She reminded herself that Megan was here. Jared had his own problems to sort out with his ex; they had a conversation to have, she suspected. Jared had said he didn't love her anymore, but it would be extremely awkward to act on any feelings she had for Jared while Megan was still here. And cruel, too.

'Megan?' Emmie called when she reached her flat, tapping on the door. She knocked a few more times before Megan answered.

'Sorry,' said Megan when the door swung open. She was bundled up in a turtleneck and a dressing gown, a bobble hat stuffed onto her head and a cashmere scarf weaved around her neck. She'd also tugged on some leg warmers. 'I was in the bedroom trying to keep warm.'

'Come downstairs,' said Emmie. 'It's only going to get colder. It's better for us all to be in one room with the fire and the cats. We'll be warmer.'

Megan bit her lip. 'But Jared . . .'

'He agreed,' Emmie clarified.

'I don't know . . .'

'You came here to talk to him, didn't you?' Emmie asked. 'Well, now you two have no choice but to talk. And I won't have you freezing up here. You're a tenant and Auntie Sylvie wanted me to look after you.' She took Megan's arm, pulling her over the threshold. 'Come on.' When Megan stiffened, she added, 'You don't *have* to talk to him. I'll make him sleep on the floor behind the armchair. You won't even have to look at him, if you don't want to.'

Megan let out a breath and finally, she nodded. 'Okay. Let me grab a pillow and quilt. There were spares, do you need some?'

'Sure.'

When Megan had collected the bedding, Emmie led the way back downstairs to the Cat Lounge, Megan padding slowly after her. Emmie snorted when she stepped inside the lounge. Jared had, in fact, set himself up exactly where she'd just joked about him sleeping. He'd piled the pillows and blankets he'd previously taken into the staffroom in the space between the armchair and the wall, so that he was tucked away in a corner. He was sitting there now, phone in hand, back pressed against the wall, and partially hidden by the armchair. Eric was sniffing curiously around his feet and the gathering of blankets, his bob tail twitching.

Jared didn't say anything, just nodded at them when they stepped inside and looked back down at the screen.

'You can have the couch,' Emmie told Megan. She stepped across the coffee table and pushed it over to one side, so there was a gap for herself on the floor. The cats' ears all pricked back when it screeched on the wooden floor. Thomas darted away from his spot near the fire, onto the back of the sofa, eyes bulging in the orange glow.

'Oh, you don't have to . . .' Megan began. She glanced uncertainly at Jared.

'It's fine. I don't mind the floor. Besides, how else will I get you to leave a five-star review after this?' she joked.

Megan smiled. 'Sorry, Emmie,' she said, so quietly that only they could hear. 'I don't usually get so . . .' She blinked away the teary sheen in her eyes, and lowered her voice. 'Well, like this. It's just uncomfortable. Not what I expected.'

'I don't think any of us expected this. Get comfy. We can heat up some leftover food if we get hungry and settle in for the—'

Before she could finish speaking, there was an almighty smash in the café's main room and Thomas mewled shrilly and bounded over the table, back into his cat-tower hiding place. Some of the other cats tipped their heads back in shock, ears at an angle. The sound was so sudden that Emmie cried out instinctively, too, not even realising she was doing it until the sound left her mouth. Jared leaped to his feet and Megan jumped about a foot in the air, clutching her heart.

All three of them rushed out into the main café, Jared yanking the door to the Cat Lounge shut behind them.

The window behind the counter had been smashed to pieces, spilling glass across the sink below and onto the floor. Some kind of debris had smashed its way through;

it looked like a chunk of grey roof slate. Tiny shards of glass had also managed to find their way onto the counter, glistening like gems. The wind billowed into the café, bringing with it a plume of snow, and a blast of ice-cold air that seared through Emmie's clothes, as if reaching for her skin. The Christmas tablecloth still spread on the tables rippled and waved.

'We have to patch it up!' Jared said, over the gusts of wind that were howling fiercely outside.

'How?' Emmie shot back.

'Find some bin bags and some heavy-duty tape! And something we can wedge in front of the window. Quickly!'

Emmie nodded. She raced to the door to the Cat Lounge first, twisting the control on the cat flap to stop it from working; the last thing they needed was a cat getting out here, or for poor Salem to panic further. She hurried off into the staffroom. Her pulse was still pounding in her throat from the sudden smashing sound – she'd imagined that scene on the news, where a thick tree had slammed into a house, almost killing the man inside. Digging around in the staffroom drawers and cupboards, she found the bin liners and tape. When she returned to the main café, Megan was helping Jared heave one of the smaller bookcases through the gate that led behind the counter.

'Unroll one of the bin bags,' said Jared. 'We'll put it over the window and tape it in place, then put the bookshelf in front. It'll help.'

Wind and snow flurried into the café, coating the tables in wet flakes and soaking the armchairs. Megan took the bin bags from Emmie and unrolled one. She and Megan held the bag in place while Jared stamped down the tape. Emmie had to work hard to ignore the frown on

Jared's face as he pushed tape down near Megan's hand, inches from her. Megan said nothing and averted her eyes. When he did the same on Emmie's side, his fingertips caught against her skin, and her entire arm tingled, electricity shooting up to her neck. She bit down on her lip as something in her lower stomach leaped.

By the time they were done, using multiple layers just to be safe, and the bookshelf was standing strong in front of their makeshift cover – wedged between the taps and the window – Emmie felt, oddly, both warm and frozen solid at the same time. Jared's solution seemed to be doing the trick, though; the bin bag was blustering about and rippling, but it was holding.

'Thank God it was only a small window,' Emmie said, getting her breath back and looking around at the snow droplets that had splattered onto the coffee machines.

'It seems sturdy enough,' said Jared.

'I'll keep the cat flap closed and move a litter tray or two into the lounge with us. I'd take the cats up to Sylvie's flat but I don't want them getting poorly, either . . . and Salem . . .'

'I'll help you with the trays,' Megan offered.

'Thanks,' Emmie said. 'Out in the main café and to the left – there's a staff door to the basement room, where we have some trays.'

When Megan moved off into the hallway, Jared stared at Emmie for a moment, his mouth a slight 'o'. He took a step forward and touched her arm. Even through the layers of clothing, his touch made her feel warm, and she swallowed at the equally warm look in his molten brown eyes.

*

Back in the Cat Lounge, they stayed bundled up in their layers and blankets for the rest of the night, and took it in turns to change the litter trays they'd dragged in for the cats. The cats were content to snooze on the back of the sofa and by the fire – apart from Thomas, who was still in his hiding place in the cat tower – and Emmie had brought in a few cat beds and an extra scratching post as well. It was cramped, but at least it was warm and they were all safe.

'Well, isn't this charming?' Emmie joked at one point, after scooping cat poop into a scented bag and taking it out to the other room before the smell killed them. 'Litter trays roasting on an open fire . . .'

Megan wrinkled her nose, clearly disgusted by the comparison, but to Emmie's surprise, Jared burst into laughter – a full-on, throwing-his-head-back belly laugh. She'd never heard him sound so entertained and a bubble of pride rose in her chest.

'Who wants a drink – tea, hot chocolate?' Emmie asked them.

'Do you have anything alcoholic instead?' Megan mumbled, drawing her knees up to her chest in her position on the sofa. 'To help with the tension . . . It's Christmas, after all.'

Jared's laughter vanished and a crease lined his brow. 'I wouldn't have thought you'd need help with that, Megan. You're pretty good at creating tension on your own.'

Megan flinched. But she chose to ignore him. 'I'm not an aggressive drunk,' she told Emmie. 'Just a giggly idiot.'

'I have just the thing!' Emmie cried, somewhat shrilly, and rose to her feet and dashed from the room, hoping they wouldn't tear each other apart if she was gone for five minutes. When she came back, she was clutching a glass bottle, with a thick bottle of Coke wedged under her bad arm – a bit of a balance, but she'd made it work. 'Jack Daniel's. Sylvie got it for me as a moving-in present.'

'I didn't have you down as a whiskey girl,' said Jared.

'I'll grab some glasses too.'

She left the lounge, returning with some glasses for them to drink from. Jared took one, filling it with whiskey and fizzing Coke, and setting the Coke down on the table so Megan could help herself, too.

'Here you go, Emmie,' said Megan, who had made Emmie a drink, too.

'Thanks.'

A tiny part of Emmie's mind couldn't help but wonder what it'd be like if Megan *weren't* here. Maybe she'd fall into Jared's arms by the fire and they'd spend a romantic evening together . . .

She hadn't even had any whiskey yet and she was already daydreaming and acting like an idiot. She needed to get a grip; she was standing here, between a gorgeous man and his equally stunning ex. It was ridiculous to even contemplate anything like that, while his ex was here. Her heart sank when she thought about the possibility of them getting back together. Maybe he'd have a change of heart while they were stuck here, and decide to take Megan back.

'What's that noise?' Megan said suddenly.

'I don't hear anything,' said Emmie.

'Shh, listen. Try to ignore the fire cracking . . .'

They all fell silent. Emmie strained her ears. Very faintly, she could hear something: a gentle scraping. As if, somewhere far in the depths of the café, someone was scraping paint from the walls.

'Do you hear?' whispered Megan, her eyes widening.

'I can hear it,' said Emmie. She frowned, listening.

'Probably just something outside,' Jared suggested. 'Maybe the wind blowing something into the walls – a branch. It's been windy as hell.'

Megan visibly shuddered and clutched her elbows. 'It's *creepy*,' she said. 'Is it haunted in here? Did someone die in the walls or something? I heard that on a podcast once. Some guy was secretly living in the walls of this family house and he died there.'

'You're actually pretty morbid, you know that?' Emmie laughed.

'I have been told that,' said Megan, sounding proud.

Silence descended over them again. Kitty hopped up onto the sofa to rub up against Megan's side, and she tickled behind her ears until the cat settled beside her, sprawled out with her paws extended, purring loudly.

'Maybe we can play a game to pass the time,' Megan suggested.

Jared raised his eyebrows.

'It could break the ice,' she added weakly. 'I'm sick of the weird atmosphere in here. If we're stuck here, we can at least not act *weird*.'

'It *is* weird. It's a messed-up situation to be in for Christmas,' Jared said. He'd scooted to the side slightly in his position on the floor, so he was more visible behind the armchair.

Megan frowned. 'Let's play a drinking game, then. At least if I'm drunk it'll take the edge off the way you're looking at me, like I'm a piece of shit.'

'I'm not looking at you like you're a piece of shit at all. I'm just here, existing.'

'I don't know . . .' Emmie began. She wasn't sure a drinking game was the way to go . . . Maybe in their drunken state, Megan and Jared might actually *resolve* things, or rekindle old feelings. Or scratch each other's eyes out. That one seemed more likely right now.

'Aw, come on, Emmie,' said Megan. 'I'm a silly drunk, and so is Jared, I remember. And it's Christmas. We're due a tipple.'

'We don't have to play a game like that if Emmie isn't comfortable,' Jared pointed out. He was sticking up for her again. Her lips twitched.

Hadn't she been telling herself earlier that she'd always been so caught up in working, in pushing herself? That she hadn't even made proper time to nurture friend-ships back home because she just wanted to 'make it', whatever that meant? Being snowed in here could be an opportunity to let her hair down a bit. It wasn't like she had to serve customers – and with the splint, drawing was more difficult anyway. And not everyone was like her brother when they got drunk. Why should she let him stop her from having fun?

'Okay. Let's do it. I don't know either of you that well,' said Emmie, 'so we could guess something about the other person, and if the guess is wrong, we take a swig?' She took a seat on the leather sofa, near Megan.

'I like that idea!' said Megan, clapping her hands together.

'I already know Megan plenty,' said Jared reluctantly.

'We get it, Jared,' Megan snapped, wrapping her arms around her knees. 'You know me, and you don't care to know me anymore, right? Well, there are things you *don't* know. You should listen sometime instead of being bull-headed!'

'I'm not being bull—'

'You two can quiz *me* and I'll quiz you both,' Emmie cut in, trying for a compromise and ignoring the mini-spat. 'No need to ask each other questions.'

'Okay then,' said Jared.

'Megan?'

She gave a half-shrug and examined her fingernails. 'Fine by me.'

'Good.' Emmie sat up straighter.

Salem was still huddled on the armchair, like a black ball of soot. Since they'd left to deal with the broken window, Lilian and Duchess had sandwiched him in like a cat burrito, and they were all sleeping now. That sounded like a good idea for an illustration. She'd have to sketch it out later.

'I'll go first and ask Jared,' Emmie said. 'I'm going to guess . . . you have a sister?'

'Wrong. Just a brother.'

Emmie mock-clapped her hand to her forehead. 'Not a good start.' She took a swig from her whiskey, the liquid scorching its way down her throat, eased somewhat by the fizzing Coke.

'Hm,' he pondered, assessing her, and grinned. 'Your parents live in Manchester. Easy one, right?'

She scoffed. 'Wrong, actually! They live in Spain. They have a school in Alcaudete, teaching English. Are you trying to get me drunk by guessing things that seem obvious because I told you I'm from Manchester? That's cheating!'

He smirked and took a glug from his glass, pushing his hair out of his eyes in one smooth movement that made her heart pound extra hard.

'I'll guess with Megan now,' Emmie said. 'You went to university?'

Megan shook her head. 'No. I never went to uni. I did beauty therapy and nails in college and then started working.'

'Ah! I assumed you met Jared at uni. I thought he did English or poetry, for sure!'

Jared tapped the rim of his glass. 'You thought *I* did English or poetry? Why?' He laughed again, and she felt that familiar swelling feeling in her chest – joy that she'd made him laugh. 'I didn't go to uni, either.'

Sipping some whiskey again, she answered, 'You look almost like a vagabond, I guess. A nomad. You know, a wanderer of the hills.'

He laughed harder. '*I wandered lonely as a cloud . . .*' he quoted. When she looked bemused – the words were familiar somehow, but she couldn't place who said them – he said, 'Wordsworth. No? Come on, he grew up in Cumbria.'

'Yeah,' Megan added. 'Tourists always come to see Dove Cottage over in Grasmere.'

'Oh,' Emmie said. 'I might have seen that on a magnet in a tourist shop . . .' The alcohol was buzzing pleasantly through Emmie already; she may as well be wandering on the clouds herself. Was she actually starting to have fun?

'You've never had pets?' Megan said, turning to Emmie, and tapping her chin. 'That's why you work here – to fulfil a dream.'

'Wrong,' she answered. 'Family cats.' She thought of Faye and laughed. 'There are definitely people working here as some kind of . . . wish fulfilment, though. Mostly because they have miserable landlords who won't let them have a cat.'

'Ha.' Megan knocked back some whiskey. 'I've had a few of those.'

They went back and forth like this for a while. She learned Jared lived in a flat in Ambleside, near a gushing waterfall – a popular spot for tourists. He liked action-based video games, where she preferred cosy ones. Megan didn't care much for games or graphic novels, but they *did* both love watching cheesy romance movies, something Jared scoffed at. Megan was also a horror movie buff, and never grew bored of them, even the ones that frightened her the most. She'd seen almost every horror series on Netflix that Emmie could think to list off. That explained her morbid sense of humour, then.

Soon, they'd all had multiple glasses of whiskey. Megan's eyes had hazed over and she'd scooted over to let Emmie sit on the couch with her.

'I want to ask Jared something,' she burst out.

Chapter 12

Jared braced himself. He'd known this would come at some point; the whiskey game had just speeded things up. He supposed it was better to get it out of the way now. If she had things to say, she could say them. They could hash things out. It didn't change anything. He wouldn't be taking her back.

'Why didn't you let me explain properly?' Megan asked. 'I tried to call. You never even gave me a *chance*. You just said we were done and blocked me.'

Jared sighed so deeply a whistling sound came from between his teeth. 'Why would I? You cheated. I found out where you'd really been, all of those times—'

'You shouldn't be so judgemental—'

He laughed then, wry and hollow. '*Judgemental?* You had a fiancé, yet you started seeing me. We were together for nine months, Megan! And I never knew! You told me you had an awkward flatmate, that your place was always a mess, and that was why I couldn't visit you, but all the while, it was because you were living with your fiancé. Of course I cut you off after that. What person wouldn't? And to make matters worse, you were viewing *wedding venues* here while you were seeing me.'

'You never even gave me chance to explain that! I never viewed venues here while we were together! I used to come here with Gran years ago, and she loved Crescent

Wood Country House . . . Ethan just happened to know that . . .' Megan's lip was wobbling.

'Oh, please,' he said, and had to resist rolling his eyes. 'Don't give me the crocodile tears—'

'They're not!' Her voice was shrill and she was sitting at the edge of the couch, ramrod straight. 'You have no idea—'

'I can guess. You wanted to have it all—'

'He was a control freak!' she cried. 'I tried to leave so many times. It started off small: he'd guilt-trip me for seeing my friends, make me feel bad about my clothes, my make-up. It got worse when he quit his job. He'd tell me he'd hurt himself if I left, that he was living *for* me. I'd wanted to leave for so long. When I met you . . .' Her chin was dimpled as she struggled to contain her emotion, and although Jared opened his mouth to speak, nothing came out. 'I thought I could work up the courage to leave him. But he kept telling me he couldn't live without me, that he'd be homeless, that he'd jump off a bridge if anything happened to us, or if I called the wedding off.' Tears were flooding freely down her face now. She was speaking quickly, as if she'd needed to get this out. 'I was so terrified he needed me and that he'd die if I left, that it would be my fault. But I wanted to be with *you*. I loved *you*.'

Emmie glanced between the two of them, her hands clasped awkwardly in her lap. Jared was still struggling for words; he imagined Emmie wanted the floor to swallow her up and spit her out somewhere where she *wasn't* stuck between him and his ex.

He'd assumed the typical cheating scenario – that Megan had wanted to enjoy both of them, without ever committing to one until she was forced to. He'd been wrong. Did that really excuse what she'd done, though, and the fact that she'd lied to him for so long?

'You never should have kissed me, taken it further with me, not while you were with someone else,' he said, but his tone was softer. 'Even when I called you my girlfriend by accident that time, you agreed – acted like we were exclusive. You should have talked to me about Ethan instead.' He was bone-tired and there was a heaviness to his limbs, an ache forming in his eye sockets because, in a warped way, he could relate to Ethan. He knew what it was like to carry around that endless, bottomless feeling, like a giant maw in the chest. But there was no defending Ethan's behaviour and such emotional abuse and control tactics. No wonder Megan was so upset, if that was what she'd been living with.

'I *know* that, and I'm sorry. That's why I came here. To apologise. To explain, and see if we still had a chance to fix it,' Megan said softly.

Jared was silent. Emmie's hand was on Megan's now, squeezing. She was stuck in the middle and she was comforting Megan. He felt a rush of something – admiration, maybe? He didn't know. What he did know was that there was nothing left for him and Megan. All he felt when he looked at her was sadness, and a sense of weariness. There was nothing positive, and besides, he would never be able to trust her again. That wasn't a solid foundation for a lasting relationship. He just wanted to put all of this behind him. And maybe he couldn't until he told her the other reason he'd been so furious with her.

'You missed Poppy's vet appointment because you were with Ethan,' he said.

She frowned.

'You were meant to take Poppy in for a scan.' He hesitated, collecting himself, keeping his emotions steady. She looked almost hopeful, her eyes glistening. 'You didn't take her. You said you forgot because your flatmate was causing some trouble at home. After you left, she got ill. She was on steroids for months; they helped at first. Until they didn't. She died a few weeks ago. The vet told me if they'd have caught things sooner, maybe she . . .'

He trailed off, unable to continue because his voice was cracking and the bad memories were coming back, of cradling Poppy in his arms as she weakened, of wrapping her in a blanket, saying his last goodbye as the vet sat solemnly in a chair in his flat. He sucked in a breath as he tried to compose himself. He'd wrestled with that decision, the euthanasia. It was one of the hardest things he'd ever had to do, but he'd known it was time, that she was unhappy, the medication no longer helping.

Megan's eyes widened and she pressed a hand to her lips. 'I didn't know . . .' she breathed. There was another beat of silence, and then: 'You blamed me?'

'I did at the time – maybe a part of me still couldn't let it go,' he said honestly. No one would ever really know what Poppy's illness was, because he couldn't afford all the additional tests, and maybe catching it earlier wouldn't have made a jot of difference. But the emotions were still tangled inside him, and Megan was wrapped up in them. 'I can't help wondering if things would have been different, if—'

'I'm sorry,' said Megan, her eyes brimming with glassy tears now. 'I'm so, so sorry. I loved Poppy too – if I'd known—'

'I know we can't change anything,' he said quickly. Guilt was clamping down on his chest, making it difficult to get the words out. She looked positively haunted by what he'd said, her cheeks drained of colour, and the look on her face caused something to shift inside him, like a stone being dislodged. Holding on to all this guilt and blame wasn't helping either of them. 'I know . . . I know it wasn't you, it was whatever was wrong with her. I was just so angry. I did everything I could and it wasn't enough. Even if I'd taken her myself that day, maybe the outcome would've been the same.'

'I'm really sorry.'

Megan blinked back her tears, hard. Emmie's hand was still resting on Megan's, but she was watching Jared closely.

'I wanted to tell you everything. You don't know what Ethan was like,' said Megan, staring at her lap.

'I know,' said Jared quietly.

'It was hell sometimes. I was trapped. I felt like . . . I felt like you saved me, in a way. But I still couldn't get myself unstuck and I couldn't bring myself to tell you either.' Her chest shuddered as she inhaled deeply. 'And that was on me.'

There was a long, pregnant pause.

'We can't fix it, can we?' said Megan, giving a shaky laugh even though her eyes were watery. 'Whatever we had before.'

Jared slowly shook his head. 'No. I've already moved on, and I don't want to go backwards. And I think you've been through enough too. Don't you think a fresh start would be better for both of us?'

Megan got to her feet, and gathered up her quilt, pillow, and hot water bottle. 'I'm going back upstairs to bed,' she said softly, hurrying to the door, tears leaking from the corners of her eyes.

'Megan—' Emmie began.

'I need to be on my own. I'll be fine.'

'At least take some of the flasks up so you have more hot water. And the first-aid blanket from the staffroom, just in case?'

Megan nodded and was out of the door so fast, she might as well have been a shadow in a darkened forest. Something twisted in Jared's chest – he hadn't wanted to make her cry, but it was all out in the open, at least. It was better that she knew everything. Closure, like Emmie had said.

Once Megan had vanished, the silence was thick and Jared's neck felt clammy. He watched one of the cats head over for a drink of water from a feeder, lapping at the liquid. Emmie rose to her feet and wedged the towel they were using by the door to block any draughts back into place. She sat back down and grabbed the whiskey bottle.

'You'll probably want more whiskey,' said Emmie, waving it at him.

He grabbed his glass and moved to join her on the sofa, so she could give him a top-up. 'You're probably right,' he said, as she poured liquid into the glass one-handed – he helped her by steadying the bottle. When she was done, he took the whiskey from her, set it down on the table, and sighed. 'I didn't mean to upset her.'

Emmie gave a half-shrug, but she shifted, looking uncomfortable. 'You needed to talk. No time like the present.'

'More awkwardness, though,' he said. 'Having to turn down my ex in front of you.'

'And the rest of the audience,' Emmie said, waving her non-splinted hand to encompass the cats gathered by the fire.

He laughed. 'They aren't so bad.'

'Will she be okay upstairs, do you think?' Emmie asked him. 'It's really cold.'

'I don't think you could persuade her to come back, after that.' He looked away, grabbing his glass again for a swig of whiskey, and lifting his eyebrows at her. 'Are we still playing the game now?'

'We can be, if you want.'

'Good. Then let me guess a few more things about you.'

They bounced questions back and forth, random facts and pieces of history and memories. He told her about his mother and her love of tarot cards and palm readings, how she found signs in the smallest of things. And she told him about her parents, how long they'd been married, how they moved to Spain a few years after she graduated.

'You feel lonely without them?' he guessed.

'I can't deny that.' Emmie seemed tipsy now, giggling at random intervals, her cheeks turning pinker. 'And maybe I resent them a little. They left me to deal with my ass of a brother by myself. They're smarter than me, though. They cut him off ages ago. And I kept him around, even though he took advantage of me. I still struggle to ignore him.'

'Why'd they have to cut him off?'

She giggled again, sagging sideways on the sofa until she was almost close enough to fall into his lap, the firelight dancing in her eyes. 'Well, because they're smarter than me. He was always drunk, gambling, taking advantage.

Sometimes you have to cut people out. Like a big, rotten tumour.' She mimed sawing something from her arm. 'Even family. I have a difficult time saying no – and he's my brother. He wasn't always this way.' She set her empty whiskey glass on the table with a clatter, and he did the same. 'I'm just your resident people-pleaser. And workaholic.'

'Maybe you've had enough now,' he said. She looked precariously close to falling off the couch.

'S'true. I'm a lightweight, really. I hardly drink, probably because of him. I don't want to be like that – like *him*. Whiskey's warm, though. Nice.'

Her eyes were hazy with the fog of alcohol. Jared was more relaxed, leaning back, one leg propped on the table; he'd had more than her, too, but he could hold his alcohol. 'Do you want some water?' he asked.

She waved a lazy hand. 'I'm good.'

'Really? You don't seem it.'

She made a *pfft* noise and tucked her hair behind her ears. 'Dustin's always criticising me, putting me down. I had all these rejections piling up from internships, opportunities . . . He said I needed to *get serious and grow up*.' She rolled her eyes. 'Ironic, really, since all he does these days is muck around and cause everyone else grief. When I got offered the picture book contract, I thought it would all work out.' She barked out a laugh. 'Obviously my brother decided I'd made it and started asking me to loan him even more money, all the time, like a personal cash machine. The publisher had other ideas too, and ditched me.'

'Ah,' he said softly. 'I'm sorry to hear that.'

Emmie rose her hands to the ceiling, the splint lifting high in the air. 'They pulled the offer. Now I make lattes and clean litter trays when I really want to be doing something more with my art. I keep positive but sometimes . . . I think, does anyone care?'

'I care,' he said. 'That drawing you did of Poppy, it meant a lot to me. You're a good artist.'

There was a pinkish hue to the top of her cheeks; he wanted to brush his fingers across the colour, trace the lines of her cheekbones and jaw.

'It meant a lot to you?' she breathed.

'Of course.'

She scooted closer to him, and her eyes were dancing with light from the wood burner and candles, as if they housed fireflies within.

'Jared,' she said softly. 'Is it really so bad to be stuck here? That's part of the game, so you have to tell the truth.'

'It depends. It'd be less awkward if Megan—'

'Not Megan,' Emmie said. 'With me. Being stuck here *with me*. You can tell me. The cats won't tell anyone, and neither will I.'

He relaxed at that, a smile tugging the corners of his lips. 'It's not so bad,' he said quietly, and exhaled deeply, a rush of warm, whiskey-scented breath. 'We're keeping occupied. And what about you?' he added. 'Is it really so bad being shut in here with . . . What did you call me? A vagabond?'

'Not so bad,' she responded.

His smile grew a few centimetres wider. She was glowing so vibrantly in the firelight, as if she'd been forged in the flame, her hair threaded with spools of gold. God, she was so beautiful. And so talented and funny – and he loved her positivity, her can-do attitude, even in the face of rejection and doubt. She didn't seem to realise how good she was. And not just as an artist – as a person. She leaned closer, glittering lights contained in her eyes, and he couldn't bring himself to move away – not yet.

'What are you looking at?' he asked, clearing his throat.

'Your skin, it looks pretty.'

He laughed, but it was edged with a hoarseness. She was too close, and he was noticing the soft heart shape of her mouth, the crinkled lines on her lips, and the barely perceptible freckles dusting her cheeks like sprinkles. 'I think you should probably get some sleep now,' he croaked.

She shuffled closer to him, ignoring the suggestion. The movement brought her face even nearer to his, and he glanced up, still and unmoving.

'What are *you* looking at?' she asked quietly. 'Is my skin all glowy too?' She patted her own cheeks.

'No, your freckles . . .'

'Oh . . .' She giggled, reaching for his hand with her good one, hesitating before grasping it in her own and raising it to her cheek. His heart cartwheeled when his fingertips touched her skin, brushing across the scattering of freckles that bridged her cheeks and nose. She felt soft, silky, warmed by the fire.

He didn't want to let go – he wanted to keep hold of her hand, keep touching her. He threaded his fingers through hers, entangling them.

One of the cats leaped up onto the sofa next to him, jarring him out of the moment as it snaked its way onto the back to settle down. He pulled his hand away from Emmie's abruptly. She'd been drinking; she wasn't thinking properly. Neither was he. He couldn't think straight when she looked at him with those eyes, and he couldn't say for sure whether the whiskey had addled his brain. And was this wrong, anyway, with his ex just a few floors above them? What if she came back down?

'Get some sleep,' he told her hoarsely.

'I'm not tired,' she whispered, even as she stifled a yawn and looked at him blearily.

She leaned towards him, glancing to his mouth, so close their noses almost touched. Her hair fell out from behind her ear and brushed his face. He reached out, tucking it back into place, his mouth very dry as his hand skimmed the soft curve of her ear.

He couldn't pull away, even though something inside him was screaming that he should put some distance between them, that Megan was upstairs and Emmie wasn't thinking straight.

'You're drunk,' he said slowly.

'And?' she prompted.

'You aren't thinking.'

'Don't be silly,' she said. She didn't move away. Her eyes were bursting with orange light, with wavering flames, making her look intensely beautiful. Emmie cupped her hand on the back of his neck, her warm touch sending a pulse through his skin, through his core. 'Of course I'm thinking. It's just that I have no inhibitions now. No wall between what I feel . . . and everything else.'

'What you feel . . . ?' he repeated. 'And what's that?'

'I can show you,' she whispered.

And then she was kissing him. And to hell with Megan and all the rest of it.

He barely remembered the last time he'd felt like this. She was right: she had no inhibitions, that was for sure.

Where he was tentative at first, she was confident, pressing her mouth into his, gripping the back of his neck. His hands rippled through her soft hair, pulling her closer to him. He could taste the whiskey on her lips, and even though it sparked a warning in his head – that maybe this wasn't wise, not right now – he ignored it, pushing it aside in favour of the fire roaring through him. His body seemed both a million miles away, light and breezy, and aflame and blazing, all at once.

A cat scrabbled loudly, kicking at the litter inside one of the boxes in the corner, jolting them apart in surprise.

The noise brought him crashing back to himself, to reality. He got to his feet at once, feeling breathless, putting distance between them. This was wrong, all wrong. If she found out about this, Megan would think he was doing it to hurt her, and Emmie might agree when she sobered up. She might feel in control now, like this was what she wanted, but how would she feel in the morning, stone-cold sober? Going any further with this wasn't right. If this was going to happen with Emmie – and God, he *wanted* it to, he wanted her – it had to be at the right time.

'We really shouldn't do this when you're drunk. You can sleep on the sofa,' he said to her, moving over to the litter box so he could clean it and take the bag away, trying to ignore the adrenaline pumping through him and the scalding heat on his lips. 'Stretch out.'

Emmie pouted at him. Her cheeks were flushed pink. All he wanted to do was kiss her again. 'Spoilsport,' she said.

Why, even as he told himself it was wrong right now, did he want to go back over there and be with her until the sun came up?

Chapter 13

The following morning, Emmie woke feeling sluggish, with a mild headache and a craving for a pizza or a cheeseburger – not that she was going to get either of those things when they had no power. She rolled over on the sofa and grabbed her phone, squinting at the glowing screen in the semi-darkness and making the backs of her eyes ache as though they were being pressed with a set of fingers. She groaned. Still no Wi-Fi, which meant no power. Binx was sleeping at the end of the sofa, by her feet, his nose tucked into his little grey tail.

She was hungover. She didn't remember the last time *that* had happened. And then she remembered the kiss she'd shared with Jared. That had actually *happened*. A rush of something – like pride – coursed through her. She may feel bad physically now, but she'd had fun last night. She'd felt a million times lighter. Although she did feel a little guilty, kissing Jared like that, with Megan upstairs. What would she think if she knew? It had been so tactless of her.

The blinds in the Cat Lounge were closed, but pale chinks of light shone through the slats. The fire in the wood burner had died down, leaving behind nothing but a pile of grey ash, and even under the thick quilt Jared must have placed over her, she could still feel the cold. It nipped at her hands and ears. The cats were all quiet and sleeping, dotted around the room – some on the back of the sofa, others on some of the floating beds lining the walls. In the corner, she could see Jared's torso poking out from behind the armchair; he was fast asleep in a cocoon of blankets with his hat pulled down over his ears, his long hair sticking out of the bottom. She smiled faintly at the sight.

Emmie sat up, adjusting her splint, which had become askew during the night. She should go check on Megan. But first, she'd start a fire and heat up some soup – perhaps take some to Megan as well. She became even guiltier when she realised she was only thinking of doing that because she felt a steady trickle of guilt about the previous evening.

She pushed all that to one side as best she could, but it still lingered there like a persistent cobweb. She cleaned the litter and filled the cats' dispensers with fresh food – prompting several of them to wake up at once and weave around her ankles.

'Salem,' Emmie whispered. He was still in his loaf position on the armchair. He'd been in the same spot last night. He'd barely moved – maybe a few inches to the side, but not much else. 'Here you go, little boy.'

She bent over and clinked her nails onto one of the food dispensers. He simply opened his eyes and blinked at her, but made no effort to move.

She tried setting some biscuits down on the armchair in front of his nose. He sniffed at them absently, and turned away, his huge yellowy eyes uninterested.

'You have to eat,' she said quietly, kneeling down before the armchair and stroking the top of his head. 'It's your favourite flavour!'

The black cat turned his head and tucked his face into his tail.

Emmie felt slightly sick, and she wasn't sure if it was the whiskey she'd drunk last night, or worry for Salem – possibly both. She tried fetching him a different type of food, and even tried offering him a few treats and cat milk. He lapped up all of the milk, but wouldn't touch anything else. At least she'd managed to get some more liquid down him, and he was drinking water too, but she was seriously worried. She crossed the room and fired off a message to her Aunt Sylvie.

> Don't want to worry you too much, but Salem is off colour and we're still stuck here. Might be nothing but he's not eating. He's had a bit of milk and is drinking water. Anything else I can do? Has he done this before? xxx

There wasn't much else she could do, so she focused on building a fire in the burner. They were down to their last few logs so she didn't put in much. When it was getting going, she fetched some leftover soup and bowls from the café, popping open the plastic Tupperware containers and pouring the liquid into a pan instead. She left the pan of soup on the wood burner – it'd take a while for the fire to build properly, anyway. With one last glance at Salem, she went to check on Megan.

Reaching Megan's door, she tapped a few times and waited. When Megan opened it, she was wrapped in a green sleeping bag and a thick winter quilt. Her hair was pulled back into a ponytail, slightly dishevelled around the edges, and faint dark circles rimmed her eyes; it looked like she'd barely slept.

'Morning,' said Emmie. 'Have you been okay up here? I'm sorry I didn't check on you last night, I fell asleep.' *And kissed your ex,* she thought, but didn't say. She was almost afraid the words would come rushing out of her lips, and pinched her mouth together.

A memory flitted across her mind – inching closer to Jared, the firelight dancing across his cheeks and making them shine amber, how close she'd been to him. Her mouth on his, gooseflesh all over her skin. Guilt crawled up her spine.

'I've been okay. I used the first-aid blanket and refilled the hot water bottles with the flasks, so it wasn't too bad . . .'

'You really don't have to stay up here—'

Megan was shaking her head. Emmie could tell she'd been crying during the night, and her stomach clenched. Her eyes were puffy and surrounded by purple and red broken blood vessels. For the first time, she looked unpolished.

'I'll manage,' Megan reassured her. 'I don't really want to be down there with Jared . . .'

Emmie sighed. 'It probably doesn't make much difference anyway. There isn't enough wood for the burner.'

'Really?'

'Yeah, I was an idiot and went to town on the cat supplies and everything else – but not the wood. I didn't realise Sylvie had none left.'

'It's not your fault. If it helps, there's another first-aid blanket in here. I totally forgot about the first-aid kit

Sylvie mentioned was in here. I didn't think I'd need it.' Megan stepped back from the doorway. 'Come in, I'll give it to you.'

Emmie stepped through the door and followed her into the lounge. The blinds were thrown open, revealing an endless white sky and a flurry of frantic snowfall. Storm Marie really was in full force, a tangle of flakes and wind gusts. While she was here, Emmie took the chance to peer out through the glass, squinting through the snowy chaos to get a look at lower ground. It was tricky to make out, but she could just about see the mountainous snowdrifts trapping them inside – although it was difficult to estimate how tall they were from here, in all the wild flurries of the storm.

How much longer would they be stuck at the café? She needed to get Salem checked out, to make sure he was okay.

'You're really not going to come downstairs?' Emmie asked, turning her back on the windows.

Megan shook her head. 'He said he wants to move on . . .' Megan drew the quilt tighter around her shoulders; it was so large, it trailed the floor behind her like a wedding train. 'I guess I can't make him change his mind. I should have known. Maybe I shouldn't have been holding on so hard.' She took a long, shuddering breath, released a laugh on the exhalation. 'It was such a messed-up situation anyway. And that was my fault.'

'Don't be so hard on yourself,' Emmie said. 'It's tough, when you're dealing with someone like that,' she added, thinking of her brother. Sometimes, people got their claws stuck into you so deeply that it was hard to wrench them free, even if you knew it was for the best. Especially when they were family, or a fiancé, in Megan's case.

'Thanks,' said Megan. She crossed to a dresser, opening a drawer and digging around until she produced a first-aid kit in a green packet. 'Here it is. The blanket's in there.' She turned and passed it to Emmie.

'I'm making soup on the wood burner,' said Emmie. 'You should eat something hot. I'll bring some up.'

Megan nodded, a smile ghosting her lips. 'I'd like that. You know . . .' She paused again, clutching at the quilt gathered around her. 'I didn't expect you to be so nice to me.'

'Why not?' *Would she think I'm being so nice if she knew I'd kissed Jared last night?* Emmie almost wanted to admit it, because she felt terrible now, standing here in front of Megan. Even though she didn't regret the kiss, not at all.

'I don't know – I mean, what I told you about everything, with my ex-fiancé and Jared, how I lied to him—'

Emmie cut across her. 'Hey, I don't believe in all this stupid rivalry between women. You had your reasons.' She shrugged. 'And anyway, I know what it's like to deal with someone like your ex-fiancé. I don't just mean the usual annoying little brother, either. I'm talking a professional emotional con man, at times.'

'Professional emotional con man?' Megan's eyes widened, then she burst into laughter. 'God, I needed that,' she said, when she'd laughed for a solid minute and had wiped the corner of her eye. 'Sorry,' she added. 'I shouldn't laugh.'

Emmie grinned. At least she'd managed to make her smile. 'It's fine, it's better than crying. Come downstairs if you change your mind.'

'I will.'

She turned, and was halfway to the door when Megan said, 'Emmie?'

'Yeah?'

'Just so you know. Jared's not an emotional con man. He's . . . a really great guy, someone who's worth having in your corner. He treated me like a queen.' Megan turned her attention back on the snow. 'I know it's over between us, but . . . any girl would be lucky to have him.'

Chapter 14

While she was upstairs, Emmie took some painkill-ers for her mild hangover and quickly changed into some fresh clothes she retrieved from the wardrobe in her flat – a thick pair of grey leggings, a warm black dress and a red jumper printed with white stars. It took longer than it normally would; it wasn't exactly easy to get dressed while wearing a splint. Her cheeks flushed when she imagined asking Jared for help, but she dis-carded that particular daydream – that would only lead to one thing, and *that* wasn't going to happen with Megan here. When she returned to the Cat Lounge to check on the soup, Jared was awake and stretching his arms over his head. She headed over to the wood burner to give the soup a good stir, trying to ignore the way her insides were swirling like milk poured into tea.

'Morning,' Jared said, stifling a yawn. 'Are you . . .' He trailed off.

'Morning,' she said, avoiding his gaze when she thought of the way she'd been last night. Being tipsy made her more forthright – to say what was on her mind, to be more open with her opinions and true feelings – but perhaps it hadn't been a good thing, not with Megan here. Should they discuss it? She didn't know; he seemed just as unsure as she did. 'Do you know if Salem's eaten anything?' she asked instead. She motioned at the black cat in the armchair, the biscuits still positioned close to him, as she swirled the spoon in the broth.

He shook his head. 'I didn't see him eat anything. He did get down to drink some water, though.'

Emmie frowned. 'He hasn't been eating at all. I thought it was a hairball at first, but he hasn't brought anything up that I can tell. I messaged Sylvie about it, but . . .'

Jared shifted in his stack of blankets. 'Not eating is a serious symptom for cats.'

'I know. But it's still snowing. It's really coming down, and the storm's going to be here another day at least. Even if we *could* dig ourselves out today, it's Boxing Day, and travel might still be iffy. How would we get over to the vet in this weather?' Even as she spoke, her stomach twisted at the thought of Salem going more time without food. 'Do you want some soup?' she asked Jared.

Jared nodded. The blankets rustled as he got to his feet. Jess watched him from the back of the sofa with interest, her big green eyes following his every move.

The kiss between them lingered in Emmie's mind, and she couldn't help but imagine his lips brushing hers, what it had felt like. She pressed a hand to the side of her face, stirring the pan with the other. And the way he'd looked when she'd given him her sketch of him and Poppy – the way he'd squeezed her hand, said *It's perfect*. He had looked at her drawing – and her – like they were jewels poking unexpectedly from a craggy wall.

Megan's words floated into her mind. *Any girl would be lucky to have him.*

Emmie shook her head slightly to clear away the thoughts. That *hadn't* been an invitation from Megan to help herself to Jared. It was just a statement, letting Emmie know Jared wasn't toxic. She wouldn't want Megan to think she was throwing herself at her ex-boyfriend to hurt her. There were more important things to think about, anyway. Like Salem's health. And getting out of here. Kissing could wait.

'Are we going to talk about last night?' said Jared carefully.

'I don't know . . .' She pulled in a lungful of air, concentrating on stirring, the heat rising from the pan. But he was behind her now – she could feel the heat of him against her back. And all she wanted to do was place her hands on his chest and kiss him again; her palms tingled with the urge. 'With Megan here?'

'I know. But you seemed pretty sure last night . . . Was that just the whiskey?'

She let go of the spoon and turned to face him. God, he was gorgeous – the way the stubble scattered across his jawline, his hair brushing his ears and highlighting the planes of his face. He looked hurt at the possibility that she'd only kissed him because of alcohol, and her chest squeezed.

'I was sure. I am,' she said, raising her hand, brushing her fingertips against his chest. She felt him stiffen beneath them. Her mouth became very dry, and she had to swallow. 'It's just . . . now's not the right time. If Megan knew, she'd think . . .'

'I know. We're on the same page,' he answered. He reached up, clasping her fingers to his. He looked over to the door. Then, subtly, he planted a kiss on them, sending sparks through her. 'But we'll talk about it? When this is all done with?'

Emmie nodded. All the air seemed to have left her lungs. She turned back to the soup, otherwise she might not be able to avoid glancing at his lips. And that was dangerous.

Her phone pinged. Glad of the distraction, she grabbed it, scanning through the message list. Sylvie had been in touch.

> Try the home-visit vet tomorrow when the storm starts to clear. He can check Salem. I'll be making my way home in a few days as soon as the weather clears up. Thanks so much for holding things down, Em x

Emmie shot back a reply:

> I'll call the vet tomorrow, first thing. I'm sure Salem will be okay xx

She set the phone back down and poured some soup into bowls.

'Here you go,' she said, offering one of the steaming bowls of thick chicken soup to Jared, the aroma rising up to her nose and making her stomach rumble. 'I promised Megan some as well, so I'll take it up.'

★

Jared pushed open the door to the storeroom – they'd run out of litter bags, so he'd come to get fresh ones. It was cold in here, the air pluming in front of him thickly, and despite being wrapped in his coat, a pair of gloves, and his hat, the cold air felt as though it were getting into his very bones. He crossed the storeroom, rubbing his gloved hands together and blowing on them.

As he scoured the shelves, he heard it. That *scritch-scratch* sound Megan had first pointed out. He paused, listening. He was sure he'd heard a squeak as well, something that sounded alive. Holding his breath, he edged across the room, towards the sound in the corner.

Scritch-scratch. Eek.

That didn't sound like a branch. Did Sylvie have mice in the walls, or something? He frowned, pressing an ear to the wall between two shelves, the wallpaper and brick on the other side freezing cold against his skin.

Scritch-scratch. Eek.

He couldn't make out what it was, even as he strained his ears to breaking point. He tapped on the wall.

All went quiet.

Jared straightened up, frowning at a tiny hole in the wallpaper. He wished he could see what was on the other side.

He'd heard mice before. Their squeaks sounded high-pitched; this sounded like something completely different. More like a whimper or a grizzle.

He went back through to the Cat Lounge, frowning, and asked Emmie to come listen. She set down her portable console and followed him.

'Not you too,' said Emmie, on the way to the storeroom. 'Do you think this place has a ghost as well?'

Jared snorted. 'I'm not my mother.'

'What?'

'Oh, well, you know how she does tarot readings for work? She's into spiritual stuff. If you asked her, she'd probably say it was the ghost of some cat who lived here . . .' He trailed off, realising what he'd said, thinking of Poppy and then remembering the drawing he'd rescued off the floor at the winter fair, the one Emmie had done. He hadn't even mentioned it to her, but she didn't seem to miss it much.

He was quiet as they passed into the storeroom, acutely aware of the narrow spaces and how closely they had to walk. When they approached the wall where he'd heard the sound, his arm was almost brushing against hers. Boxes were stacked on the shelves all around them, making it feel even more claustrophobic. He hadn't even *felt* claustrophobic – he didn't mind cramped spaces – until she came close to him. The back of his neck felt unnaturally warm, given the cold air in here.

He caught the sound again, but it faded instantly, much quicker than it had earlier.

'Listen. Do you hear that?' he said to her.

They were quiet for a while, listening. Jared was half convinced the sound wouldn't happen again, just to prove him wrong. Emmie shifted on the balls of her feet, and her shoulder brushed his, making a burst of something tingly rush up his neck and down his spine. He needed to get a *grip*. He knew he was attracted to her, felt it tugging at him the more time he spent around her – but he couldn't give in to that feeling, not here. Inviting another relationship into his life could mean inviting more drama, and he wasn't sure he was ready for that. He focused his attention on the quiet again, listening.

A few seconds later, there it was. *Scritch-scratch. Eek.* He shifted closer to the origin, straining, pressing his ear against the cold wall.

'I heard it,' said Emmie quietly, taking a step forward. 'Something outside? Sounds like squeaking. On the other side of that wall, there's the mural some children painted for us, and then one of the streets breaks off into some fields and woodland. It's likely just an animal . . . Oh my God!' she cried suddenly. 'What if it's that stray cat? What if he's trapped somehow?' Emmie paused, listening again. 'It sounds like squeaking, like a cat!'

Jared's eyes widened. 'It could be. Is there any way it could get into the wall?'

'I don't know – I mean, I don't think so. Unless there's been some damage during the storm that we aren't aware of . . .'

'It might have found a way in, to shelter from the weather. A hole or something,' he suggested. 'We can't do anything to help it while we're stuck here though.'

'But . . . what if it's hurt?' she said, sounding crestfallen. 'And Salem seems unwell too . . . We have to help them.'

'We will. We'll do what we can,' he promised. 'Once we get ourselves out of here.' And in the meantime, until they got out, he had to tamp down on his growing feelings towards Emmie.

★

'You can't?' Emmie repeated, aware she was sounding horribly whiny, like a child denied sweets, but if she was honest, she hadn't expected the home-visit vet to even answer her call. It was the following morning, the day after Boxing Day, and her phone was pressed to her ear underneath the bobble hat she'd tugged on to keep her head warm. She was pacing the café by the counter. They'd spent yesterday eating leftovers and hunkering down, watching over Salem and prompting him to drink from a dish of water. Megan was keeping out of the way in her flat. And Emmie was trying desperately to contain herself whenever she thought about that kiss. They'd had no firewood left, and nothing left to burn, so they'd loaded up on even more blankets. Luckily, the power had come back on today, the news promising that the worst of Storm Marie was over. And she'd finally managed to get hold of the home-visit vet. He didn't bring good news.

'But . . . I'm really worried about him,' she continued. 'Isn't not eating a bad sign? He's really lethargic.'

'It's not ideal, no, but it could be caused by any number of things,' the vet said. 'Keep encouraging him to drink water. I can't get out for home visits at the moment. We've also had a power cut and the van was crushed by a tree.'

'What about tomorrow?' she said.

'It'll take time for us to sort the van issue,' he said. 'I can't say when we'll be sorted again.' His voice was kindly, like a friendly schoolteacher, and yet, his next words sounded urgent: 'Your best bet is to take him to the out-of-hours clinic, as soon as you get out of the café. Go straight there. I'd say a normal bricks-and-mortar vet, but you're unlikely to get an appointment at such short notice and if he's not eating, and hasn't eaten properly in a while, you want to get him seen right away.'

'The out-of-hours place – that's Pinnacle Veterinary, in Penrith, right?' she asked. Sylvie had pinned the address and details to the staffroom fridge and made Emmie aware of it when she first moved in.

'That's the one. They have twenty-four-seven services for emergencies.'

There was just one more problem. She'd known not having a car, not driving, could be an issue, living somewhere like the Lake District. Sure, there were buses, but how many would be timetabled, after the worst storm in decades? She wondered if the taxi services were back up and running yet. She hoped so.

'Thank you,' she told the vet. 'I'll figure something out.'

'Let me know how you get on?'

'I will,' she promised, and hung up.

★

There were four full bars of signal in the top corner of Jared's phone; no more need to rely on his data to send a few texts, which had also been patchy. He hadn't meant to sleep in so long; it was already almost eleven. Clambering to his feet and kicking aside the blankets, he hurried across the room and tried the light switch. It spilled a yellow-amber glow across the ceiling and walls.

He breathed out. They finally had power again. He swiped open the family group chat.

> *Jared:* We have power! I might be leaving soon
>
>   *Mum:* Aw, I can't wait to see you
>
>   *Shane:* Can we have another Chrimbo dinner?
> To make up for the one we missed?
>
>   *Mum:* You're a greedy sod. We still have a pile
> of leftovers

Jared glanced across the room; Emmie wasn't here. The large quilt she'd slept under had fallen onto the floor, and Lilian was sitting on top, tail curled around herself, large splodgy body rising and falling with her soft breaths. Some of the other cats were dotted around the space: on the back of the sofa, on the arm of the chair.

The door creaked open slowly, and Emmie stepped inside. 'Oh,' she said softly, when she noticed that he was awake. 'Morning.'

'Morning,' he said hoarsely.

'Good news – we have power,' she said.

'I noticed. You put the heating on – I can already feel the difference in here.'

'And I made coffee,' she added, with a smile. 'Clearly the number-one priority now we have power.'

Her grin disappeared, replaced by a look of concern as she looked at Salem, a little black blob with his eyes shut. He'd not moved all night.

Moving across to the blinds, Jared poked his fingers into the slats, peeking outside. The snowfall had finally stopped, the air no longer a tumultuous combination of flakes and fierce winds. Things looked calmer, the layer of white overhead clearing to make way for a patch of greyish sky, like a glimpse of another season. It was trying to rain, drizzly wetness coming down and soaking into the snow.

'Doesn't look so bad out there,' said Jared.

'I know. They said temperatures are picking up a little too. We're over the worst of it, thank goodness.'

'We can dig ourselves out today, I reckon,' said Jared, turning back to Emmie. 'It'll be a rough job – there's a lot of snow. But the rain'll help.'

'Good idea. Salem really needs to get looked at, and we need to see about that stray. Have you done this before?' Emmie asked. 'Dug yourself out? I have no idea how.'

'Yeah, it happened to us at home once or twice when I was a kid.'

'I bet it was more fun back then.'

'It was. Our mum used to make us hot chocolate and we'd build a blanket and pillow fort, have a movie night – if the power was on,' Jared said. 'She'd read our palms, tell our fortunes.'

'Sounds like fun.'

Jared snorted. 'Yeah. She really believes she can do it. We used to eat all that up, back then. I don't believe in any of it now.'

'I've never had my fortune told before.'

'You haven't? Not even at a fairground?' he asked, and when she shook her head, he said, 'Maybe she can read yours.'

As soon as the words left his mouth, he could have kicked himself, because he'd just implied she could *meet his mother*. That wasn't even something he said to someone on a first date, so why did it feel so natural to suggest it to Emmie? The truth was, he felt like his mum would like her – they were both creative types. He shifted his feet awkwardly.

'I'd like that,' said Emmie, oblivious to how he was feeling. 'I hope my fortune would be something like . . .' She held out her one functioning hand in an L shape, as if framing an imaginary movie screen, and put on a low, mysterious-sounding voice. '. . . I foresee cats in your future, ones you actually own. They will be white and fluffy like ghosts. You will live in a castle with them and do your illustrations from there.'

Jared laughed. 'What? A castle?'

'My unobtainable dream home.' She grinned again. 'Perfect for white, ghostly cats. Not in a creepy way – it'd be like . . . an animated movie. A fairy tale. And I'd have a big studio for drawing. A library . . .'

'Sounds nice,' he said.

'If we're digging ourselves out, I should ask Megan if she'll come down and help.'

Jared sighed.

'I know.' She reached out and squeezed his arm, and he tensed, that tingling sensation spreading over his arm, his stomach jerking. 'I know it's hard having her here. I can't imagine being stuck here with an ex. But it'll be faster with three of us, and then you don't have to see her again.'

Jared wanted to object, but there was no getting around it. 'You're right. It will be faster.'

Emmie smiled. She squeezed his arm one more time and left the room.

When Emmie came back, she'd changed into fresh clothes – a pink baggy jumper that brought out the colour in her cheeks, and made her look sweet and pretty. Megan was at her side, also dressed warmly in leggings, thick leg warmers, and a long-sleeved jumper. She avoided looking at Jared, and hooked her hand onto her elbow. Awkwardness settled over him like cling film, making the room feel like it lacked air.

'What do we do to dig ourselves out?' Emmie asked Jared.

'I'm sure Sylvie has a shovel or two somewhere for digging out cars in the winter,' he said. Being practical was the only way to get through this. 'We'll find some tools. Buckets, too. We can transfer the snow to one of the bathtubs upstairs and turn up the heat to melt it.'

'We have to haul snow upstairs in buckets?' said Megan, sounding incredulous. 'My arms are too puny for that . . .'

'And mine are a bit useless. Well, one of them is,' said Emmie, looking down at her splint.

There was no lift in the café – just the flights of stairs. Two café floors, one floor for Emmie's flat and another for Megan's.

'You two can be on digging duty at the front door,' said Jared. 'I'll be on stair duty.'

Chapter 15

Jared eventually decided he'd help them dig as well as carrying the buckets of snow upstairs. Emmie was using her good hand to chip away at some of the snow in the doorway, dumping chunks into buckets they'd found in the kitchen. Megan was hacking away more fiercely, out of breath. In between carrying ice and snow upstairs, he helped them remove big chunks from the doorway. Sylvie was well prepared for thick snowfall, at least; they'd found some shovels in a tool cupboard by the back door, along with some other car tools and canisters of de-icer. It wasn't the easiest thing to do, but the rising temperatures were helping the snow to melt – as well as the bits of rain attempting to fall – and they'd made some progress, starting from the top down. Already, there was a sliver of milky daylight visible at the top of the door. Their first sign of freedom.

A small part of him wondered how often he'd see Emmie, once they'd freed themselves. Would he be fired from the café when Sylvie found out he'd lied? He found he wanted to stay, to keep working here, and that he had more questions for Emmie that he hadn't asked during the whiskey game. There was so much more he wanted to know about her. What would happen when they finally discussed that kiss? Was he even ready for another relationship?

'Okay, you can take that upstairs now,' Megan said, out of breath, pushing her hair out of her eyes and motioning to the filled buckets.

'Right,' said Jared, not keen on taking orders from her, but not wanting to start an argument, either. He knew she was still upset about the outcome between them.

'Thanks,' said Emmie. She'd rolled the sleeves of her jumper up and there was an adorable pink flush over her slightly pointed nose. They'd decided to dump all the snow in her bathtub where it could melt, then Megan's when hers got full.

He hauled the buckets away. It was a pain, having to drag these buckets through the various latched gates and doors and to the stairs like this. He was fit enough to hike around the Lakes and through the surrounding forests with Shane on the weekends, but he was still breathless when he reached Emmie's flat. The buckets were *far* heavier than they looked. He paused, stooping over to catch his breath, a stitch in his side throbbing in protest. When he'd recovered somewhat, he pushed open the door to Emmie's flat and pulled the buckets of snow over the threshold. He couldn't help but stop to take in where she spent her time.

To the right was a wide window spanning the wall, the blinds rolled up to show a view of the white sky and the hodgepodge rooftops of Oakside, all coated in snow. A desk sat underneath the window, with a laptop covered in stickers of animals, an external screen, and a gaming keyboard and mouse. In the middle of the room, she had a glass coffee table and a two-seater cream sofa, a TV mounted opposite. The sofa cushions were all shaped like stars, avocados, and video game characters. He smiled.

Megan had never really shared his interest in video games; she'd sometimes been offended when he wanted to spend a few hours playing in the evening, instead of watching TV.

There was a kitchen over to his left. Even that had hints of Emmie's personality scattered everywhere, in amongst the regular furnishings: classic Game Boy stickers on the fridge, a mat in front of the cabinets covered in cartoon strawberries, a collection of spoons shaped like white cats poking from a glass jar.

Jared carefully carried the buckets to the bathroom, dumping them on the tile. He passed her bedroom on the way. The door was cracked open, and he glimpsed her lilac bedspread. He wondered what her bedroom looked like. But it was too invasive to look, so he focused instead on emptying the buckets out into the bathtub and searching for the controls for her heaters.

Once the heat was on, he took one last glance around the flat and left, feeling, oddly, as though he'd just got to know her a little better.

*

When Jared came back downstairs into the main entrance, Megan was still hacking away at the snow at the door. She didn't say anything to him, and the awkwardness settled over him like a layer of low-hanging mist.

'Alright?' he asked her.

'I'm fine,' she said, without turning round from her work. 'Emmie's in the Cat Lounge having a rest – I said she should go easy, with that wrist. This bucket isn't full yet.'

Jared took that as his cue to leave. He found Emmie in the Cat Lounge, kneeling in front of the armchair. The central heating was doing a fair job of keeping the chill off, now that the power was back on. Emmie was stroking Salem, who was sitting on the armchair, paws tucked underneath him and his head nestled to the side.

'Is the vet coming out today?' he asked her. With everything that had happened, and the mysterious scratching, he'd completely forgotten to ask how the call with the home-visit vet had gone.

She turned to him. 'No, he said he couldn't come. Their van was crushed by a fallen tree.'

'What?' Jared said, his skin prickling with heat. The animal hadn't been eating and it had barely moved the whole time they'd been stuck here. 'Isn't it his job to come out? He should sort another van out, and come right away!'

'He suggested taking Salem to an out-of-hours service, but—'

'But?' Jared prompted. He was thinking of Poppy, and how an earlier vet appointment could have saved her life. 'We should do *everything* we can to get him there. It could be serious.'

'I know. But I don't drive, Jared, remember—'

'Then we'll get you a taxi or a bus as soon as we get out of here,' he interrupted. 'You should have mentioned the vet couldn't come. We could have been working faster!'

She spluttered something incomprehensible, looking confused. 'We've been working as quickly as we can, and I didn't want to stress everyone out. And I'm not sure if transport is back up and running again. Unless we can use Megan's car?'

They had to dig themselves out and get Salem to a vet at once, Jared decided. That was all there was to it.

'We'll have to ask her,' he said. 'We have to make sure Salem is going to be okay.'

Her expression softened. She got up, crossed the room, and squeezed his hand tightly. 'We will. I promise.'

Chapter 16

They were still chipping away at the snow in front of the main door, and Emmie could tell that Jared was upset about what was happening with Salem, even if he didn't vocalise it. She was touched by his concern for a little cat that didn't even belong to him. Jared vanished upstairs to empty a bucket into the bathtub, and when he returned, he grabbed a shovel and launched a fresh assault at the blockage.

Megan shot Emmie a questioning look when Jared wasn't looking. *What's wrong with him?* she mouthed at her.

Salem, she mouthed back.

Emmie was equally worried about him – if not more so, because Sylvie had placed her trust in Emmie to look after things. Worry and doubt niggled away at her insides like wood chewed on by a mouse. Soon, she couldn't stand the silence any longer.

'You're quiet,' she said to Jared, standing up straight and wiping her hair from her eyes. She was sweaty with the exertion of their work, but they'd cleared snow from at least half the doorway now. Soon they'd be able to get out.

'Just busy, and staying focused,' he huffed, hauling another shovelful of snow into the bucket, which was half filled. His hair concealed most of his face as he bent over, so she couldn't tell what he was thinking. 'This snow should be cleared soon if we keep at it.'

Megan shot them both a look, and Emmie heaved a sigh, rubbing her fingertips against her temple. Her wrist was throbbing, she was tired, and she was concerned for Salem. The awkward atmosphere here wasn't helping matters, even if it was to be expected, now that Jared had made his feelings clear to Megan.

'Let's just keep working,' said Jared, as if reading her thoughts.

'I'm taking a break,' Emmie said. They'd just have to put up with each other while she rested her wrist, and checked on Salem again.

She went into the Cat Lounge, where Salem was still sitting in the same position on the armchair, curled into a fluffy ball. She petted him softly, and he stirred, shuffling slightly at her touch. Even his fur was looking bedraggled – there wasn't a shine to it, like there usually was, and it stuck up slightly along his back in little spikes.

'Hey, little guy,' she whispered. 'We'll get you looked after soon, don't worry. Everyone is working as hard as they can.'

She spent some time stroking Salem's head. She was becoming increasingly worried about him, and despite them digging their way out, she didn't know how she was going to get him to the out-of-hours service. She'd have to ask Megan about borrowing her car. But still, she couldn't drive it. Maybe Megan would drive her there. She'd offer to pay, if necessary.

Emmie tried Salem with some food from the dispenser again, but he barely budged, just blinked open a lazy green eye and stared at the food, not interested. At least he was still drinking.

She messaged Sylvie.

> We're digging out now, almost clear. I'm going to take Salem to out-of-hours vet. Home-visit vet isn't an option. I checked. Will let you know what happens. xxx

Emmie waited for a response, but Sylvie didn't reply. She clicked her screen off. It was the afternoon now, and she was probably busy with Emmie's grandparents. She'd sent a text to Emmie earlier to say that she would be driving home with them in the coming days – they'd missed Christmas, but her grandparents still wanted to see her and the café, and would spend the remainder of the year here.

She checked the weather updates. The snow had stopped in most parts of the country now, and it wasn't forecast to be anywhere near as bad from here on out. Storm Marie was officially over.

Emmie left the Cat Lounge and made her way back into the café. Megan was sitting at a table with a mug of coffee. Jared wasn't there; he must be at the front door still, working on shifting heaps of snow into the plastic buckets.

'Megan?' Emmie said, sliding into the seat opposite her. 'I need a huge favour.'

'What's up?' she asked, draining her coffee mug and setting it back down.

'I don't drive, and we really need to get Salem to the out-of-hours place when we've dug our way out. I tried the home-visit vet yesterday, but they can't make it.'

Megan clutched her mug and twisted it between her hands. 'I hardly know the roads round here and the conditions are still going to be pretty hazardous.' She bit her lip. 'I'm a nervous driver . . .'

'But Salem really needs to go. I don't know if I can rely on taxis and buses so soon after the storm. Please?' She could text Faye, but she lived over near the university. It could take her ages to get here – that was if her own car wasn't buried ten feet under snow as well.

'I . . . Okay, I'll take you,' said Megan.

Emmie leaned back against the seat in relief, hand against her heart. 'Thank you.'

She'd have to leave the other cats here for a few hours while they got Salem looked at. Would Jared stay and look after them? She was sure he'd agree, if she asked.

A plan in place for the journey at least, she got to her feet. She was finally starting to feel like she'd found a place for herself here at the café. She'd known what to do in a violent storm; she'd looked after the animals for Sylvie. There was no Dustin leaning over her shoulder, with alcohol-tinged breath.

She'd do what she could for Salem, too. She had to.

*

A few hours later, they'd successfully cleared all the snow from the front doorway, and Emmie let out a deep exhalation. She'd never been so glad to see the opposite side of the street. Jared was clearing a path down the drive, occasionally looking out at the whiteness coating everything like low clouds. The road was indistinguishable from the footpath and the trees across the way were thick with snowy mounds, their branches weighed down like drooping necks. Megan was standing at Emmie's shoulder, watching him.

'Thank goodness for that,' said Megan. 'We're free again.'

'I know.'

'I phoned someone else about the van – a local garage,' said Jared, wandering over to them. 'They're nearby and willing to come today since the snow has slowed and the storm's set to be ending. They'll tow it.' He leaned the shovel against the wall. They both stepped aside to let him pass into the entryway. 'Salem?' Jared prompted.

'Megan said she'd drive me to the out-of-hours place in Penrith—' Emmie began.

'Megan will?' He raised a single eyebrow. 'Are you sure?'

Megan shifted from foot to foot uncertainly and closed the door after Jared to keep the bite of the cold air out. 'It's just . . . I really don't know the roads, or how to get to Penrith, and with the weather being so bad . . . It'll be getting dark soon,' she said.

'I can't drive myself,' Emmie said, worried that Megan would go back on her word now. 'And someone needs to stay here and mind the café and the animals.'

'I'll drive you,' Jared said at once. He rubbed the back of his neck, side-eyeing Megan. 'Look, I know you're nervous about being on the roads at the best of times. And that's fair, the roads'll still be snowy. If you don't mind me taking your car . . . ? Mine's at home.'

Megan shook her head. She looked relieved at the prospect of not driving, despite him asking for her vehicle. 'I'm booked in at the flat for a few more days, so I can stay here for now . . . Just bring her back in one piece. I'll go get the keys for you.'

'Kitty needs medicine while we're gone,' Emmie blurted. The other cats would need looking after, too. 'Pills. Later on. There are notes on the fridge in the staffroom.'

'Okay. Don't worry, I'll look after everything here.'

'I'll check the roads and whether there are any closures. You might want to call ahead to the out-of-hours place and let them know we're coming,' Jared told Emmie.

Emmie nodded, heading off to do just that, grateful that they could all finally work together.

★

Jared rolled the car slowly to the front of the café, parking up at the kerb and winding down the window. Megan drove a baby-blue Fiat, and a sparkly pink crown-shaped air freshener hung from the display mirror above him, smelling faintly of pineapple. A fluffy white scarf was discarded in the back seat, glittering faintly. Jared turned on the car's heater and waved at them both out of the window.

'Grab Salem and let's go!' he called across to Emmie.

Emmie gave him a thumbs up, disappearing inside the café. When she returned, she was wearing a blue coat over her jumper and jeans, and was carrying a soft black cat carrier, fully zipped up. Salem was practically invisible inside, camouflaged by the black fabric, the only hint he was there the glint of his yellowy-green eyes as Emmie walked forward. Emmie paused to say something to Megan at the door, before hurrying down the path – it was still fringed with tall stacks of snow either side.

'It's okay, Salem,' Emmie crooned as she clambered into the back seat, positioning the cat carrier next to her, so she could see him through the mesh door. She clipped her seatbelt in place. 'We're going to make you better!'

Through the mirror, he saw her wave at Megan, who disappeared inside the café again.

With Salem tucked safely in his carrier and Emmie buckled in, Jared attached his phone to the suction stand near to the wheel and tapped the screen to open up Google Maps. 'Can you give me the postcode of the place?' he asked Emmie. 'I've never been to the out-of-hours clinic. And I've only been to Penrith itself a couple of times.'

'Sure,' said Emmie, digging around in her pocket and producing a slip of lined paper.

When she'd read out the postcode to him, and he'd typed it into Google Maps, Jared pulled away from Cat-purrcino.

'Thanks for driving me,' said Emmie, head still angled down to focus on Salem.

'It's no problem,' he said, thinking of that crease on Emmie's forehead, the way she'd kept checking on Salem over the last few days, muttering soft words to him, trying to make him eat. And the way the cat had looked, so lethargic, so similar in demeanour to Poppy, even down to the refusal to eat.

Jared wound the car around the roads leading back through the town of Oakside. Salem was mewling softly in the carrier, and Emmie was mumbling soothing words and crooning to him to try to calm him down.

'It's okay, little guy,' she hushed the cat, and when Jared glanced in the mirror briefly, he could see her leaning over, poking her finger against the carrier's mesh door, wiggling it in front of his tiny black nose. 'I wish I could explain it to him – why we're taking him out like this,' she said to Jared. 'Hush, Salem, it'll be okay.'

Jared swallowed. The memories of losing Poppy were all too fresh in his mind – it had only been a few weeks ago, and his stomach was churning at the thought of being back in a vet's office, as if he were anticipating bad news already. He'd felt the same way as Emmie every time he'd taken Poppy to the vet, or given her medication.

'It's a shame they don't speak,' he said quietly. 'Or understand us.'

'They know we love them,' she said. 'If he gets medicine and starts feeling better, he might understand that it's for his own good.'

Her words stirred something in his chest that he tried very hard to ignore, his throat feeling hot.

He was driving slowly, carefully, crawling through the snowy streets. The road in front of the car was coated in snow, as were the buildings lining the road; roofs were thick with it, and as they passed the playground, the equipment was barely visible under the dusting. Someone had built a giant snowman in the middle of the park, complete with a carrot for a nose. The angled rooftops and buildings appeared postcard-perfect, an image fit for a gift shop. A huge, thick tree had fallen right into one of the roads up ahead, blocking it, and destroying a bus stop opposite. Glass was smashed and scattered everywhere; all that remained of the bus stop was the post displaying the numbers and routes, and the small wooden seat.

Jared turned off down a side street to find another route through, and the app began to correct his course.

'I wonder how much more damage Storm Marie did,' Emmie pondered aloud. 'We'd best be careful on the roads.'

'I'll take the route through Ambleside and Grasmere, not up Kirkstone Pass,' said Jared. 'We'd better avoid that.'

'What's wrong with Kirkstone Pass?' Emmie asked, hushing Salem again as he uttered a long, worried mewl.

'Well, it often gets closed by the local authority when the weather's bad. It's a nightmare at the best of times,' Jared said, as he manoeuvred the car around a few narrow side roads, with squat brick buildings either side, their gardens piled with snow and empty plant pots. 'My brother Shane's wife – Danni – she broke down up there once and got stuck in the dark on her own for hours. Round here, they call the route up there from Ambleside the Struggle.'

Emmie laughed. 'The Struggle? Yeah, that does sound as though it'd be best avoided. We've got enough struggles already with this little guy.' Her voice softened and she mumbled soothing words to the cat again. 'At least we're on our way, now.'

'It's been ploughed apparently, the Struggle,' said Jared. 'And it's open right now. I checked. But they're advising people not to use it anyway, as it's still icy.'

The satnav chattered away in a mechanical female voice, directing them. Soon, the sprawling Lake Windermere was on their left, the fells hovering behind it dusted with heavy snow, flecked with dark patches marking trees and rocks. Afternoon light from the sun was trying to push through the clouds overhead, lighting the icy lake up with patches of yellow, the surface shining like splintered glass. Branches were held in place in the water, suspended, heavy with snowfall. Jared continued to crawl forward, mindful of the icy and snowy conditions. In the silence of the car, he thought back to that kiss, to her pressed against him, lips touching lips and fire in her eyes . . . Should he bring it up? They had a poorly cat to think about. And did he need more time to think, to gain some space – now that they weren't trapped – to think about whether he was truly ready to try again with someone else?

'Wow, it looks gorgeous,' Emmie breathed. 'Like a work of art.'

The catch in her voice made him glance back into the mirror. Her expression was one of wonder, her eyes widening as she tucked her hair into her hat and leaned closer to the windowpane, examining the lake. A smile tugged at his mouth as he returned his attention to the road.

'Maybe you can put it in one of your drawings,' he suggested.

'I might do. You can see why the poets found this place so inspiring . . .' Emmie cleared her throat. 'But the snow around here is on another level,' she added quickly, her words rushing out. 'I bet you can make a mean snowman.'

'You probably can.'

'Or a good snow angel.'

'Can't say I've ever done one. It's too bloody cold to lie down in the stuff.'

Emmie laughed. 'What? You've never done one? It's like a rite of passage when it comes to snowy weather! Not even at Christmas?'

'Nope.'

'What, just because it's cold? I didn't know you were that much of a wimp,' she said, her tone light.

'I'm not!' he said, but he couldn't help laughing too.

'Right, that's it, then,' she declared. 'You have to do some snow angels and send me a picture.'

'Why do you get out of doing them, if you love having fun in the snow so much?' he asked, snorting. 'Maybe they aren't so much fun after all!'

'Okay,' she said, 'I'll do them with you. Maybe we can make them look more like snow-cats to bring in customers at Catpurrcino . . . We'd have to improvise with the tail, though, maybe use a scarf . . .'

That made him laugh again. And it came from low in his belly. The kind of deep laugh that made you feel as though you'd just exhaled. And when he was finished, his entire torso felt lighter, as if he'd cut off a dead weight.

For a moment, the only sound was Salem's cries and his scrabbling to get free of the cat carrier, which reminded him of taking Poppy to the vet. Right away, he felt irrationally guilty for laughing, when two weeks ago he'd lost the one creature that had given his life so much meaning, saved him.

Emmie murmured wordlessly, trying to soothe Salem.

'Have you done much sightseeing, since you got here?' said Jared, trying to distract himself from Salem's mewls and scrabbling.

'Not much, really. I've been too busy working – at the café, on my art . . .' She sounded almost regretful. Her voice brightened. 'But I *love* Beatrix Potter. I've been meaning to go see Hill Top Farm and the museum . . .'

'You should. It isn't good to work all the time. You said you were a workaholic.'

She was quiet for a few minutes – a glance at her expression in the mirror showed him she looked slightly sad – then she shushed Salem again, making kissing noises at his carrier. Jared wondered why she looked that way – was it because she was worried about the vet visit? Or was it because he'd mentioned what she'd said about being a workaholic?

'There's a lot of inspiration to be found here,' Jared found himself saying, and an invitation was on the tip of his tongue: to offer to take her to the farm, to drive her around, show her all the natural wonders on display here. 'There are some amazing hikes, great scenery. You should make the most of your time here. It's a good place for artists. You can't get inspired if you don't take a break sometime.'

'You're right,' she said. 'I guess . . . I don't know how long I'm going to be staying. It was just supposed to be temporary, you know? I've been trying to get my art career going, so I can figure out what to do from here . . .'

'Oh. Really?'

He hadn't known that. Something suspiciously like disappointment hung over him – temporary could mean another few weeks, or another few months. Her smiling face popped into his mind, her light-hearted tone as she drank whiskey and asked him questions. The drawing she'd done of him and Poppy, the soft words, her kindness. That *kiss*, the one that set his insides alight.

Stupid. He was being an idiot. He'd only just managed to resolve things with Megan. He had money issues to sort out, besides. And if she was leaving anyway . . .

They continued up the winding, weaving roads, the hills towering either side, thick with snow and looking like the peaks of a great wedding cake. Great, now he was comparing things to wedding cakes. What the hell was the matter with him?

He had to stop thinking like an idiot. Being cooped up with his ex and Emmie, who he was attracted to, had clearly scrambled his mind.

★

'Finally!' Emmie said, as they pulled into the wide car park at the side of the out-of-hours clinic. It had taken them a little over an hour to get here and she'd been anxious the whole drive – a drive that Jared said should normally take forty-five minutes, if you weren't worried about skidding into a tree or a brick wall and smashing up your car on the way. Each mewl from Salem along the way had added a fresh layer of concern to her already stacked-up worries; she hated how upset the poor cat sounded. Her shoulders and jaw ached with the tension. A huge sign overlooking the car park read PINNACLE VETERINARIANS in bold letters, with a logo of an intertwined dog and cat, shaking paws.

'Thanks so much, Jared,' said Emmie, as she shoved open the car door. 'I owe you.'

Jared waved her comment away, clicking the engine off. 'It's okay,' he said.

She clambered out of the car, extracting Salem awkwardly with her good hand, who was still trying desperately to escape from the carrier, shoving his tiny black nose into the door. Her heart ached for him. Jared followed her out and locked the car doors.

'I'll come with you,' he said, his voice hoarse.

'Are you sure?' she said, surprised. 'You don't have to. I know it might be hard for you, after . . .'

'No, it's okay. I'll come inside. You shouldn't go in alone, just in case . . .' He trailed off.

With a lump in her throat, Emmie nodded. She hadn't even thought about that, but he was right. And the appreciation she felt threatened to knock her from her feet. She clung to Salem's carrier more tightly.

'Here, let me,' he said, taking it from her gently. 'You've been doing too much with that wrist lately.'

The vet had agreed to take a look at Salem when Emmie had called ahead earlier, but she was still pent up, wondering what the outcome would be. She crossed the car park with Jared, heading for the main entrance – it was a small alcove built into the side of the building, with a porch jutting out, with snow-coated flower pots either side of the steps. White, frosted farmland stretched either side of the building, a mound of hills and mountains in the distance. A collection of brickwork buildings, fields, gates, and stone walls surrounded the vet office. It was fairly isolated and more on the outskirts of Penrith – they'd hardly passed anything except a garage and a bunch of houses on their way here. A large white van and a few other cars were dotted around, parked under trees.

When she reached the main porch, Emmie pushed an intercom button to the side of the door and was greeted by a metallic buzz. Moments later, it crackled to life, and a woman's voice spoke.

'Hi, can I help you?'

'I've come with Salem,' Emmie explained.

'Ah yes, come on in. The vet's expecting you.'

A deep buzz resonated from the intercom again, and Emmie pushed the door open, holding it open for Jared as he navigated the carrier inside. They found themselves in a bright but small waiting room. A reception desk stood against the left wall; to the right, there were shelves of medicated food for dogs and cats, as well as toys, bowls, and supplements. Leaflets and colourful noticeboards adorned the area around the window ledge.

Emmie approached the desk, Jared close behind her. The woman behind it was in her forties, with auburn hair pulled back into a neat ponytail and a make-up-free face. She wore a navy-blue shirt stamped with the vet company logo, and her head only just about popped up over the screen of her computer.

'Salem?' said the receptionist, offering her a kindly smile. 'Have a seat. Dr Frank will be with you in a moment. You're very lucky it's so quiet today.'

'Thanks,' said Emmie, and she headed across to two plastic chairs beneath the window.

Emmie's butt had barely hit the seat when a side door opened and a smiling, large man with broad shoulders and a grey beard appeared. Like his colleague, he wore navy blue, with a collection of colourful pens sticking out of his pocket and a name badge reading DOCTOR CARSTEN FRANK: VETERINARIAN pinned to his chest. One of the pens had a topper shaped like white cat ears sticking up from the top. That, along with his kindly eyes and warm smile, made Emmie feel instantly relaxed, and some of the tension she'd been carrying since they left the café drained from her shoulders.

'Salem?' the vet said.

'Yes, hi. I'm Emmie,' she said, giving him a shaky smile in return. 'This is Jared.' She motioned at Jared, who had risen to his feet behind her, holding the carrier. Salem had retreated somewhere to the back of it, cloaked in shadow.

'Come on through.' Carsten motioned towards the door.

Emmie nodded and stepped forward, entering the small examination room with Jared.

The walls were painted a pale, soothing blue, and the examination table and a set of scales jutted out, with

Carsten's computer and a collection of drawers towards the back of the room. At the opposite end of the room was another door, and Emmie could just make out a yellow wall and a gathering of notices about blood tests and injections. Her mouth had gone very dry now that she was in here. If something was wrong with Salem . . . What would she do? Aunt Sylvie would be home soon, but Emmie was now seriously questioning herself, wondering if she should have tried harder to leave the café much sooner. But what else could she have done during a storm like that?

'You can open up the carrier and get him on the table. You mentioned he wasn't eating?' Carsten asked, tugging some fresh gloves from a box nearby and snapping them on.

Jared winced at the sound.

Emmie tried to bring some moisture to her mouth. She swallowed. 'He hasn't eaten in a few days,' she explained. 'We've been snowed in and couldn't bring him right away, so I wanted to get him here as soon as I could.'

Jared set the carrier on the table and opened the door. Salem, the poor thing, was huddled at the back, refusing to move, so with Carsten's help, they upended the carrier until he was forced to drop softly onto the table below. Salem immediately clawed his way towards Emmie, burying his face in her elbow, hunched into as much of a ball as he could be.

A lump rose to her throat. 'Come on, little guy,' she soothed, trying to prise him away from the crook of her elbow, which was difficult with one hand, so Jared helped. 'Let's get you sorted.'

Jared made some crooning noises at Salem and stroked the top of his head.

'I'll take a look at him and see what's what,' said Carsten softly.

When Emmie tugged the frightened cat gently away from her arm, Carsten took over, holding on to him carefully and peering at his eyes and the insides of his ears. When he tipped Salem's head back to look inside his mouth, Emmie cringed; Salem looked petrified, but Carsten crooned to him in an attempt to calm him. Jared was studying the wall rather than watching the examination.

'There now, not to worry,' Carsten said soothingly, as he continued examining Salem. 'This'll look a bit uncomfortable, but I promise it won't hurt,' he explained for Emmie's benefit. 'Could you hold him carefully, please?'

'Can you . . . ?' Emmie asked Jared.

Jared looked ashen but he nodded, holding Salem in place as Carsten felt around his stomach and abdomen, pressing his fingers down. When he was done with that, he rifled around his desk and produced a clean thermometer from a packet. 'Now, I need to check his temperature – could you hold him, please? It'll be a little uncomfortable for him.'

Jared kept hold of Salem near his front paws. He tried to squeeze away to bury himself in Emmie's arm again, but Carsten was able to lift his tail and place the thermometer. Emmie felt the poor cat stiffen in discomfort.

For a fleeting moment, all she could think about was Jared losing his cat. She didn't know the specifics, but was this what he'd had to endure in the lead-up to her passing? The poking, the prodding, the poor cat being scared witless and not knowing what was going on? She couldn't even imagine dealing with it for an extended period of time, with an animal you'd lived with and bonded with for so long. And then to lose them, to not have been able to do anything to stop it . . . And now he was here. Helping her, in a vet's office, when he could have just as easily waited outside for them. Her throat tightened.

'Hush, little guy, it's okay, nearly done,' she soothed Salem, stroking him softly with her fingertips and making kissing noises.

When Carsten produced the thermometer and checked it, he said, 'His temperature is a little high. Could you place him on the scales over there, please?'

Emmie felt sick with dread, and Jared carried Salem across the room and set him onto the scales. It took a bit of encouragement to keep him in place, both of their hands hovering over him to keep him there long enough for Carsten to take a reading of his weight.

'We'll probably have to do some bloodwork,' the vet concluded. 'I can feel something on his abdomen but it's difficult to tell what it is without an ultrasound. It could be inflammation, or something more serious. If the bloodwork is inconclusive, I'd want to do an ultrasound and some more tests.'

Emmie's heart skittered. 'More serious?'

'I don't want to worry you just yet,' said Carsten kindly. 'We'll know more if we do the tests. Do you have insurance for Salem? I can give you options if I know your circumstances better, but I would recommend bloodwork, and an ultrasound if needed after that. I'd like to keep him here for observation as well. He may need treatment that requires fluids if he's dehydrated.'

'Do you mind if I call my aunt?' said Emmie. 'When I called, I explained that it's her cat, but she's away and hasn't been able to get back because of the storm . . .'

'Of course,' said Carsten, and the twinkling compassion in his eyes made the lump in her throat ache.

She hoped it was nothing serious.

Chapter 17

Emmie thankfully managed to get through to Aunt Sylvie, who agreed to all the testing and said she could put it on her insurance. Emmie could hear the emotion in her aunt's voice. 'I'm setting off home in the morning,' her aunt said. 'I know I should have come sooner, but some of the roads were still closed and with the weather being so bad . . . I won't be long. I feel awful . . .'

Emmie had reassured her that it wasn't her fault. Salem falling ill while she was away – and during a storm – was just bad timing. They couldn't have predicted it would all happen at once.

Emmie left Salem with Carsten, who said he'd be in touch about the blood results. All being well, and if it was something simple like an infection, Salem would receive some fluids overnight and they could pick him up and bring him home tomorrow with antibiotics.

When they clambered back into the car – Emmie sitting in the front seat, this time – Jared looked just as worried as she felt.

'Thanks again for bringing me,' said Emmie, as they drove away from the vet's office and got back on the road.

'It wasn't any trouble.'

She shook her head. 'I feel bad,' she admitted. 'After what happened with Poppy . . .'

'I know, but that's why I wanted you to have someone with you in there. It's best if you're not alone.'

God, she suddenly felt like crying at his kindness. Maybe it was just a build-up of everything that had happened recently.

'Thank you. I'm so glad he's there now.'

'They'll take good care of him. They know what they're doing,' he reassured her. 'Salem's in the best hands.'

They lapsed into silence as they drove back in the direction of Oakside, guided by the satnav and surrounded on all sides by flat, snow-crusted fields, soon replaced by rising, towering hills and craggy rocks. Some of the roads were still icy, and Jared drove slowly. The satnav spat out mechanical instructions in a monotonous voice. It was already getting dark, the sky fading to a deep blue and darkening around them, the hills like shadowy giants in the gloom. There was only one straight road stretching before them, bordered by a low brick wall piled with snow, and very few other cars on the road. Soon Jared was frowning, glancing from his phone to the road, a ridged crease on his nose.

'It wasn't supposed to bring us this way!' he said suddenly. 'We're on Kirkstone Pass! The Struggle!'

Emmie almost laughed – the local name for the road had sounded so ridiculous earlier, and how typical that they'd ended up here. But with it being so dim now, daylight almost gone, and the roads being perilous and icy, it really wasn't funny.

'You never told me why exactly it's called the Struggle,' she said, trying to keep her voice steady.

'Well, the ascent is the hardest, but it's still a bitch going down the Struggle in these conditions . . . it's steep! There are bends and climbs on the descent, too . . .' He scrolled across his phone screen, observing the map. 'There are no turn-offs anywhere nearby. We just have to carry on.'

'Take your time,' said Emmie. 'We don't have to go superfast.'

She peered out of the front window. The road looked barely wide enough for two cars to pass each other. Thank goodness Salem was no longer with them.

'I'm sorry, Emmie. I never wanted to bring us this way.'

'Don't be. It's not your fault.'

Jared was silent as he concentrated on the road, but he looked nervous, hunched over the wheel with his shoulders drawn up towards his ears. There were no street lamps around – not on this deserted, long stretch of road – and the sun vanished behind one of the giant mounds surrounding them. It was dark and cold, and a layer of mist was descending over the hilltops, encasing them like breath. Some of the bends were so sharp it was impossible to see what was round the corner. The darkness had come on so quickly, like a switch being flipped, and a shudder crawled over Emmie's neck. The only light was cast onto the road by the car's headlights, pooling out like a spotlight into a void.

They were rounding a particularly dangerous curve in the Struggle when a car came shooting from around the bend at full pelt, a blaze of headlights and motion.

It was too close. It wasn't giving them enough berth.

Jared cried out, a strangled sound like a startled animal, swerving suddenly. The fast car clipped them, thumping hard into the side of their vehicle before it vanished in a rushing glow of headlights. Emmie's heart jumped up into her throat, her chest heaving with a sudden gasp.

Their car skidded on the thick ice and snow at the road's edge, out of control even with Jared desperately trying to steer them back on track. Emmie screamed as she was banged about in her seat. Her seatbelt was the only thing keeping her in place as Jared struggled to get the car back into place.

'I can't stop it!' Jared shouted. 'Emmie—'

There was a horrible crunching sound as the car spun. In the rush of amber headlights, a wooden gate appeared, a stone wall either side, and the car smashed into it. Despite the seatbelt holding her in place, Emmie felt like she was rising, bouncing up high and away from her seat, the material cutting into her shoulder so hard it hurt as they were jostled along.

After that, Emmie didn't remember anything except blackness.

Chapter 18

It was no use – Jared couldn't prevent the car from skidding into a frenzy. As he fought with the wheel to bring it under control, he glimpsed a wide fence leading onto some farmland and groaned, twisting the wheel. If they skidded through the fence, they wouldn't smash into the brick wall running up the Pass, or hit another car when they reached the sharp corner up ahead.

Yanking at the wheel, exerting all his strength, he controlled the spin until they slammed through the wooden fence, the wood smashing to one side. He caught a glimpse of two white sheep scattering. Emmie was screaming beside him, the sound of her terror enough to curdle his blood. The car jostled over the moor and the side of his face was slammed into the steering wheel painfully. He felt one of his teeth crack and a burst of agony in the side of his mouth like a mini explosion.

They rolled forward, bounced along and dropped. And they were falling down briefly, until the car slammed to a stop on a patch of snowy ground, and his teeth were rattled around his skull like marbles. More pain seared across his jaw. Both airbags had burst into life to protect them, huge and white and glaring, but too late to save his tooth.

Jared groaned, leaning away from the inflated airbag. 'Emmie?' he croaked.

There was no more screaming. All he could hear was the *baa* of a sheep outside and a horrible silence. The drop hadn't been very far down. She *had* to be okay. He peered around his airbag to check on her.

She was slumped forward into the airbag.

'Emmie?' he tried again, reaching for her shoulder. As he moved his own arm, a shooting pain speared its way upwards and he winced. He ignored it, gently patting at Emmie's shoulder to draw her attention in case she was injured. 'Emmie, can you hear me? Are you hurt?'

No answer. She must be unconscious. What if she . . .

Jared's heart was thumping, each beat resonating through his broken tooth and intensifying the pain in his arm. But he was fine; he wasn't seriously injured. He was more worried about her.

He yanked out his seatbelt, fishing into his pocket for his phone – the harsh glow sending fresh pain through his jaw – and checking the bars. There was no signal.

'Shit,' he hissed. He held it up, as if that could improve matters, but there was nothing.

Outside, it was pitch-dark. He couldn't see much further than the cluster of scattered plants and grass visible in the headlights. He glanced over to Emmie, still quiet, her hair fanned around her face like reeds. He should . . . *Shit*. He reached out, feeling for her neck, checking. A heartbeat, pulsing beneath his fingers. And he couldn't see any blood. He breathed out. But her passing out wasn't a good sign.

He clambered out of the car, into the cold. The wing mirrors were destroyed and smashed, the glinting glass visible in the snow beneath his feet. He shivered, glancing up the way they'd come, at the incline back up to the road. He was right – they hadn't dropped much, just a small dip in the land. Thank God.

Jared hesitated, turning back to the car, his chest twisting with uncertainty. He didn't want to leave her but if she was injured, he couldn't move her. He might make it worse. He leaned back into the car, paying no heed to the intense, knifelike pain in his arm and the throb to his tooth.

'I'll be back for you, okay? Promise. Emmie, stay with me. Please.' A small part of him hoped she could hear, somehow.

He steeled himself, drawing himself back and closing the door. Leaving her behind felt like wading through water, like abandonment. What if something happened to her? But if he stayed here, he couldn't get help, and she needed it.

Jared cradled his bad arm against his side and began the trek up the moor to the road. There must be better signal up there – the satnav had worked on the road. If not, he'd have to walk back to the inn that they'd passed at some point, ages ago. He'd do it, if necessary, and try to flag down another car on his way for help.

Hang on until then, Emmie.

Climbing back up the hill with a dodgy arm – which he now suspected was broken – was not easy, and he used his phone as a torch. He clambered and skidded over the snowy earth, using rocks to find his footing. At one point, he reached the top of an incline and slipped, skidding all the way back down, almost landing on his injured arm and twisting to avoid it at the last moment. He cursed, seething, hauling himself upright and clamping his mouth down – the icy-cold air was whistling through his teeth, making the pain there worse. He set off again, moving at an angle this time.

By the time he reached the top of the incline, and the roadside, he was panting, his breath coming in white plumes. The smashed-up wooden gate was to his right, visible in the torchlight from his phone, some of the debris scattered in the mounds of snow and the rest hanging precariously off the main structure.

In the blackened sky, the moon was visible, a thin slice surrounded by dotted stars. Jared held up his phone, tapping in 999 without even checking the signal. It wouldn't go through.

He uttered a stream of curses, glancing over his shoulder. Down the hill, he could just about make out the shadowy form of the car, headlights still aglow, illuminating the white snow and the pockets of bracken sticking out at intervals.

'Hang on, Emmie,' he whispered, and began to make his way up the road.

*

He'd walked for ages and felt like his feet were bleeding when he finally managed to find a spot where he had mobile signal and could call for help. It had felt unnerving, walking with the stone wall to his left, only the shadows and his worry for Emmie for company. He was concerned he might get hit by a car on his way. After making the phone call, waiting for the emergency services to come was even worse – standing in the pitch-dark, his phone flashlight on, a little voice in his head telling him that he'd left Emmie behind, that she might not be okay. His teeth were chattering so hard in his skull it felt like his entire brain was vibrating, and his feet were numb and aching.

It was the Mountain Rescue Team who came out – because of the weather and road conditions. He heard the wailing of the sirens before he saw the flashing blue lights and the two massive crewed Land Rovers, which screeched to a halt nearby.

'*Jared?*' His brother Shane came charging out of one of the Land Rovers with the other members of his team. Jared had never been so relieved to see his brother's face before, and his knees finally gave way beneath him.

'Whoa, easy!' Shane rushed forward and grabbed him, steadying him. 'Where's the other person, and the car? Are they hurt?'

'Emmie,' he croaked weakly. 'I don't know . . . She was unconscious.'

He had to direct them to the car. It felt like fog was blanketing everything, making time move differently, turning his mind sluggish – would he look back on this day, years from now, as one of the worst days of his life? One where he'd made a monumental mistake . . . got someone he cared about grievously injured, or worse . . . ? He couldn't stop shaking and he didn't know if it was entirely to do with the cold.

He barely remembered the rescue team getting to Emmie, freeing her from the car, before he was bundled into one of the vehicles alongside her. She looked so vulnerable and fragile on the stretcher, her hair fanning out at the sides. All he could think about was how this was his fault, how she might not make it. He'd been driving and so he was responsible. How could he have let that happen?

Jared kept his hand gripped tightly on Emmie's as they drove. It was cold, and she didn't move, but at least she was alive. She was breathing. Shane sat beside him, and kept shooting him worried looks.

'Don't worry,' said Shane, as they sped along as fast as the icy conditions would allow, sirens screaming. 'We got to you quickly – we'll get her checked out and—'

Jared could barely process his brother's words of reassurance. He nodded lamely.

He moved in a daze from the Land Rover to the hospital when they got there, the movements of the paramedics and Emmie's stretcher a blur around him. He answered questions, but felt like he was doing it from outside of his own body, a wandering ghost. Shane stayed with him. The nurse said he must be in shock; the words registered, but only just. He had his own assessment with the nurses while Emmie was whisked away, having his vital signs checked – his heart rate, blood pressure, among other things. It seemed to go on forever. Again, he didn't feel present as they poked and prodded and questioned him. He only wanted to know if Emmie was okay.

'Emmie,' he said repeatedly. 'Is she . . .'

'Let's get you sorted out first, love, then we can find out,' said one of the nurses kindly. Shane hovered in the background, a look of deep concern a permanent fixture on his face.

They cleaned some of the lacerations on Jared's cheeks, which stung, and pressed a bandage over them. Jared barely remembered being ushered into a green plastic chair and handed a strong cup of tea and a biscuit for the shock. His hands were shaking and he held the cup tighter to keep it steady, but only ended up sloshing tea down his jeans.

'You're lucky,' said the nurse. 'You have some lacerations, a broken tooth, and your arm is broken, but it could have been much worse. We'll get a cast on that arm for you, and you'll need to be referred to a dentist for that tooth.'

Jared nodded numbly.

'For the lacerations, you'll need to change that dressing and clean them every few days. And we'll give you some antibiotics to prevent infection . . .'

She continued, telling him about more procedures and processes. The words were hazy – at least Shane was listening. But he didn't need to remember them in the end. She tapped a few things into her computer until the printer churned on the desk behind her, spitting out a summary of what she'd said. There was tinsel strung around her desk, Christmas cards on the walls. He couldn't believe this had happened when not long ago, he'd rustled up a Christmas dinner for them all back at the café.

When the printer was done churning out papers, she handed him the sheets and smiled, the corners of her eyes crinkling. 'I know, it's a lot to take in and you've been through the mill tonight, haven't you? Let me see if I can find out about your Emmie for you and then we'll get your cast fitted.'

Your Emmie.

His Emmie. He shifted in his seat. He didn't correct the nurse. Did he want her to be his Emmie? It seemed like things had come sharply into focus now that she was hurt.

He turned to his brother, who looked tired and was clutching a plastic coffee cup. The agony in Jared's chest felt like it was going to crush all of his bones – like these feelings of guilt and pain were a disease, spreading everywhere.

'I should call Mum . . .' Shane said hesitantly. He must have been sitting on these words for a while now, waiting until Jared was done with his own assessment.

'Don't,' said Jared quickly. 'Not yet. She'll want to come here and it's still icy. I don't want her to get into an accident as well.'

'But—'

'I . . . can't lose Emmie,' he said, his thoughts cartwheeling away from his mother, and back to her. 'I can't.' Jared's voice cracked, and he cupped his head in his hands, scraping his fingertips through his hair. He felt utterly useless.

'Does she know how you feel?' said Shane, dropping the subject of their mother – for which Jared was grateful. He couldn't stand another person getting hurt tonight.

Jared said nothing in response, only stared at the tiled floor. He'd put Emmie in danger. What did *his* feelings matter now?

'When she wakes up, you can tell her,' Shane encouraged him. 'I'm sure she'll want to hear it.'

You hear that, Emmie? Jared thought desperately. *You can't go anywhere, not when there's still so much left for me to say.*

*

Jared clambered out of the taxi outside the cat café. Services were finally back up and running, and instead of going home, he'd come back here. He couldn't sit around doing nothing while Emmie was in hospital; the guilt was eating at him, the self-blame. He had to do *something* productive to stop himself from going crazy and stewing in his thoughts. And he'd remembered the stray cat. In the rush to get Salem to the out-of-hours clinic, and with the accident right after, they had forgotten to go and look.

Behind him, the taxi driver pulled away, crawling back down the hill. Jared's van had already been collected and taken away; Sylvie had appreciated him calling for help when it had broken down, but she was able to resolve it through her own insurance and it would be fixed and taken care of. The car park was empty, quiet, with only the soft whistle of the wind to fill it.

He circled round to the front of the café, and around to the side wall, pausing in front of the huge mural painted there in bright reds, yellows, greens and oranges. He hadn't seen it before, although Emmie had told him about it: a huge wild garden painted on the bricks, with crude-looking cats painted around the bottoms of the flowers, with big yellow eyes and long tails. There was no sign of the stray cat itself, and he nearly turned around and walked away, but his gaze snagged on something on the ground that stopped him in his tracks.

A trail of feathers.

He moved forward, following the trail closer to the wall, until he spotted a dead bird – or what was left of it, which wasn't much at all.

As he got nearer, he noticed there was a hole in the wall on the far left side of the mural. Jared pulled his phone out of his pocket, switching on his torch as he approached. It was a long hole, going into the wall quite deeply, and when he knelt down to look, shining the bright light of the torch inside, his breath hitched in surprise. There, inside the hole, was a black cat, curled into a ball.

It lifted its head, hissing at him, baring its tiny white fangs, eyes wild. Below its chin was the tell-tale white beard Emmie had mentioned.

'Found you,' he said quietly, smiling to himself. Poor little thing.

The cat was shrinking away against the back of the hole, but there was nowhere else for it to go – and it wasn't going to shoot out of the hole, not with him standing here, a potential threat.

'It's okay, little guy,' he told it gently. 'We'll get you looked after.'

Pulling up Google on his phone, he found the number of the cat shelter and gave them a call. With that, all he had to do was wait for them to come out. He'd wait as long as was necessary for the cat to get the help it needed.

*

When Emmie's eyes fluttered open, she felt as though she'd been sleeping for weeks, and her head and neck ached. Her body felt almost weighed down, and she realised she was in a bed, covered and wrapped in blankets. She blinked to clear the fuzz from her vision, and a white ceiling and a bright light swam into view.

She shuffled up, the coverings rustling around her. They weren't the familiar winter quilts from the café but white sheets and a heavy green blanket thrown over her legs. And there was an oak-brown door nearby, with a tiny window. She was in a hospital bed, wearing a hospital gown.

It all came back to her, in fits and starts. The trip to the vet, with Salem. The drive home, with Jared. And the snow, the skidding, the spinning . . .

It made her dizzy thinking about it. She took a few deep breaths.

Emmie turned, expecting to see Jared by her bed, but an empty plastic chair was pushed against the wall. To her left, there was a set of oak drawers, and a huge bouquet of pale pink and cream roses sitting in a clear vase, interspersed with curving green leaves. Her phone was set on the table beside them; it didn't look damaged since it had been tucked in her coat pocket.

Immediately, her heart kicked up in her chest, as if prompting her to action, to questioning everything. *Jared.* Was he okay? What had happened to him? Where was he? What if he . . . A series of images skittered through her mind, laced with fear – Jared being taken away on a stretcher, in a hospital bed with tubes sticking out of him, in intensive care being operated on. Or worse . . . No. She couldn't imagine that. It made her chest hurt, her heart physically aching with the weight of it. She had to find out if he was okay.

Someone bustled into the room then. Emmie turned quickly, which made her neck hurt. She rose a hand to it, touching the back.

'Be careful,' the nurse who had entered advised her. She was dressed in scrubs and had sunshine-blonde hair tied in a neat ponytail. 'How are you feeling?'

'Sore. Where's . . . the man who was in the car with me – Jared?' Her voice was hoarse but she rushed on anyway. 'Is he okay? Is he hurt? Did he—'

'He's absolutely fine, darling, don't fret. No serious injuries – I think you fared the worst, but you'll be okay.' The woman smiled down at her. 'Do you remember what happened to you both?'

The relief that Jared was unharmed lifted all the weight from her heart, turning it featherlight. All the tension drained from her clenched shoulder blades. Emmie held back from nodding and instead rasped, 'Yes. Most of it.'

'You've been unconscious for a while since the accident, and we've had you on fluids. Here, let me help you sit up.' The nurse helped to move Emmie forwards, and propped up her pillows behind her so she could lean back more comfortably.

Emmie sighed at the comfort of the pillows against her back – they were soft and squidgy. 'Thank you. How long have I been here?'

'Since yesterday evening. We've been running some tests, and couldn't find any serious signs of trauma from the accident, so we believe your fainting was shock – but it's possible you may have whiplash too, if your neck hurts.' She smiled, gesturing to the splint, which still rested on Emmie's hand and wrist. 'You're lucky you didn't break your wrist, with you already having an injury. The healing process for that should be able to carry on as normal.'

'I . . . see. So . . . what . . .'

'I know it's a lot to take in. Don't worry. We'll keep you in a few more days to make sure you're on the mend. We'll need to run some more tests and do another assessment now you're awake, just to check your head. You're probably hungry.'

Emmie thought longingly of the Christmas meal leftovers, back at the café. 'I'm starving.'

'Great, then I'll sort you some food.' The nurse offered another smile, her ocean-blue eyes twinkling. 'Jared left you a card.' The nurse bustled to the other side of her bed and plucked a card from among the brightly coloured flowers – Emmie hadn't noticed it sitting within the leaves and petals. 'Here you are. Your aunt is here too – she just went to get a drink from one of the machines.'

The nurse handed her the card. Emmie turned it over. Her name was written on it in sloping capital letters.

'You're fortunate to have him,' the nurse told her. 'He walked all the way up the Pass until he was able to call for help.'

'Oh. We're not . . .' Emmie trailed off, deciding not to elaborate because coming up with a response made her head hurt and she still didn't know *what* they were to each other. But he'd done all of that, for her? Her cheeks blazed with heat as she folded open the card and read the message inside.

> *Emmie,*
> *I'm really sorry you got hurt. We never should have*
> *ended up on the Pass. I hope these make up for it.*
> *Rest up.*
> *Jared x*

Flummoxed and flustered in equal measure, Emmie snapped the card closed and huffed out a breathy laugh. He could have got her phone number and texted her – instead he'd given her flowers. No one had done that for her before. When she set them down on the table, she couldn't help but press her hands to her cheeks, smiling.

'I'll see about getting you something to eat,' the nurse said kindly. 'Your aunt should be back soon.'

'Thank you.'

The nurse bustled out, and Emmie was left with the flowers. She couldn't stop staring at their cream and pink splendour, the flowers huge and bright in the simple, clinical hospital room. It cheered the whole place – and situation – up. She couldn't believe they'd ended up in an accident. Her memories of the event were patchy, and trying to remember things clearly sent a pounding through her forehead. She pressed her fingers to the bridge of her nose. What she did know was that the Pass was treacherous, and it wasn't Jared's fault she'd ended up there. She needed to let Jared know she didn't blame him, not in the slightest. In fact, she was grateful for everything he'd done, from the dinner he'd cooked them to helping her with Salem and everything in between and after.

The door creaked open. 'Emmie?' said a voice.

Emmie looked up to see her aunt framed in the doorway, her auburn hair scooped high into a messy bun on her head. She looked exhausted, her face colourless – and it looked like she'd thrown on the first set of clothes she could find: a baggy button-up shirt with a hoodie tugged over the top, and loose-fitting jeans. When she saw Emmie was awake, her face broke into a wide smile.

Her aunt came hurrying over, setting a plastic coffee cup on the side table. 'I just saw the nurse and she said you're awake – how are you feeling, love?'

'A bit headachy, and my neck hurts,' said Emmie.

'That's to be expected. I'm so glad you weren't seriously hurt.' Sylvie leaned over and gave Emmie a kiss on the head, smoothing her hair back. Her face was lined with worry, and pale as clouds; her aunt hadn't been inside this hospital since Uncle Bennie had passed away.

'Jared brought those for you.' Sylvie tipped her chin at the flowers.

'I know. They're gorgeous.'

Sylvie stepped back and shook her head. 'He blames himself, you know – Jared. I told him not to. It was so icy on the roads.'

'You're right. It *isn't* his fault.'

'He was hiding it well, but I could see he was beside himself. He really cares for you, Emmie.'

Emmie shifted against the cushions, something inside of her swooping at Sylvie's words. 'I know,' she said gently. 'I care for him, too.'

'There's no rush, but when you get out of here . . . I think he needs to hear all of this from you.' Aunt Sylvie swallowed, and looked as if she were fighting back emotion. 'Life's too short to hold yourself back, love.'

Emmie swallowed. 'You're probably right.'

And perhaps life was too short to be so consumed by achieving, by becoming successful, by working herself so hard. She suddenly felt a fierce rush of gratitude for everything she had: for her aunt and the café, her colleagues, the beautiful surroundings she'd failed to explore because she'd been so consumed by work. For Jared, and his kindness and encouragement. For her grandparents.

'Where are . . . Gran and Grandad?' she asked, looking over Aunt Sylvie's shoulder.

'At mine. They came while you were still asleep but I took them home earlier to get some rest. Your gran barely slept, worrying about you.'

'I can't wait to see them.'

'Your grandad couldn't stop shaking Jared's hand, when he learned what he'd done to help you.'

'Did Jared really . . .' Emmie began, struggling to form the sentence when her skull was starting to pound. 'Jared walked up Kirkstone Pass until he could call for help? In the cold and the snow?'

Sylvie nodded, her expression warming. 'He did. Walked a long way until he got mobile signal to call for help. He hated leaving you, though. He wasn't sure if he was doing the right thing, but I think he did right by you.'

Tears sprang into Emmie's eyes. He'd walked and walked to get help – for her? And he'd driven her all the way to the vet's office with Salem, even coming inside with her after what he'd been through.

'Salem!' Emmie gasped, sitting forward suddenly. 'Is he—'

'Don't worry,' said Aunt Sylvie, pressing Emmie's shoulder gently so that she was leaning against her cushions again. 'Salem is fine. I went to pick him up while you were asleep.' She gnawed her lip. 'I didn't want you waking up with me gone, but . . .'

'No, you had to get him. Is he okay? What was wrong with him?'

'They think it's an infection of some sort, causing him gastric issues, so he's on antibiotics and he's had plenty of fluids. We'll see how he gets on with those. Hopefully he'll be on the mend.' Sylvie's lips twitched. 'Like you.'

Emmie exhaled a long breath, letting her shoulders relax into the squidgy cushions. 'That's a relief.'

Aunt Sylvie's eyes fell on the flowers again. 'Jared's a good lad,' she said. 'I'm glad he was here to look after you – both you and Salem – when I couldn't be.'

Nodding, Emmie felt that familiar inflating feeling in her chest, as if she was filling up with hot air, expanding. There was gratitude in that feeling, but something else, too, something that made her feel floaty and happy, fired up with possibility.

Am I . . . Could I be . . . falling for him? she wondered, because what she was feeling – it felt very much like love.

Chapter 19

Jared's mum lived in a white-painted semi-detached house in Ambleside – the type of place she'd been able to get with a no-deposit mortgage when he was small, and had almost paid off. These days, there was so much red tape if you actually wanted to buy a similar place, and on his income – part freelance to boot – he stood no chance of ever being lent enough money. He envied her that, even now, as he stood on the doorstep ringing the bell. All the money worries he'd had lately, the stress and the strain . . . He couldn't even imagine being half a year away from paying off a mortgage and owning a place outright. Then again, did that even matter? His worries seemed pale now, since the accident, like bright clothing faded in the wash. He was alive; he was healthy. And so was Emmie. It could have been so much worse. He smiled to himself. Emmie seemed to have rubbed off on him.

'Love!' his mother cried when she opened the door, embracing him and planting a kiss on his cheek. He winced as she came close to the cuts and wounds, still not quite healed. 'I'm *so* glad you're alright. You look like you were mauled by an angry chef, though!'

Once he was sure Emmie was okay, he'd called her to let her know what had happened, and she'd immediately started to panic. 'That's why I got out of kitchen work,' he joked. 'All the angry head chefs running around with cleavers. It's not as bad as it looks.'

'You should have let me come to the hospital—'

'Emmie was in a worse state than I was. She didn't need all the fuss, and besides, she was sleeping.'

His mum's expression softened. 'Come in. I'll put the kettle on. How is she?'

'Recovering. Sylvie said they were keeping her in longer to be sure.' He stepped over the threshold. He'd brought a bag of Christmas presents from his flat that he hadn't been able to share with her until now.

He loved coming here; it was coming home, brimming with nostalgia. There were bad memories, too, of course, but they'd faded and worn over time, like aged paper. Inside, everything was green and white and wooden, and filled to bursting with plants and family photographs, pictures of him and Shane and his mother lining the hallway into the living room. He let his mum potter around the kitchen as he pushed through the purple hanging beads in the living room doorway and got himself comfortable on the settee.

Everything in here was adorned for her work. Thick fluffy rugs, illustrations of the moon and the stars on the walls, glass cabinets filled with crystals and salt lamps, currently switched off. On the far side of the room, she had a round oak table set up, covered in a purple satin tablecloth, and two chairs. An old CD player he'd remembered using as a kid sat on a shelf nearby, racks of discs and CDs beside it.

His mum returned carrying two steaming mugs of strong tea. He set down the bag of presents by the flashing Christmas tree in the corner, and she handed him a mug that read *POSITIVI-TEA*.

'Trying to tell me something?' he joked, raising it to her.

'Don't be daft,' she said, carrying her own tea over to the green armchair by the little window partly concealed by heavy, frilly net curtains. She deposited her tea on a side table, sitting on the edge of the armchair and studying him, a crystal necklace dangling forward from her chest. 'Are you really okay, kiddo? Heavens, it must have shaken you, being in that accident.' She shook her head, pressing a hand to her heart. 'I'm so glad you're both safe.'

'I'm fine, honestly. I'm glad, too.'

He drank a gulp of the hot tea. She must have been burning incense somewhere in the house, because it smelt of sandalwood, the scent tickling his nose. When he and Shane were children, she'd always had a vague interest in the spiritual – a crystal here, visiting a psychic there. After she got up the courage to leave his father, she'd fully embraced it, even turned it into a business. He didn't believe in it, but she did, and it comforted her, and that was fair enough. Sometimes he wished he had that kind of outlet or coping mechanism; mostly he just plodded along, as if he were groping around in the dark for a light switch.

'You've been through a lot lately,' said his mum gently. 'First Poppy, then getting snowed in at work, and now the accident.'

'I know.' Jared sucked in the heady, sandalwood-infused air. 'I haven't been to the hospital today,' he admitted, lowering his chin, preferring to look at the swirly patterns in her tasselled rug, which looked vaguely like a magic carpet. 'I left flowers, but . . . I haven't seen her, and Sylvie said she's awake now.'

His mum leaned back in her seat; he heard the armchair creak beneath her. 'You blame yourself?'

'How can I not? I took Emmie on Kirkstone Pass. She's in that hospital because of me.'

'You have to stop blaming yourself for things that are outside of your control,' she said. 'It doesn't help you. You did it with Poppy, with Emmie . . . You've always done it.'

He winced, and he wasn't sure whether it was the reference to Poppy, or the way his mother could look right through him and pull out the truth like a spool of loose thread.

'Poppy wasn't your fault,' she continued gently. 'You did everything you could for that cat, to make her well, but it was her time, and you gave her a gentle end. A kind end.'

Christ, he could feel the backs of his eyes burning, a heaviness pushing on his ribs. A flash of the vet coming into the house, a weak and tired Poppy held in a blanket in his arms before the end. He blinked the emotion back, trying to push it down where it couldn't reach him.

'Don't fight the emotions, Jared,' she advised him, leaning across to squeeze his hand. 'It does more harm than good.'

'I shouldn't be this upset anymore,' he blurted, swallowing down the clogging sensation in his throat. The words lacked authenticity, felt hollow in his mouth – hadn't he told his brother off, for suggesting Poppy's death meant less, because she wasn't a person? And now he was giving himself some kind of time frame for getting over it?

Her hand clenched his even tighter. 'You've been through a lot these past few days. And grief is a strange thing. We visit occasionally, it comes and it goes. We sit with it, but we don't dwell there permanently. Remember that. There will be good days and bad.'

A throaty laugh escaped him. 'You know, I do love having a wise woman as a parent.'

'Wild woman, some call it. Emmie sounds like one, too,' she replied, a mischievous twinkle in her eye. She let go of his hand and leaned back again. 'As for Emmie . . . you didn't *mean* to take her on the Pass. It's not like you drove her through a gate intentionally, or wanted to land her in hospital.' There was a smile in her voice, soon spreading to the corners of her lips. 'Unless my son has become the lead in some twisted Netflix series and hasn't told me about it yet?'

He snorted. 'No, I haven't.'

'Well, then. There's nothing to worry about. It wasn't your fault.'

He nodded. He feared Emmie blaming *him* for the accident, and obviously, he hadn't intended to hurt anyone. Now he knew how Megan must have felt, when he told her about Poppy. Megan hadn't set out with malice in mind, either. She'd lied about Ethan – that was a fact. But she hadn't harmed Poppy. He was suddenly glad they'd talked it over while they were stuck at the café.

'But what if . . .' He couldn't finish. Everything felt tight – his shoulders, his neck. He twisted, trying to release the tension.

'What if she blames you?' she asked.

He nodded.

'My dear, you're sitting here, looking angsty, all in a tizzy, worrying about whether she'll blame you, feeling guilty for what happened. If she feels even a degree of

265

what you clearly feel for her, she won't blame you. She'll want you to be at her side.'

'I have . . . baggage,' he told her, the sweetness of the tea she'd made him suddenly sickening. 'You know that. She might not want that.'

'What? Your mental health?' She reached for her tea again, draining some of the liquid. The winter sun was trying to push its way through the net curtains, casting dappled light onto the rug. 'We all have issues, Jared, things we deal with. Relationships aren't about two people being perfect together. They're about choosing to be together in spite of those issues – and deciding which ones you're willing to work on together. And which ones are deal-breakers.'

He fell silent. She wasn't looking at him – she was watching the net curtains, her gaze falling to the row of photos lined up on the windowsill, all of Jared and Shane, young and fresh-faced and smiling. There was no father figure in any of them, and he knew she'd plucked that wisdom from her own life like a pearl, learned from finally deciding to leave their dad.

'What if I *am* her deal-breaker?' he said quietly. 'If she doesn't want to put up with my shit?'

His mother's lips quirked. 'Then she'd be a fool for overlooking all your wonderful qualities. But you'd deal with it. You'd move on, and carry on. As we all do.' She raised herself to her feet, crossed the room, and planted a kiss on his forehead, smoothing back his hair as if he were five years old. 'Wait there. I have something for you. I put it to one side so I could make sure I watched you open it.' She pushed her way through the purple beads in the living-room doorway.

266

Puzzled, he sipped at his tea, listening to the stairs creak as she went up into the bedroom. When she came down again, she was clutching a brown-paper bag – a square-edged shape was sticking up from the inside.

'Happy Christmas,' she said, holding it out.

There was white, reindeer-etched tissue paper wrapped around a silvery box. He opened it as she settled back into her armchair. Jared carefully guided out the object: a picture frame with a shiny silver border.

He thought it was going to be a photo, but when he turned it over in his hands, his chest caught. It was a sketch. Rough pencil strokes formed fur, whiskers, big green eyes and pointed ears. Poppy's tell-tale orange mark above her eye had been carefully coloured in. She had that same gentle, loving expression on her face that he'd missed so fiercely recently.

'Mum,' he said, his voice hoarse. 'This is amazing.' His thumb moved over the signature in the bottom right. 'You did this?'

She nodded, smiling widely. 'I've been playing around with sketching again, so I thought I'd draw her for you.'

'I love it.' He set it carefully to one side and got up to give her a hug, feeling equal parts choked with emotion and touched that she'd do this for him – just like Emmie had when they were snowed in. Her wiry orange hair tickled his chin as he squeezed her close for a moment and whispered, 'Thanks, Mum.'

'There're more presents for you under the tree,' she said, pointing. She rubbed her hands together eagerly, like a child who had been waiting for Santa to clatter over the roof. 'And I want to see what mine are!'

It was clear to him that he was incredibly lucky to be surrounded by people who were so supportive and caring. And, he realised, Emmie was one of those people. He wanted her in his life, and he might just be falling in love with her.

★

Jared had messaged Sylvie and told her he needed to speak with her, and she'd agreed to meet him at a small Oakside café. The café he'd chosen was a tea room down the road from Catpurrcino, tucked away across from the local library. Snow was still stacked on rooftops and lining pavements like white garlands, but it was beginning to melt, and the gritters had been out in full force clearing paths on most of the roads.

Sylvie was already there when he stepped into the tea room, a bell tinkling over his head. She waved at him from a back corner by a window, and he hurried across to sit down. The window looked out across a car park and a collection of brickwork buildings and distant hills, the white snow fading from their peaks.

'Thanks for waiting. Have you been here long?' he asked, slipping off his scarf and coat and hanging them on the chair.

'A few minutes. I haven't even ordered yet.' She gestured to the laminated menu on the table. She beamed up at him. 'I'm so glad you managed to find that stray. Did the shelter come to pick him up, then? I hope it wasn't too bad on your allergies?'

Jared nodded, but inwardly, he was wincing at her comment, which was why he'd wanted to talk to her.

He'd mentioned the stray when he'd texted her but not the other reason for this conversation. 'I waited until they got there. They'll do what they can to find the owners. They said it's about a year old or so. And it's a female.'

'Goodness. Maybe it escaped from home, got lost. I'm glad she's in their hands now.'

While she perused the menu, he sucked in a lungful of air. He'd promised Emmie he would tell the truth and now was the time.

'Shall we order first, then we can talk about whatever you wanted to chat about?' she asked him. When she glanced up at him, her eyes were kind, and she was smiling, the movement etching a wrinkle into her cheek.

'Sure.'

Sylvie ordered a pot of tea and one of the lunch specials. Jared didn't feel much like eating, but since she was, he ordered a latte and a bacon muffin. When their drinks arrived, the waitress depositing them on the table and telling them the food wouldn't be long, he added sugar to his latte and stirred it into the froth, wondering where to even start.

'I owe you an apology,' he began.

Sylvie lifted her eyebrows in surprise. She concentrated on pouring tea into her cup and swirling in the milk. Finally, she raised her cup to her lips. 'Why? You helped Emmie while I was gone, and when she needed to get Salem to—'

'I'm talking about before that. When I took the job with you.'

'Oh?'

'I lied to you from the start. I know it sounds like I'm making excuses but I did have reasons.'

'Lied about what?' she said, sounding cautious.

'I'm not allergic to cats.'

She stared at him, her teacup still hovering in the air, forgotten. 'What?'

'I'm not allergic.' He grasped the handle of his mug, for something to do with his hands. 'I told you that because I didn't want to come inside the building.'

The further he got into this conversation, the more he was realising he didn't *want* to get fired. It was no longer just about paying his rent and bills. He liked the work, liked driving around with the radio on past the sprawling countryside, and bumping into Emmie at the back door of the café when he picked up orders. It was laid-back, not too much pressure, just what he needed while he found his feet with his freelance work again. And he really wanted to stay.

'I don't understand,' said Sylvie.

He heaved in another lungful of air, his gaze on the hills outside the window and the pale sky. Birds were wheeling across the rooftops in spiky V shapes.

'I lost my cat. A few weeks before I took the job with you. I know it sounds stupid to most people but it's been hard. I didn't want to be around the animals.'

It all sounded so ridiculous. He shook his head, but there was that weight in his throat again, pressing down, reminding him how much he missed her, even now.

'She saved me,' he added.

He waited, forcing down a swig of his coffee, as she considered his words.

Eventually, she set her teacup down. 'Jared,' she said, and her voice was soft. 'Is that all? You could have told me that from the start, you silly lad.'

Jared almost got a crick in his neck, he looked up from his latte so quickly. 'What?'

'You didn't have to lie to me about that.' Sylvie shook her head, and her gentle smile was back.

There was a pause, during which the waitress brought their food, setting down the plates and adding some condiments to the middle of the table. Sylvie thanked her, and she went back across to the tills. Jared was still processing what she was saying.

'I know what cats – what pets – mean to people,' Sylvie continued, reaching for the salad dressing and sprinkling some onto her plate. 'I know it better than most. I've had so many cats over the years, even before I owned the café. And you know, I've always believed in how healing animals can be. It's part of why I opened the place. Maybe I should have told you about Bennie from the start.'

'Bennie?'

'My husband,' Sylvie clarified. 'I moved to Oakside with him, years ago, and he always loved cats – same as me.' The corner of her lip tipped into a smile that didn't quite reach her eyes. 'When he passed away – cancer – and his life insurance paid out, I bought that building in Oakside, and turned the café that had closed down there into Catpurrcino.'

Jared couldn't believe what he was hearing, and he felt like an idiot. All this time, he'd been so focused on people *not* understanding, that he'd overlooked the fact that Sylvie might know exactly how he was feeling.

'Our cats . . . they really helped him, at the end. They were lying with him as he passed peacefully at home.' Her eyes took on a sheen, and she blinked a few times to clear them. 'Listen to me, getting sentimental. I'm only telling you because I understand. You needn't have hidden that from me. I would have made accommodations for you.'

'I . . .' He trailed off. He had no idea what to say. 'I'm sorry about your husband.'

'It's alright.' Sylvie smiled softly. 'I'm not a schoolmarm, Jared. What did you think I was going to do, set the cats on you?'

'Uh . . . fire me?' Jared suggested, smirking. 'Maybe I shouldn't be giving you ideas.'

'Ha! No. I don't want to fire you, Jared.'

Jared drank some more of his coffee, relief seeping into his bones. The idea that had been percolating in his brain now came to the forefront. Emmie was her niece; surely she'd be on board with it?

'If I'm not fired, maybe I can give you an idea?' he said. 'For the café.'

She picked up her knife and fork, spearing them into her salad. 'I'm listening.'

Chapter 20

Emmie had finally been discharged after several mind-numbingly boring days in hospital, making her realise just how maddening it was if she weren't kept busy. She'd had to spend New Year's Eve there, and the following day, but it hadn't been so bad; her grandparents had come along to have a bit of an early celebration and she'd loved seeing them after so long. The rest of the staff from Catpurrcino had all signed a get-well card for her, and Clem had even baked her a special batch of cookies, which made up for all the not-so-satisfying hospital food.

Today, Aunt Sylvie had kindly offered to collect Emmie from the hospital and bring her home to Catpurrcino. When she arrived to pick her up, Emmie was half-hoping Jared would be with her, and had to resist craning her neck to check – the nurses had told her she didn't need to wear a brace, but she did need to be careful and move slowly to begin with, as she healed. She stood on her tiptoes instead. To her disappointment, Jared wasn't there. She sank back down onto flat feet. Had he decided he didn't want to speak with her, after all? Were they ever going to address that kiss, and what they were to one another?

'Emmie, love!' Sylvie enveloped her in a warm hug, her flowery perfume surrounding them. 'I bet you're glad to be getting out of here.'

They headed out to the car, Sylvie tapping away on her phone. As they drove back to Oakside, Emmie explained that it was fine for her to return to work soon. Keeping active and returning to work was apparently beneficial for whiplash recovery. The wrist fracture, though, was more of a problem, and the splint was as clunky as ever.

'Not to worry,' said Aunt Sylvie. 'Faye and I will be there to support you.' She beamed across at Emmie from behind the steering wheel. 'I'm so proud of you.'

Emmie waved the comment aside with her good hand.

'I mean it. You really did take care of things while I was gone, in the worst possible circumstances. I knew I could count on you.'

'Thanks.' Emmie returned her smile.

There was snow covering the hills and fields as they drove back into Oakside and through the streets. The snowfall had eased, though, with only a few minor flurries passing over since Storm Marie. But reminders of the storm were everywhere: in the leftover fallen trees with their roots sticking into the air, in bent lampposts, in the shops that were still closed. The harsh nip of winter clawed at skin, but the sky was no longer entirely white, clearing the way for patches of sky blue and the promise of brighter, snow-free days ahead. Emmie smiled to herself as they rolled up the hill to Catpurrcino, the building framed by the segments of blue sky. She hadn't been away for very long but she'd missed it.

It felt like home, now, she realised, as she clambered out of the car. She slammed the door shut with her good hand.

When she looked up, she noticed the café appeared to be at capacity, people seated at tables and chairs. The string lights in the window were glittering like icicles, and Emmie spotted Faye mingling. She wasn't wearing a café apron, but was more dressed up, in a sparkly pink jumper and bright yellow hoop earrings. Emmie turned to Aunt Sylvie, who had just climbed out the other side of the car and locked it. Come to think of it, under her coat, Sylvie looked almost dressed up, too. Emmie could see a necklace sparkling at her throat and she was wearing her nice heeled boots with the shiny gold buckles.

'Why's everyone so dressed up?' said Emmie. 'Faye isn't in uniform.'

'Come on,' said Aunt Sylvie, winking. She threaded an arm around Emmie's shoulders.

Before they could head inside, someone called, 'Emmie!'

They turned, and Megan was waving at them from the opposite corner of the café, bundled up in a chunky hat, her coat, and a pair of leather gloves. There was a bag slung over her shoulder.

'She checked out this morning,' Sylvie explained. 'Are you leaving, love?' she called across to Megan.

'Yes,' said Megan. 'Can I have a word before I go, Emmie?'

'I won't be a minute,' Emmie told Sylvie. Her aunt hovered near the café door while Emmie headed to the street corner to speak to Megan.

'I'm all packed up now,' Megan said, hefting her bag further onto her shoulder. 'Calling a taxi soon.'

'I'm so sorry about your car—' Emmie started.

Megan shook her head. 'Don't be, it'll get sorted with my insurance. I'm just glad you're both alive! I wanted to talk to you before I left, so I've just been exploring the town. Sylvie told me you were on the way back.'

'You waited around just to talk to me? You didn't have to do that. You could have just asked her for my number, or something.'

Megan shifted from foot to foot, biting her lip. 'I don't think it's a good idea.'

'Okay . . .'

'I feel like we could have been friends,' Megan admitted. 'But I'm not an idiot – I see how Jared feels about you. I don't want to come between that, for either of you.'

Emmie didn't know what to say. All the signs had been there for both of them, and they'd both been holding back – first, Emmie had held back because she'd come here to focus on work and to escape her brother. Then, because she didn't want to upset Megan. But now nothing stood in her way. She wondered if Jared would still be holding back or not.

'I know what you mean,' said Emmie. 'For what it's worth, I think we could have been good friends, too.'

Megan's eyes brightened. 'Right? We would.' The solemn look returned to her face. 'But we should all move on, me included. I didn't want to leave without saying goodbye though.'

'Well, can I give you a hug, at least? An awkward one.' Emmie glanced down at the splint encasing her hand. She held her arms apart clumsily.

'Deal.' Megan grinned, the strands of her dark hair tickling Emmie's cheek as she embraced her and then drew back. 'Take care of yourself, Emmie.'

'You too.' Emmie paused, thinking of her brother, and of Megan's ex, Ethan. They'd both dealt with difficult people; maybe that was why there seemed to be a silvery thread of understanding between them. 'You'll get there, you know,' she added. 'You'll find your person.'

'I know.' Megan offered one last smile and waved, lifting her phone to her ear to call a taxi.

★

Sylvie was still standing outside Catpurrcino, waiting for Emmie. Emmie was about to follow her inside when someone pushed their way out of the café doors behind her aunt – someone who made her chest leap uncomfortably, made her feel sick and hot and light-headed all at once.

Dustin.

He strode around the side of her aunt. When Emmie saw him, she gasped. Because he looked *different*.

Her brother had always been tall and broad – she'd called him a bear, when they were little – but since he'd started drinking and gambling years ago, he'd become thin and pallid, favouring alcohol over food. His hair – the same shade as hers – was closely cropped. When she left home it had been long and unbrushed, tangled. His blue eyes seemed changed, too. There was a shine in them that hadn't been there before. He wasn't staggering or swaying, and he wore smart dark jeans and a long thick coat.

'What's going on?' Emmie said, dumbfounded. 'What are you doing here?'

Sylvie's eyes narrowed. 'You're not supposed to be here, Dustin,' she said.

'I came to see Emmie. To support the event,' said Dustin. He wasn't slurring his words, either.

'Event?' Emmie repeated, picking out the word in amongst the confusion. 'What are you talking about?'

277

'I know you didn't invite me, Em. But I tried to visit you in the hospital – Grandad told me about the accident – and Sylvie wouldn't let me come. I was really worried about you.'

Emmie shot her aunt a questioning look.

Aunt Sylvie looked crestfallen and touched Emmie's arm lightly. 'I'm sorry. I was trying to protect you, love. I thought he might turn up drunk and you needed to rest—'

'I wouldn't have,' said Dustin. 'I swear. I haven't had a drink since the last time I talked to Emmie on the phone.' Dustin shoved his hands in his pockets and his Adam's apple bobbed as he swallowed. 'I got on medication to help me go cold turkey. I'm in counselling.'

Emmie opened her mouth and closed it again. She couldn't quite believe what she was hearing. All those times she'd encouraged Dustin to get help, to see a doctor or a counsellor, he'd brushed her off. Her eyes skimmed over him again, taking in his neat clothes, his close-cut hair. He'd even had a shave.

'I'll follow you inside, Auntie,' she said to Sylvie.

'Are you sure?'

Emmie nodded.

'Okay . . .' Aunt Sylvie squeezed her elbow and moved away, but hesitated partway to the café doors. 'If you need me . . .'

'I know.'

The café doors banged shut after Sylvie, and Emmie was left alone on the pavement with her brother.

'Is all of that true?' she asked him, taking a few steps closer. 'You're getting help?'

He nodded. 'It's true. I have the emails and letters to prove it to you – and I wouldn't blame you for asking.'

He sighed, the cold making the breath plume like a bright cloud in front of him. 'I'm sorry. I just came here to tell you . . . I know you blocked my number, which was fair enough, and I didn't think you'd believe me if I emailed. I had to show you that I've cleaned up my act. I've treated you and everyone else like rubbish. I've . . . lied, manipulated you. I see that now.'

'Why now?' Emmie breathed. 'I kept telling you to get help—'

'I realised . . . When you said you never wanted to see me again, I . . . I guess it hit home, that I'd lost so much of my family.' She opened her mouth to reply, but he was already speaking again. 'You don't have to say anything. I just thought, maybe if things carried on, I really *would* lose myself. My family, and then myself. Maybe I'd get more violent than just punching through a wall. Everything about me would just be . . . taken away, and for what? Honestly? It scared me.'

Emmie didn't have any words left. She hurried forward and enveloped him in a hug. He was taller than her, and he closed his arms around her.

'I'm proud of you,' she whispered.

'Got you, little bear,' he said in her ear.

'Dustin, what *happened* to you?' she said, her throat clogged with emotion. 'You've never told me why all this started.'

She'd never understood all this – what had prompted him to turn to drinking so heavily in the first place, why he became so entrenched in it. For years she'd wondered, and he'd never opened up to her. She'd felt like she'd lost her brother, like she'd grieved for the person she'd lost – because it wasn't him. She'd known something had happened – something to fundamentally change things, to break something. She just didn't know what.

'I should have talked to you all,' he said thickly, swallowing again. 'I was talking to Gran and Grandad, inside. I . . . I just don't know if I have the words to explain it yet. I'm still . . .' His chest shuddered as Emmie drew back from his embrace. 'Still working on it, in counselling. But I . . . I lost someone. Someone close to me, in the worst way. I don't know if I can talk about it yet.'

She grabbed his hands and squeezed them tight. 'I'm here, no matter what it is, whenever you want to talk to me. And for the time being, you can join us for whatever this *event* is.' She offered up a watery smile, tears clouding her eyes.

'I'd like that,' he said.

'Come on, then. Let's go in together.'

She tugged her brother towards the café entrance, through the separate door into the gift shop and reception area, and then into the main café, through the latched gate.

When they stepped across the threshold, everyone turned, laughing at the look on Emmie's face. There were colourful lights arranged in lines across the ceiling, out of reach of the cats, and someone had created a bouquet of cat-friendly shiny balloons in a vase on the counter by the till. The chalkboard – which usually announced the menu to customers – read *EMMIE'S GALLERY* at the top, in bright, block letters. A crude-looking cat was drawn underneath it, with a big smile and long whiskers.

'I don't understand,' said Emmie, confused.

Then she glimpsed them, the finer details. There were framed pictures on the walls that weren't there before, each frame a different pastel shade – lilac, yellow, peach, cream. And sitting in the frames were her own colourful cat illustrations, depicting each of the café's resident cats. She'd been working on them in her room in the evenings, and Sylvie must have taken them from her sketchbook and framed them. Emmie spluttered out a wordless exclamation when she realised what was going on.

'Those are . . .'

She looked around at all the gathered guests. Faye was waving at her from near the counter, a toothy smile fixed in place, her hair gathered back in a sleek bun, and their receptionist Kaitlyn was beside her in a pretty dress. Her grandparents were huddled together in a corner, and they waved, her grandad pulling a silly face at her, as he always did, making her laugh. And there were other faces she recognised, seated at the tables and chairs around the edges of the room. The elderly couple who always came into the café once a month, on a Wednesday, were at one of the tables, sitting in front of a teapot. Thomas was sprawled on a table next to them, pink paw pads extended. A few of the staff from the cat shelter they partnered with had come, too. And a couple of customers she'd served regularly were seated at the tables. Sophie and Miles waved at her from the corner, both beaming and dressed smartly. The only person of note who was missing was Clem.

To Emmie's right, nestled in an armchair atop a plump cushion, was Salem, dozing and looking quite content.

'Salem!' she cried, bending down to scratch him behind the ears. Within mere moments, he was purring; she could feel it vibrating beneath her fingertips. 'Hey, little guy.'

'He's been enjoying the attention today,' said Sylvie, at Emmie's shoulder. 'And the antibiotics have been working a treat. The vet thinks he's going to be just fine.'

Faye was calling for quiet now, hushing them all.

Emmie's heart skipped. Jared emerged from the crowd – she hadn't even noticed him – wearing a dark blue jumper and a pair of black jeans, his long hair scooped behind his ears, ruffled slightly. His beard was freshly trimmed yet he still managed to look rugged. He looked smart, and downright gorgeous, even though his arm was in a cast. His eyes moved from her brother to Emmie, and he gave a small nod of recognition. Had they talked, perhaps, before Emmie got here?

'Emmie!' he called. 'Welcome back. All this here, is for you.' He gestured around. For the first time, Emmie could pick out the cats sitting on some of the wall shelves or the cat towers. Jess was weaving between tables in search of a food dispenser, eventually flopping down underneath a chair and receiving a scratch on the head from the woman sitting there. 'I know you've had your confidence knocked with your art, and the last event – the winter fair – didn't exactly go to plan. So, we thought we'd do something else for you.'

'We?' Emmie croaked, glancing at Aunt Sylvie.

Sylvie nodded. 'All this was Jared's idea, but I was in total agreement. You should be proud of your work, Emmie, no matter what. So I've hung it here for everyone to see, and if you're okay with it, Jared was thinking we'd auction it off tonight. Donate the proceeds to the shelter.' She glanced at the two staff members from the shelter, who beamed back at her and nodded. 'Everyone here is very interested in getting their hands on some of your art.'

'I . . .' Emmie could barely speak around the lump rising in her throat. The way she'd felt when she woke up in the hospital – that she needed to put less stock in working so hard toward some arbitrary level of success, rose inside her again. *This* was the definition of success, wasn't it? It didn't matter if she wasn't working for a company as an illustrator, and it didn't matter if she never got a picture book contract. She could love her art and enjoy her creativity regardless, and even if only a few people appreciated it – people she cared about and loved – then that was a form of success in itself.

'I'd love that,' she managed.

'Good. Because this auction is my way of saying thank you, for looking after the café and Salem.' Aunt Sylvie hooked her arms around Emmie's shoulders.

Emmie's chest squeezed. She couldn't think of anything to say. Jared had thought of all this? He'd known how much the failed winter fair had upset her, and he'd planned all this. She was touched by the gesture, her heart fluttering.

Her eyes found his, and the way he was looking at her . . . had *anyone* ever looked at her like that? As if she were the only person in the room?

'Emmie,' he said hoarsely. 'You've done a lot for this place. And for me.' He cleared his throat. 'You deserve this.' He motioned to the café once again, at her drawings on the walls, and there were a series of smiles and nods from those gathered. 'And I . . . being honest, I feel like I belong with you. If you'll have me.'

Her mouth was dry, and even though she knew what her answer was, she hesitated, feeling shy in front of all of these people. Her palms were hot, clammy with anticipation. But when Faye called out, 'Get on with it, then!' she laughed.

'Of course I'll have you,' said Emmie. 'But you'll have to catch me first. You owe me a snow angel.'

With that, she darted through the latched gate, through the reception area, and out into the street.

*

There was a patch of woodland a short way up the hill from the café, a popular spot for dog walkers that led into a small stretch of forest. Emmie raced outside, giggling, heading up towards the hill, Jared calling after her. She could hear him laughing, asking for her to come back. She smiled to herself. There was *no way* she was going to kiss him in front of all those people. She wasn't one of those proposal-at-the-airport types. Not that she expected a proposal at this stage, but any romantic gesture was better to her when it was away from so many observers. And he *did* owe her a snow angel, and a bit of fun out here in the leftover snow, not that she could do much herself with her neck still healing.

'Emmie, you'll end up breaking your other wrist!' Jared called, sounding out of breath as he followed up the hill behind her.

'I'll be fine!' she yelled back.

His laugh pealed its way up the hill. 'Can we just stop? Hey, if you think you belong with me, running away isn't really the right course of action . . .' He sounded out of breath.

She smiled, didn't answer, and instead turned onto the forest path, picking her way through the bracken. Finally, she was in the field, surrounded by bulky trees on all sides, the area quiet. It was like a postcard here, the chalky snow beneath her trodden by a dozen feet and paws, building a path into the forest beyond. Milky sunlight broke through the trees, spilling down, warming the side of her face and shining onto the remaining snow.

Jared caught hold of her good wrist, tugging her gently by the sleeve. 'Hey,' he said, voice as soft as snowfall itself. 'Caught you.'

She turned to face him. His cheeks were flushed pink with exertion and she smiled. The sun made his skin look golden, as if flecked with honey-drenched stars.

'Why did you run?' he asked her.

'Because I wanted to be away from prying eyes,' she said, stepping closer to him. 'I don't like having an audience for this kind of thing.'

'Sorry about that.' He smiled, scratching the back of his neck. His expression was earnest when he met her gaze again and drew in a long breath.

'I'd wrap my hands around your neck to make this extra romantic, but I'm a little . . . incapable.' She held up her splint.

'Me too.' He held up his cast, and they both laughed.

Jared reached out, taking her good hand in his, lifting it, placing it on the back of his neck, where his skin was warm to the touch. His hair covered her fingers, tickling her knuckles, and he leaned down towards her, cupping her face with his fingertips tenderly, as if he might break her.

'Is your neck okay . . . ?'

'It's fine. They said movement is good, you know, for healing,' she breathed. 'So . . .'

'Good,' he answered.

He kissed her, and she sank into it, tasting coffee and sweetness and longing all at once. His lips moved against hers and her grip on the back of his neck tightened. Dizzy with joy, with the feel of his soft lips on hers, she could barely think. His hands were cupping her waist now, drawing her nearer still, the sudden warmth of the sun encasing them.

When they broke apart, the sweetness lingering on Emmie's mouth, making her want to kiss him again, he smiled against her mouth and pressed a finger to her lower lip, keeping her close. 'Finally,' he murmured. 'Now, shall we get back to your guests?'

'They can wait another two minutes – it's good for my neck, after all,' she said. And she kissed him again, tasting coffee and joy and a future spent together.

Chapter 21

April, four months later

Bluebells and daffodils had sprouted up across Oak-side, marking the start of spring with their bright colours and swaying heads. The cherry tree outside the cat café was in full bloom, too, spilling its petals across the roadside and the tables and chairs set up outside under the awning, making everything look like a children's storybook, awash with pink. Emmie smiled, inhaling the fresh air as she walked away from the café after her morning shift, waving to Faye one last time through the window as she went. She only walked for ten minutes before she arrived at Jared's new flat, which was tucked away behind the church building and graveyard, and shrouded in the shade of a huge tree.

When she headed up the steps and to his flat, she buzzed for Jared to let her in. Once she'd stepped into the hall and closed the door behind her, it wasn't long before pattering paws greeted her, and a small black cat bounded down the hall-way. The air smelt delicious: of meat, garlic and heady spices.

'Hi, Nova,' Emmie crooned, bending down to stroke the black cat's silky back. The cat erupted into happy purrs as she brushed against her legs. 'Did you miss me?'

'Hey,' Jared called. He was framed in the doorway at the end of the hall, a tea towel in his hand, grinning at her. The green T-shirt he wore brought out the golden hue of his hair. She hurried forwards, unable to resist weaving her arms around his waist and nuzzling close.

'Hey yourself,' she said, and pressed her lips against his.

He kissed her back, hands finding her hair, and when they broke apart, he was smiling widely again. The tea towel had somehow ended up on the floor and Nova was inspecting it, attempting to bat it away with a paw.

'Something smells nice,' Emmie said, her mouth watering at the mingling scents in the air.

'I thought I'd make you some food – you said you'd be busy this morning. I'm doing the *fanciest* turkey burgers you'll ever eat.' He turned and hurried back into the kitchen to check on the food. 'And sweet potato wedges!' he called.

Emmie beamed, following, Nova at her heels, chasing the hem of her long dress. A pan was bubbling on the stove, and two slabs of turkey were sizzling on the grill. Some glazed burger buns had been set out on the counter, with a collection of salad and sauces. The radio was playing through a speaker on top of the fridge, cycling through a playlist, mostly indie and folk rock bands that she'd come to enjoy herself. Jared kicked a toy mouse across the kitchen and back out into the hall. Nova didn't waste any time and charged after it, a blur of black fur as she dashed away.

'I'm so glad you took one of the kittens,' Emmie said, crossing the kitchen to stand beside him as he checked on the burgers, flipping them over. The cat shelter had never found an owner for the cat after Jared discovered her in the wall – they'd tried everything, and she had no microchip. *And* she'd been pregnant. In the end, Jared had adopted one of her kittens. The others had found homes too – one with Sylvie at her own home. Sylvie had also adopted the mother.

She was glad Jared had found this new home, too. The flat was being rented out by one of their regular customers. Emmie had known Jared was unhappy at his old place, filled with too many memories, not only of Poppy but of his time with Megan – a time spent struggling. Being here in this new place had helped him to put the past behind him, given him a fresh start. She knew it would never be that simple – that there would be ebbs and flows, always – but seeing how content he was here, and spending time with him and Nova, made her happy, too.

'Nova?' he said, and when she nodded, he smirked, turning towards her. 'She's not the only one I'm glad to have found, Em. Do you know how hard I've fallen for you?'

He reached for her hips, pulling her towards him quickly, as if they were engaged in a dance, and she squealed with laughter, melting into his kiss.

'Of course,' she said. 'The only one who fell harder was me.'

'Debatable. You know,' he murmured against her mouth, planting kisses along her jawline and making her skin tingle and her insides shudder with delight. 'You really should have your own key to this place.'

'I'd like that, not the least because it means more of your great food . . .' she whispered back, and laughed as

Nova came trotting back into the kitchen with her mouse gripped between her teeth. It was one of her favourite toys, and it had been a gift from Dustin. He'd found work at a huge pet chain and he got discounts on some of the best goods.

Jared held on to her more tightly, his breath on her neck as he leaned in for another kiss, and peppered them down the side of her neck. 'You need to stop being so irresistibly distracting or I'll burn our lunch in favour of something *more* delicious.'

Emmie grinned and disentangled herself so he could get on with it, her neck shivering with gooseflesh. 'Go on then, Chef,' she said, giving him a playful tap on the bum. 'We can save that for the bedroom – *after* lunch.'

'Dessert, then?' His eyes glittered.

Later, Sylvie came over to see Nova – the café was closed today, as it was a Sunday – and they left her with the cat while they drove over to Jared's mum's place. Emmie had been here on several occasions now – she'd even had a few palm and tarot readings, where she was told they'd have a long and happy future together, though she wasn't sure if that was just his mum's biased interpretation of things, rather than the truth. She'd even told Emmie another crucial relationship in her life was on the long road to being healed, and Emmie thought at once of Dustin, who still hadn't touched a drop of alcohol – or logged in to an online gambling site. He'd even reached out to their parents again, and joined some of her video chats with them. Things weren't perfect, but she was glad they were on the road to being mended.

The white-painted house was awash in the bright spring sunshine when they arrived, pink flowers and green leaves snaking up the sides of the front door. While Jared's mother boiled the kettle and puttered around in search of ginger biscuits, they made their way into the back garden.

It was a reflection of Jared's mother out here, everything vaguely witchy and spiritual. A cobbled path led up to a patch of trimmed grass and a small shed, the roof covered in moss. Beyond the shed, she'd created a circular space of climbing plants that snaked up the back fence, and an array of flower pots filled with black, red and orange flowers. Wind chimes twinkled in the soft breeze and sun catchers shaped like stars threw rainbows onto the exposed fence. There was enough room for a small bench, and near the flowers, his mother had created a wooden plaque, painted black and inscribed with the word *Poppy* in gold.

They stood there, before this little garden, Jared clutching the green tube of Poppy's ashes. He'd already had some of her ashes made into things he could keep – a ball-shaped necklace that hung at his throat, and a wooden cat ornament that sat on his bookcase, so there would always be a part of her with him. But the rest of her would live here, in this little spiritual space.

'She liked it out here,' he said. 'She was never an outdoor cat, but when I lived here for a bit before moving to a different flat, she liked to come and sit in the wind, roll about in the sun. I used to sit with her sometimes, bring my laptop and do some work.'

Emmie took his hand and squeezed it; her wrist had healed now, although it sometimes felt weaker than the other one. 'Well, you can come back here whenever you need to, and she'll be here.'

Jared nodded, stepping forward with the tube, removing the lid. 'Now you can enjoy the breeze as much as you want, Poppy,' he said, and he scattered her ashes across the garden, into the flowers and into the wind.

Emmie put her arm around him, and he reached across her shoulder, drawing her close. A butterfly fluttered down into the garden, its colours suspiciously familiar, black and orange and a splodge to the side of its wing.

It was almost, Emmie thought, as if Poppy had come to be part of the moment, too – to say, not goodbye, but *hello, I'm still with you*. She watched the butterfly dance across the flowers and rise back into the open blue sky.

Acknowledgements

The road to signing a book deal was a long and complicated one for me. I'm so lucky to have my wonderful agent, Thérèse Coen. I can't thank you enough for believing in me – even when I didn't believe in myself – and for sticking by me for so long. I'm incredibly grateful for your advice, cheerleading, editorial help, and nudges in the right direction (and the excited cat GIFs when we sold this book). We did it!

To Cara Chimirri, my editor, your lovely letter was one of the best Christmas presents I've ever received, and your understanding of Jared's character and his grief was how I knew I'd found the perfect home for my cats. Thanks also to the rest of the Hodder & Stoughton team for falling in love with the cat café as much as I did, and for bringing Catpurrcino to readers. And to Kelley McMorris, whose beautiful work I'd admired long before I found out she'd be illustrating my cover – I was completely overjoyed you came on board to work your magic on the cat café.

Writing and publishing can be challenging, and I'm so grateful to my writer friends for being there for me. First, to Dandy Smith – you steered me towards writing this book when I felt lost and unsure of myself. Thank you for encouraging me to take a chance on something new. To Maria Kuzniar, for being so kind and lovely, and always lending an ear and offering wisdom when I need it. To Dave McCreery and Isabella Hunter, for the writing chats over coffee and bowls of ramen, for being such good friends, and alerting me to any available opportunity to grab Final Fantasy VII merch along the way. Thanks for being some of the first people to celebrate with me. To Molly Aitken, who has believed in me ever since we first met at a writing group years ago – anyone can count themselves lucky to have you as a friend. To the other members of that group, we may have since disbanded, but you were a wonderful bunch, and I'm not sure I'll ever find another writing group to match up to you lot.

Amita Parikh, Aisha Bushby, Rebecca Gibson, and Bryony Leah Smith have sent me so many encouraging messages to commiserate over writing and publishing – I'm so thankful for your support. Thanks as well to Una McKeown, whose early feedback on this book – and help with complicated foreign tax forms – was much appreciated. And to Jody Wenner, who critiqued an early version of my opening chapters.

A special shoutout to Cat Café Liverpool, which I visited to get a feel for a cat café's layout and how it all works, and Sheila's Cottage in Ambleside, which is in fact a real place. Shau Mei Yau, who shares in my cat obsession, kindly took the time to visit Liverpool with me and made it doubly enjoyable with her company.

Mum, thank you for raising me to do what makes me happy, no matter what that is, and for the lovely mother-daughter trips to the Lake District and beyond. I wouldn't be here without everything you've done for me. And to Glynn, Joe, my grandparents, my dad, and the rest of my family (cats included), your support means everything. I've been so lucky to grow up around people who only ever encouraged my love of storytelling.

Endless gratitude and love to my husband, Neil. I'm so lucky to share this life with such a wonderful human. Thank you for reminding me of my dreams, even when they seemed lost to me, for bringing me surprise snacks while I write, and for always putting a smile on my face. And even though they can't read this, much love to our cats, Haru and Jesper, who bring me so much joy. I'm sure Haru contributed a letter or two to this book by walking across my keyboard.

This book wouldn't be the same without my sweet calico Lily, who passed away in January 2023, after fourteen years together. She meant more to me than words can truly describe and is missed every day – but her memory lives on in this book.